Auth...
NATAL...

ultimate...

Pointe and Shoot

A JENNY T. PARTRIDGE DANCE MYSTERY

BERKLEY
PRIME
CRIME

$6.99 U.S.
$7.50 CAN

ISBN 978-0-425-22128-0

5 0 6 9 9 >

S ⊳ EAN

**Pima County
Public Library**
www.library.pima.gov

Berkley Prime Crime Titles by Natalie M. Roberts

TUTU DEADLY
TAPPED OUT
POINTE AND SHOOT

The shape didn't move.

"Police! I said get out of the vehicle now!"

Still nothing. My breathing had not improved, my head began to swim, and I watched as though from a long way away as they crept up on the vehicle, guns aimed, and quickly opened the door. The big shape fell out and hit the ground with a large *thunk*.

"It's a gorilla," Officer Willie said. He reached down and with a few good yanks pulled the mask off. A beelike buzz filled my ears and brain as I stared at the dead man. The cops' flashlights illuminated that same feral face I'd seen just hours before, delivering a Gorilla-Gram. Albert Cunningham.

The other officer was feeling for a pulse, but I knew there wasn't one. I'd never been this close to a dead body before—unless you counted the time I fell into the Dumpster on top of a dead hip-hop teacher. Hmm, I guessed that counted, but it had happened really fast and I don't remember a lot about it—but I'd watched enough television to know that wide-open, glassy eyes meant dead.

"Do you know this gorilla, er, man?" Officer Willie said to me just as the buzzing in my head grew louder. I started to sway, but then I felt a strong hand ease me to the ground.

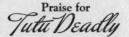

Pointe and Shoot

NATALIE M. ROBERTS

BERKLEY PRIME CRIME, NEW YORK

THE BERKLEY PUBLISHING GROUP
Published by the Penguin Group
Penguin Group (USA) Inc.
375 Hudson Street, New York, New York 10014, USA

Penguin Group (Canada), 90 Eglinton Avenue East, Suite 700, Toronto, Ontario M4P 2Y3, Canada
(a division of Pearson Penguin Canada Inc.)
Penguin Books Ltd., 80 Strand, London WC2R 0RL, England
Penguin Group Ireland, 25 St. Stephen's Green, Dublin 2, Ireland (a division of Penguin Books Ltd.)
Penguin Group (Australia), 250 Camberwell Road, Camberwell, Victoria 3124, Australia
(a division of Pearson Australia Group Pty. Ltd.)
Penguin Books India Pvt. Ltd., 11 Community Centre, Panchsheel Park, New Delhi—110 017, India
Penguin Group (NZ), 67 Apollo Drive, Rosedale, North Shore 0632, New Zealand
(a division of Pearson New Zealand Ltd.)
Penguin Books (South Africa) (Pty.) Ltd., 24 Sturdee Avenue, Rosebank, Johannesburg 2196,
South Africa

Penguin Books Ltd., Registered Offices: 80 Strand, London WC2R 0RL, England

This is a work of fiction. Names, characters, places, and incidents either are the product of the author's imagination or are used fictitiously, and any resemblance to actual persons, living or dead, business establishments, events, or locales is entirely coincidental. The publisher does not have any control over and does not assume any responsibility for author or third-party websites or their content.

POINTE AND SHOOT

A Berkley Prime Crime Book / published by arrangement with the author

PRINTING HISTORY
Berkley Prime Crime mass-market edition / May 2008

Copyright © 2008 by Natalie M. Roberts.
Cover art by Ben Perini.
Cover design by Rita Frangie.
Cover logo by axb group.
Interior text design by Kristin del Rosario.

ISBN: 978-0-425-22128-0

BERKLEY® PRIME CRIME
Berkley Prime Crime Books are published by The Berkley Publishing Group,
a division of Penguin Group (USA) Inc.,
375 Hudson Street, New York, New York 10014.
The name BERKLEY PRIME CRIME and the BERKLEY PRIME CRIME design
are trademarks belonging to Penguin Group (USA) Inc.

PRINTED IN THE UNITED STATES OF AMERICA

10 9 8 7 6 5 4 3 2 1

This book is dedicated to Makinzee Kemp, Savanna Kemp, Courtney Kemp, Josie Kemp, Anna Kemp, Raegan Kemp, Kenley Thiel, and the honorary Kemp, my own daughter Cambre. It doesn't matter where you dance—the music is always the same.

ACKNOWLEDGMENTS

First of all, I must thank Shannon Bryant, who suggested the awesome title for this book. Thanks, Shannon! As always, I must thank Calista Cates-Stanturf. She is my second pair of eyes, Jenny's biggest supporter, and a dauntless cheerleader and friend. I also am grateful for the Murdershewrites.com ladies, Jennifer Apodaca, Allison Brennan, Deborah LeBlanc, and Karin Tabke, for supporting me when the chips are down—and especially to Jen and Karin, who never fail to encourage me to continue writing the JTP books. Thanks also go to Gary Tabke, Officer Friendly, who never hesitates to take time out of his day to answer my "cop" questions, even when he would rather be watching football. Or coaching it. Or something like that.

My lovely editor, Sandra Harding, and my wonderful agent, Karen Solem, always get kudos, because, of course, they deserve them.

And to my daughters, Carissa and Cambre, who really are my reason for getting out of bed every morning. Even when it's really, really cold out there . . .

ONE

ONE OF THE MOST HUMILIATING CHILDHOOD experiences I can recall revolves directly around dance. In fact, it was so bad that I'm surprised I can still shake my groove thing without having flashbacks. My dance teacher, Miss Larae, was tall and skinny and regal with long ballet arms and legs, a sharp pointy nose, and small beady eyes. At least that's how I remember her. She resembled my weird teenage neighbor's ferret.

"Jennifer T. Partridge," she would say, in her low, nasal voice, "buttocks tucked under. Tummy in. Fifth position." And I would try, but I had a hard time tucking my tummy in—even back then. It just naturally wanted to poke out. I was, after all, only six. But I stood with my left hand on the barre, holding the position, trying as hard as I could to suck my stomach in, praying she wouldn't notice me. She always did.

I was midway down the barre, trying to blend in with the line of little ballerinas, all dressed in pink leotards, pink tights, and pink ballet shoes. Then she spotted me, her ferret eyes zooming in on my form.

The ferret had found its prey. Me. She swiftly headed toward me, carrying the long pointy stick she always had in her hand, and I cringed and tried to stay perfectly still, perhaps to camouflage myself. Nature's trick did not work. So much for all those documentaries my science-teacher dad made me watch.

"Jennifer T. Partridge, what is this?" she said, in her harsh, strident voice, and she pushed on my tummy with her pointy stick. It didn't hurt. And it might not have been so embarrassing, except I had been concentrating so hard on using the right form, the right turnout, everything taut and tucked in, that it didn't take much but that little poke to knock me off balance, and over I went—and in turn, each of the other girls in line toppled, too. Just like the dominoes I sometimes played with my dad.

"It could happen to anyone," my mother reassured me. But I was having none of that. My career would have to start over somewhere else—because even then, I knew I was born to dance.

I didn't leave the state, or even the city. In fact, I had to deal with Miss Larae for four more years before my mother moved me to another, more progressive studio that also offered jazz, tap, and modern in addition to the standard ballet. You already know my name is Jenny T. Partridge, and you probably figured out I'm a dance teacher. I own a studio in Ogden, Utah, which is home to a couple of pretty good ski resorts, Weber State University, Ogden's historic 25th Street—where my studio is located—and not a whole lot else.

Don't get me wrong. I like Ogden. And I've lived here all my life. But it is not high on the list of the nation's cultural hot spots. Still, there is plenty to do, and after a bum knee cut short my dreams of the stage and films, I settled in here. It was my fate.

Today, I watched poor Whitney Forrest—among the worst of the balance challenged—cry as the little girls around her giggled and pointed. This time she'd landed flat on her butt. The other girls had learned pretty quickly to move out of her way when she was doing a turn. She usually started in Ogden, but was so wild, her arms flailing as she moved, I half expected her to end up in Salt Lake City. But my job was to teach her, and teach her I would.

I grabbed Whitney by the hand and pulled her to her feet. I put all the girls back in their line and turned on the music, Whitney dried her eyes, and soon practice was back under way.

It was early April, and there was just a little over one week before our first competition, after all, and I wanted to do really well this year. I had plans to grow my studio, and Marco and Jack, my landlords who had a business downstairs, had offered to give me office space on their floor, in a small room, so that I could turn my larger upstairs office into a dance store.

This was a big step, and I knew it. It would require a substantial investment, and even though my parents had offered to help me, I was leery of placing their life savings in my less-than-capable hands.

But I was tired of getting by foot to mouth. I was also tired of trying to find a decent costume designer who didn't attempt to strengthen her moral fiber by covering my dancers from head to toe. We did live in the land of Mormons, but it was dance! The costumes were supposed to be a little brief.

"All right, girls," I said, clapping my hands together. "That's good for today. We only have three more practices until competition, and you know that great big trophy they give at the Dance-o-Rama? For the overall winner?"

"Oooh, yeah, I like that one," Whitney said, her earlier embarrassment forgotten. From the other room I could hear the noises of the next arriving teams—the Smalls and Petites.

"Well, if you girls do really good and you win that trophy, then we will have an ice cream party!" Squeals of glee erupted from them, their eyes sparkling with the thought of ice cream. My eyes sparkled, too. I wasn't squealing, though. That was *not* me.

"What's all the fuss about?" asked James, who taught for me and was also a friend—and a thorn in my side, due to his constant shenanigans. He'd sauntered in followed closely by Sal Tuatuola. Sal was subbing for Amber for the next eight months, while she worked on a cruise ship doing musical productions. While she was off sipping exotic drinks in foreign parts—or was that ports?—I was contemplating ice cream parties with six-year-olds. Oh well. I liked ice cream more than alcohol anyway.

"Just trying to jazz them up for next week's comp," I said.

"Ice cream party?" James asked.

"Yup."

"Jennifer, you are so predictable."

"Everyone likes ice cream."

"I like ice cream," Sal added helpfully. Sal was a very large, tall Samoan with warm cocoa brown skin, a flat nose, big brown eyes, and the dance moves of some of the best choreographers in the business. He just didn't look the part. When I first met him, he'd had a very short haircut, but in the past few months he'd started growing his hair out, and now he was sporting a pretty decent Afro. He looked like he should be cracking heads at nightclubs. Instead, he was really good at teaching dance to kids. I knew he was probably destined for bigger things, but for now, he was stuck here, because he hadn't really been dancing that long, only since he had bolted from his Mormon mission and showed up on my doorstep begging me to let him teach dance. The man had a mission all right, but it was not to preach the Mormon gospel. And that whole thing was actually working out really well for me, except I was sure I was on some list somewhere at the Mormon Church headquarters.

It was just going to have to be that way, because I had bigger chickens to fry. As surprised as I was to admit it, I needed Sal. After the Dance-o-Rama, I had exactly one week until the Ultimate Dance Championships, otherwise known as UDC. Trophies were nice, but I already had a lot of them. I'd run out of room to display them at the studio and had taken to giving them away to different girls after each competition. But at UDC, they gave away something more than trophies—the top team took home twenty-five hundred dollars! And I was determined to win that cash. In the world of dancing kids, the prizes didn't get bigger than that.

With that money I might be able to start up my little dance store, without so much help from my parents, and maybe, just maybe, for the first time in my life, have actual groceries in my fridge and cupboards, instead of Top Ramen and mac and cheese. That was my goal.

"So, what's the plan, Jen?" Sal asked. I stared at him for a moment, wondering if he had heard those wheels turning in my head, then realized he meant for class. And of course he would be the one to ask. James never actually went to work until he was directly told, but Sal was an eager beaver.

"James, you take the Smalls and clean their jazz and hip-hop routines. Sal, you are with the Petites. That jazz routine is looking really rough, and it needs serious cleaning. The hip-hop is stronger, so concentrate on the jazz first."

"Follow me, Petites," Sal hollered, and the girls gathered around him, chattering excitedly. The Smalls looked really disappointed they were stuck with James. Sal was a bit more fun, and James was a rough taskmaster, but the man knew dance.

"Let's get going," James said, sashaying to the front of the room. "Stretching out. Straight lines."

I walked into my small office and sat down for a moment, closing my eyes and allowing myself to dream of winning that money. I really, really wanted it. No, I needed it. I needed a change. I loved dance, and couldn't see myself doing anything else but teaching—and I was woefully unqualified for any other job—but I just wanted to do it more . . . successfully.

"Uh, Jen?" I opened my eyes to see Marlys, my friend, dance mom, and general john-of-all-trades. You name it, she did it at the studio, and I'd be lost without her. And I helped her out by trading her for dance lessons for her two daughters, Carly and Maribel. "There's a gorilla out here and he says he has a message for you."

"A what?"

A vision from a bad late-night movie stepped into the doorway, and I did one of those classic double takes. "Gorilla-Gram, ma'am," said a muffled voice through a ratty-looking gorilla mask. The whole costume was pretty ratty looking actually, and this particular ape was in some serious need of grooming, but I suspected no self-respecting female primate would get within ten feet of him.

Lucky me. But why was he here? It wasn't my birthday, there was no major holiday right now, and I had certainly not accomplished anything that would entitle me to a Gorilla-Gram. I hoped, anyway.

"You must have the wrong person."

"You Jenny Partridge?"

"Well, yes, but I can't imagine why anyone would possibly send me this, uh, Gorilla-Gram thing today. So it has to be a mistake."

"Look, lady, I make minimum wage and I have to wear this stinky, smelly, stupid gorilla suit all day, so just let me deliver the message and be on my way, okay? And a tip would be nice, too."

This gorilla had attitude. And he didn't wait for my answer.

"Jenny P., Jenny P., I have to say, long time no see," he sang in an off-tune voice, trying to do a few dance steps at the same time, and failing horribly. "You think you're great, but you're second-rate, and now I'm back to pick up your slack. Look out for me, Jenny P."

The gorilla did an awkward little two-step, then stood with one hand up and one down, like he was Fred Astaire or something. Marlys and I both stared, trying to figure out what the heck we had just heard.

"Can you sing that again?" Marlys asked.

"It'll cost you," Apeman said.

"Who hired you?" I asked. I tried to do a quick rundown of my enemies, particularly those who might think I was second-rate. It had to be someone in the dance world, right? I didn't do much outside of teaching dance, and everyone knew that a lot of those people were seriously whacked. But you could call me second-rate in just about anything else and be right. Just not in dance. So if this was about dance, it was definitely a message from a whack job.

"Yeah, who hired you?" Marlys demanded. She was looking pretty aggressive, hands on her hips, mom face on. In fact, I thought I saw her eye twitch.

"They wanted to remain anonymous," he answered.

An anonymous whack job. My favorite kind.

"Look, Sasquatch, you tell us who hired you, or I'll rip that mask off your head and shove it . . ."

"Whoa, Marlys," I said, staring at her aghast. "Not drinking coffee again?"

"Yeah. Does it show?"

"Yeah, just a bit."

"Look, I'm done. I delivered the message, so let's get this over with so I can go to my next gig."

"Gig," Marlys said with a disdainful snort. "You call this job a gig?"

"Look, lady . . ." The Apeman took a step toward her, and Marlys's face changed into her "bring it on" look. Scarier than the mom face. And it was twice as scary when she was craving caffeine. This guy did not know who he was messing with. She wrangled psycho dance moms on a daily basis. A scrawny guy in a bad gorilla suit was no match for her.

"Fine, I'll leave then. And no tip?" Apeman said, apparently catching that crazed gleam in Marlys's eye through the eyeholes in his mask. "Cheap jerks."

"Why would I tip you for that? That was *not* a nice message you just sang to me. And you're not good at singing. You should get a new job."

"I'm not good at singing? Well, apparently, you suck at dancing, so I guess we're even," he shot back.

This time, *I* was going to rip the mask off his head and shove it . . .

"Wow, a gorilla. That's unusual, even for you," Tate Wilson said as he walked through the door. "Part of a new routine? George of the Jungle?"

"Gorilla-Gram," Marlys corrected him. "Not a very nice gorilla, either."

"Yikes, the cops," said Apeman, apparently eyeing Tate's gun. "Gotta split. Pun intended."

"Wait a minute. Stop him, Tate. I need to know who sent me this nasty message and he won't tell me."

Tate Wilson was my sorta boyfriend and an Ogden City Police detective. He'd been around me enough to know that my life was somewhat unusual. I seemed to be a weird magnet. That didn't seem to bother him. Tate was also fairly tall, with a wicked-handsome face, a dangerous-looking scar over his eye, and a very hot body. That part didn't bother me. At all. He was also "independently wealthy," something I had never been, thus I really didn't understand what it entailed. And he didn't do a lot of explaining about anything. That bothered me a bit.

"So, Mr. Gorilla, what's the story?" he asked, using his cop glare. But I knew him well enough to see the glint of humor in his dark blue eyes.

"Look, I'm just doing my job, trying to earn an honest living. Someone gives me the message, pays the money, I deliver it."

"I think I'm going to want you to take the mask off," Tate said.

"Hey, I have four more Gorilla-Grams to deliver. This thing is murder to get on and off. I really need to go."

"Take the mask off, now, please." Even though Tate's words were nice, his tone was not. Apeman got the message.

He pulled the mask off to reveal scraggly brown hair, wet with sweat, feral eyes, pockmarked sallow skin, and an angry slash of mouth. The mask was better.

"Now, what was the message you brought to Jenny?" Tate asked harshly.

The Apeman sighed impatiently. "Do I have to sing it again?"

"Please don't," I·said. "Just recite it."

"It doesn't have the same impact," he protested.

"We'll get by," I said.

"Jenny P., Jenny P., I have to say, long time no see. You think you're great, but you're second-rate, and now I'm back to pick up your slack. Look out for me, Jenny P."

"Heartwarming," Tate said. "And who is this from?"

"He won't say," Marlys said, pointing an accusing finger at the Apeman.

"The sender wished to remain anonymous," he insisted stubbornly.

"What kind of a business are you running, anyway?" Marlys asked, her voice strident and harsh. Definitely needed caffeine.

"Wished to remain anonymous as in paid you on the side and told you to keep the change?" Tate asked drolly.

"Something like that," Monkey Man muttered.

"Male, female, tall, short?"

"Female, medium, blond hair, nice looking, big . . . uh, never mind."

"Age?"

"Dunno. Around thirty or so. Drove a nice ride. Big old Hummer."

Hummer? Hummer! A chill ran from the top of my head down my neck and I shivered. I'd had some real problems with a silver Hummer for quite a while now. First shots were fired from a silver Hummer at me and some friends, and then what I swore was the same vehicle tried to run me off the road. This could not be a coincidence, could it?

"Silver Hummer?" Tate asked. He knew all about the deadly vehicle, too.

"Hmm, yeah. Silver. Drove by me on the street, about a block from here. Saw me walking and pulled over. The lady scribbled the note, passed me a fift—er, twenty, and then told me where to deliver the Gorilla-Gram."

"Anything else you can think of?"

"Nah, man."

"Okay, I'm going to need your name and address, and phone number."

"What for? All I did was sing a stupid song, man. This is getting ridiculous."

"In case I need to contact you again," Tate said shortly, without a smile.

"Fine. Albert Cunningham, 6520 Madison. Number's 555-0987."

Tate scribbled down the information on his always-present notepad. "Okay, scram."

"What, still no tip? After all that info?"

Tate slipped a five into his hand, and the gorilla man disappeared, pulling his mask back onto his face as he left.

"Well, that's just great. The darned silver Hummer again. I was hoping that was just a bad nightmare from the past," I said.

"Well, actually, we have a few solid clues now. We know the driver is a thirty-something blond woman, she doesn't think much of your dance ability, and apparently, she dances, too." Tate frowned. "Does this ring any bells for you?"

There were all kinds of bells going off in my head, but they were more of the alarm variety, not the "Wow, I know who that is" kind.

"I figured this was all over, done, past, you know? I'm not really up for more of this kind of drama," I said, aware I was talking *way* too fast, but unable to slow my words down. "I just want to have a nice, calm competition season, and maybe win that overall money prize from UDC, and start my own little dance store so I can outfit my girls and maybe make a little bit of money, and then, maybe . . ."

"Jenny?" Tate said gently. He put a hand on my shoulder, and I stopped rambling. "It's going to be okay. As long as I'm around, no one is going to hurt you again, okay? I won't let you out of my sight. In fact, I think that you better come stay with me tonight. I'll pick you up when your last class is done. Six o'clock, right?"

"Right, six. No, wait! It's seven. The Seniors get done at seven." His touch could do that to me. Calm me down and scramble my brains all at the same time.

"Okay, I'll be here at seven."

"Jennnnnifferrr," I heard James call from the other room. "This is a mess, simply a mess. You *must* come fix it."

"Duty calls," I said with a sigh. Tate leaned down and kissed me softly and then waved good-bye to Marlys, who stood there with a slack-jawed, uncomprehending look on her face. She was really not dealing well with the caffeine withdrawal. This was worse than usual.

"Hey, wait," I hollered after him. "Why did you come by?"

"To tell you I was going to pick you up after you got off dance," he said smoothly, with a slightly wicked smile. Then he left. Boy, did that scene work out so I played right into his hands. What did I care? I was Silly Putty when Tate was around. Most of the time.

"You need caffeine," I said to Marlys, pushing her toward the door. "Go. I'll take a double skinny mocha latte, sugar free. I need caffeine, too."

"But I'm trying to quit."

"You can't function. And what's the big deal with a little caffeine, anyway?"

"They say it's not good for you."

"Who is 'they'? And what the heck do 'they' know, anyway? Name one good thing you ever learned from a 'they.'" She just stared at me, and made my point. One for Jenny! "You need caffeine. And I need a poppy-seed muffin, too."

She quit arguing and left. She knew she needed caffeine as much as I knew it.

I hurried in to help James with his "emergency" and tried to put the Gorilla-Gram and the silver Hummer out of my mind. But it wasn't going to be easy.

Someone really didn't much like me. And that same someone was getting even more aggressive.

I was awfully glad Tate was picking me up after dance.

Two

BELIEVE IT OR NOT, GORILLA-GRAMS, SIL-
ver Hummers, and mysterious enemies were the least of
my problems.

The Seniors dance needed help. Serious help. And I was
stumped as to how to fix it. James had a hot date—of
course—and had left, but Sal had spent quite a while with
me, trying to fix the problems. And it wasn't working. Marlys
had taken off when the Petites were done—but not before
giving me my latte and poppy-seed muffin, bless her heart.

Now, the studio was empty save Sal and I, and it seemed
to echo with the foretelling of my upcoming failure. If I
was going to win that money, all of my dances had to be
special, because judges were funny. They might like the
older girls, or they might like the younger ones. You just
never knew. But whatever they saw from our studio, it had
to be unique, innovative, and the best it could possibly be.
The kind of stuff that sent chills up your arms. So far, I
couldn't think of one routine that qualified. And I could see
that money just slipping out of my grasp.

Sal gave me that puppy-dog look that told me he felt as though he had failed me. I hated that look.

"It doesn't look good, does it?" he said glumly.

"The problem is, it's not unique, or special. It's good, but not good enough. I need spectacular. That one amazing routine that just wows them. And none of these are it."

I sat down on the hardwood floor, and put my head in my hands.

"I'm sorry, Jenny. I really tried."

I looked up at Sal. "Look, Sal, this is not your fault. I just have a lot riding on this, and you're pretty new to the business. You are incredible, don't get me wrong, and with a few more years behind you, I know you are going to go places."

"But that doesn't help you now." I swear, he was going to cry, and I did *not* want the big Samoan blubbering.

"I'll think of something. Don't take this personally. You're doing a great job."

"Are you sure?" His eyes still looked pretty moist.

"I'm sure."

If Sal were a puppy dog, he would have had his tail tucked between his legs as he left. It wasn't his fault. He was a product of his environment. Frankly, so was I. This needed something unique and unusual.

"Hey, I have an idea," Sal said, causing me to jump. Since I thought he'd left, he surprised me. The man moved like a cat, amazing for a man of his size. But then again he danced that way, too.

"What?" I asked, as I rose from my sitting position on the floor.

"Let's do a Company routine. You know, an audition routine. Only the best dancers from each team. Everybody can try out, but you only pick the best ones."

"Are you trying to get me killed? Have you met these moms?" I saw nothing but grief in this idea. Tell a mother her daughter isn't the best, and watch the claws come out.

And yet . . . If I put a few of my strongest dancers together, girls like Carly Fulton and Annabelle Hilton and Ashley Franks, and added a few strong Seniors and gave small parts to some of the better little girls . . .

"Yeah?" Sal said expectantly. "You're seeing it, aren't you? We can find a cool hip-hop mix, maybe with some classy jazz thrown in, and whammo! Fabulous routine."

"This could work. Every mom whose daughter doesn't make it will want my blood, but the better we get as a studio, the better they look. And I really want to win that money."

"Then let's do it. I'll spend the night finding the perfect music mix. I do that, too, you know. We can work on choreography tomorrow morning. Say, ten-ish?"

"Ten-ish it is. You're an interesting man, Sal."

"I know. It just used to be hidden behind a name tag, a white shirt, and a short haircut. If I never ride a bicycle again . . ."

He shook his head as he turned and walked away, then he stopped and turned back to me. "Oh, hey, Jenny, should I stay and walk you out? It's getting dark out, and you seem to be a magnet for crazy people."

"No, Tate is coming to pick me up. But thanks, Sal. I'll see you in the morning."

I followed him to the door, and turned the dead bolt after closing it behind him. I might be a slow learner in some things, but the past few months had made me very safety conscious. After I locked up, I walked through the studio picking up stray bobby pins, ballet shoes, gore boots, and various other items like jackets and sweatshirts—things the girls always left behind. My lost-and-found pile was huge. Time to give a warning and then take whatever was left over to the Deseret Industries, the local thrift store run by the Mormon Church. I hoped my picture wasn't on a bulletin board there, like the ones they had in the post office for America's most wanted.

As I worked, my mind buzzed with ideas for a Company routine, and I wondered what Sal would come up with for music and moves. After I finished cleaning up, I ran a broom over the two studio floors, then gathered up my purse and keys, and looked at my watch. It was 7:20 p.m. Where the heck was Tate? I fished my phone out of my purse. Great. It was dead. I'd managed to keep ahold of this one for quite a while, a feat for me. However, the darned things only worked well if you kept them charged. I couldn't remember the last time I'd plugged mine into the charger at home. Maybe it was subconscious, so I could avoid the zillions of phone calls from psycho dance moms.

But Tate knew my studio number, and I hadn't heard that phone ring, either. I walked into the office and flipped on the light, and immediately saw why. There was no handset in the base. One of the girls had come in here to use the phone—despite my strict rules against it—and carried off the handset. Who knew where I would find it? Once it was in the bathroom garbage, another time in the base of a fake potted palm. I didn't really get some people's children.

I searched both of those places but couldn't find the handset. I hit the Page button on the base and listened closely, but heard nothing. I couldn't remember the last time I used the phone in here. Usually, Marlys was right on top of those things, but she'd been pretty distracted today, what with major caffeine withdrawal. I don't know why she read those women's magazines. Always gave her crazy ideas, like the day she decided we were going on the liver cleanse diet. Lemon juice, maple syrup, and cayenne pepper? *Yeesh.* I might have to make do with something like that during the lean times, when I had no money and no food, but I sure as heck wasn't going to do it on purpose.

I searched a few more places for the missing handset, then gave up. My answering machine had been appropriated by the police during an investigation into some dancers who went missing from the Hollywood StarMakers Convention and Competition, and even though Tate had given it back, I'd never bothered to hook it back up. Just one more way for the psycho dance moms to reach me. So there was no message. Even if he had called, I wouldn't know it. The phone *did* have caller ID—located in the missing handset, of course.

Tate had probably encountered yet another one of his endless emergencies (him being a detective had some downsides), and so I was on my own.

I shut off the studio lights, unlocked the dead bolt, stepped out the door, and turned and put my key in the lock, clicking it. Just then, I heard a high-pitched, bloodcurdling scream, and I turned to see a huge form streaking toward me, fast—really fast. The hair stood up on the back of my neck. Instinct kicked in and I quickly inserted the key back in the lock as the figure bounded up the metal steps leading to my studio, the entire staircase bouncing and reverberating as the monster headed toward me. I heard the click of the lock, pushed the door open, and tried to step inside just as a hand grabbed my arm and a voice screamed, "Jenny!" I screamed right back and turned, pulling my arm from the intruder's grasp, then watched as the figure went head over heels down the metal staircase.

"Ohhh," came a moan, one I recognized. The blur of the intensity of the moment began to fade, and I realized that form had seemed mighty familiar.

Sal!

I bounded down the steps two at a time to the motionless and crumpled form on the ground. "Sal? Oh my God, Sal, what were you doing? Are you okay? Oh my God."

"Is everything all right, lady?" came a voice out of the darkness, and I jumped and turned to see one of the many homeless people that populated Ogden's 25th Street.

"No, can you go call 911?" It was a long shot, but I had to get help for my unconscious friend.

"Doncha have a cell phone? Ever'body has one of them," said the man, stepping a bit closer. Sweat broke out on my forehead. I was alone here with an injured Sal, no phone, and the place was pretty deserted. During the weekend people were always entering and exiting the restaurants and bars that populated our street, and even though the entrance to my studio came out on the back end of 25th, most of the restaurants had back entrances. We also faced the Marriott Hotel's big parking lot, which meant people were parking and coming and going—but not tonight.

"I . . . I . . ." I had to protect myself and Sal. "Oh, wait, here it is," I said, reaching into my purse and grabbing my cell phone. I pretended to dial 911 and spoke into the phone hurriedly as the night denizen hurried off, scared away by the word "police."

When I could see him no longer, I looked back down at Sal. His eyes were wide open and staring at me. "Whoa, are you okay?"

"Who are you?" he asked. "My leg hurts. Can I get some aspirin?"

This was just great.

"Which leg?" I asked. The headlights of a car pulling into the Marriott parking lot illuminated the darkness, and I yelled for help. A young woman came running over, and I recognized the special events manager who had helped me to organize Bill Flanagan's Hollywood StarMakers competition, right before the whole thing blew up—kinda literally. That was at the same time my answering machine was appropriated. Long story.

"Oh, it's you," she said, her eye twitching. I guess I could understand that.

"Can you call 911 please? He's fallen down the stairs. He doesn't seem to know who he is and he says his leg hurts."

She pulled her cell phone out of her purse and quickly dialed, efficiently telling the dispatcher what was wrong and then asking me a quick series of questions, which I relayed to Sal. Most of them were answered with a "Who are you? Can I have an aspirin?"

If he started asking for his Book of Mormon, we were in real trouble.

The lights of a police cruiser soon bounced off the surrounding buildings, and I heard the wail of an ambulance siren. Within a few minutes, Sal had been assessed and strapped onto a gurney.

"Is he going to be okay?" I asked Bones, the paramedic I knew from ride-alongs I'd gone on back when I was still trying to play with grown-ups in the real world and had worked briefly at the sheriff's office as a 911 dispatcher.

"Yeah, he'll live. That leg is going to take some healing, though. Busted in two places. Compound." I winced. I knew what that meant. Oh why did I have to learn that? "And he keeps asking who we are. Maybe some temporary amnesia."

I hurried over to the stretcher and said, "Sal? Sal, are you okay? I'm so sorry."

"Who are you? Can I have an aspirin?" he asked, and then he winked. I swear to God, he did. A quick wink, his eyes sharp and alert, and then he went back to moaning.

"Sal, stop it. Right now. You don't have amnesia and you know it. If you don't quit faking it, I'm gonna call the Mormons and tell them you've changed your mind and want to finish out your mission." That did it.

His eyes opened wide, and he said, "Okay, Jenny. Okay. *Sheesh.* Don't do that. I just always thought it would be cool to have amnesia." Sorta like it would be cool to be a dance teacher. What was next? An astronaut? I shivered. "It really does hurt, though. Good thing I have a high pain tolerance."

"Good thing he's on morphine," Bones added.

"Sal, why did you come screaming toward me? Why did you scare me? I don't understand."

"Screaming?" He was getting pretty woozy now. The morphine was kicking in. "Oh yeah. When I was driving home, I checked my cell and I'd missed a call from Tate. He left a message asking me to walk you to your truck and follow you, and make sure you got home safe, since he got called out on a case. So I turned my car around and came back. I parked next to your truck. When I got out, I saw this big furry creature in your front seat, and it was staring at me. I swear, it looked like Bigfoot. It scared me. So I ran."

And screamed. And scared me. And I knocked him down the stairs. I sighed. Then his words hit me.

Big furry creature? Bigfoot?

"Sorry, Jen, but we really have to take him now," Bones said, and they wheeled Sal off and into the ambulance. There were still plenty of police officers around, but I wasn't sure I wanted to explain to anyone that Bigfoot was sitting in my truck and I needed some assistance getting him out.

Could Sal have just seen a shadow? That scream of his was pretty high-pitched. He was a little high-strung. Maybe he was seeing things.

Finally, I decided my reputation was probably already well cemented with anyone within thirty miles of Ogden, due to my encounters with some crazy psycho dance moms and some crazy psychos in general, and so I approached the police officer who had taken the report on the incident. His name tag said Officer Willie. He was young and tall and stout. He also had a lot of hair everywhere but on his head. He'd given me a lot of suspicious looks as I'd explained what had happened. I couldn't blame him. It seemed suspicious; Sal had better cut out his amnesia act and back me up, or I was going to break his other leg.

"Officer Willie, Sal just told me that he parked his car next to my truck, and when he got out, he saw a big furry creature in my front seat, and that's what scared him. I told you he came toward me screaming, and that's what startled me."

Officer Willie slowly turned his head toward me. His eyes blinked, slowly, and he didn't smile, just stared at me.

I turned my head a little bit and offered a faint smile, like I'd seen women do on television when the hard-nosed detective was staring them down. It didn't phase him. Apparently, I was not one of *those* kind of women.

"A big *furry* creature?" he finally said, not breaking the stare. Blinking only occasionally. Enough to make me think he was planning to send me to the gas chamber.

"Um, yeah, that's what he said." I did the half-smile thing again, but again it had no effect.

"Where is said vehicle?"

Said vehicle?

"Uh, over here." I pointed to Bessie, my father's old truck. I'd been driving her since I'd lost my Pepto Mobile in a firebombing. More of those psychos. Officer Willie followed me while speaking into his radio, and he motioned to another officer, who came toward us as we headed to the truck.

As we drew closer, I could see there was indeed something inside my car, passenger side, human size. My stomach clenched, the hair on the back of my neck stood up, and I stopped dead in my tracks. I tried to breathe, but my heart was racing in my chest. Officer Willie looked at the other officer, and they told me to get back.

They both drew their weapons, and Willie yelled, "Police! Get out of the vehicle now, hands up over your head."

The shape didn't move.

"Police! I said get out of the vehicle now!"

Still nothing. My breathing had not improved, my head began to swim, and I watched as though from a long way away as they crept up on the vehicle, guns aimed, and quickly opened the door. The big shape fell out and hit the ground with a large *thunk*.

"It's a gorilla," Officer Willie said. He reached down and with a few good yanks pulled the mask off. A beelike buzz filled my ears and brain as I stared at the dead man. The cops' flashlights illuminated that same feral face I'd seen just hours before, delivering a Gorilla-Gram. Albert Cunningham.

The other officer was feeling for a pulse, but I knew there wasn't one. I'd never been this close to a dead body before—unless you counted the time I fell into the Dumpster on top of a dead hip-hop teacher. Hmm, I guessed that counted, but it had happened really fast and I don't remember a lot about it—but I'd watched enough television to know that wide-open, glassy eyes meant dead.

"Do you know this gorilla, er, man?" Officer Willie said to me just as the buzzing in my head grew louder. I started to sway, but then I felt a strong hand ease me to the ground.

"Head between your knees. This is not the time to pass out," Tate's strong, warm voice said.

THREE

TATE CONFIRMED THAT THE DEAD APE WAS indeed Mr. Gorilla-Gram, aka Albert Cunningham. Officer Willie gave me a very hard look, which Tate was kind enough to return for me, since I was currently out of hard looks and was just trying to keep from passing out. The uniformed policeman's eyes swung from me to Tate, and it was a standoff. Officer Willie looked away first. I was proud of Tate, although I had no idea why.

As the two of us stood there, I heard Officer Willie radio for a crime-scene unit. The reality of the situation was sinking in. Once again, I was in a bit of a jam, which would require paperwork, and paperwork, and mountains of more paperwork, and time, and there was dead body, and . . . Oh, my head was starting to buzz again.

"Stop thinking," Tate ordered me; Officer Willie gave him a funny look, and then his lip twitched. He never smiled, though. This was one serious cop. He turned away and walked over to the body, presumably to await the crime-scene investigators.

"You just told me not to think in front of another cop," I said to Tate. "I'm thinking that wasn't a compliment."

"I just meant I could practically hear the wheels turning in your head, and I didn't want you to freak yourself out and pass out."

"Oh, what's to freak out about? Just a dead gorilla in my truck, Sal on his way to the hospital, my career on the brink of the toilet again, and who knows what will happen next?"

"Perhaps you should have thought about it before you made your career choice and entered the dangerous world of teaching dance."

"Funny."

"Seriously, Jenny, I don't know how you find yourself in these situations," Tate said softly, his compassion undoing me inside a little, making me melt. "Now what's this about Sal?"

"Sal got your message to see me home after he'd already left, so he came back and parked next to Bessie. He got out, saw the gorilla in my front seat, thought it was a visitation from Bigfoot, screamed like a little girl, and came running up the stairs just as I was locking the front door and heading down. He scared me with the scream, and I didn't know who it was. Then he grabbed my arm, I yanked it back, and he fell down the stairs."

"Ouch."

"Yeah, ouch, two compound fractures."

"Double ouch."

"What's going on here, Tate? Why would someone kill that Gorilla-Gram guy and put him in my truck? It couldn't be to frame me, because I have forty kids and two teachers who can give me alibis. It must be a warning. But what? Stay away from the zoo? Don't go on a hunt for Sasquatch?"

"Well, the gorilla was the link to the Hummer. Whoever is inside that Hummer obviously doesn't want to be found, but still can't keep from tormenting you, too."

"I don't think I like this at all."

"Me, either," Tate said grimly. "Let's finish up the paperwork and get you out of here. Your truck is evidence, so we'll have to get it later. I'm taking you home to my place."

Tate's condo was safe. And comfy. And he had real food there. The only bad thing that had ever happened to me at Tate's place was an inquisition by the local Mormon mission leaders when Sal had gone on the lam after deciding he didn't want to be a missionary anymore. Going to Tate's place sounded like a good idea to me.

I SPENT A LONG TIME IN TATE'S BIG SHOWER, letting the hot water beat down on my very tight shoulder muscles. This dead-body business was hard on a girl. I'd invited Tate to join me, but he declined, saying he needed to make a few calls and then he'd fix us some dinner.

I was a little miffed, but I wasn't really in the mood for hanky-panky anyway, not with all that had happened. Poor Sal was still in surgery when Tate called the hospital inquiring about him, and it would be early morning before he would be coherent, so Tate convinced me that going to the hospital now would be useless. Still, I felt like I should be there.

I reluctantly turned off the hot water, got out of the shower, and dried myself with a warm, fluffy towel. Everything that Tate surrounded himself with was nice, and warm, and comfortable. Stylish, too. With the possible exception of me. I was the thorn in the lily bush. That and his job.

I didn't want to wonder too deeply about that tonight, because I wanted the comfort of his arms around me. I was seriously spooked by the dead gorilla guy and mysterious Hummer.

I dressed quickly in a pair of sweats and T-shirt I had

stashed over at Tate's, ran a comb through my hair, which was already curling despite still being wet, then pulled a small bottle of moisturizer out of my purse, which I had carried to the bathroom with me. I'd come prepared. I wasn't getting any younger. The face needed moisturizer. Especially my redheaded, china-doll face. After that, I padded out to the kitchen. The elegant tile was cool on my feet, and the smell of cooking food was enticing.

"That took some time," Tate said from the stove, where he stirred something that smelled like marinara sauce. I could smell garlic, and a steaming pot of noodles sat on the counter, so I knew I was right.

"I was pampering myself. I'm not getting any younger, you know. You have to pay attention after you turn twenty-five."

He gave me a sharp look.

"I didn't say I *was* twenty-five, I just said that you have to pay attention," I protested.

Sheesh. The man was severely hung up on honesty, even when it consisted of conveniently phrased words.

"Dinner's ready," he announced.

The table was nicely set with what looked like real china—it sure wasn't something from Wal-Mart, or the mismatched set of my mother's old dinner plates that sat in my cupboard, gathering dust.

The silverware was all from the same set, and there were cloth—*cloth!*—napkins on the table. I stared at it in awe. I was properly wowed—and another twinge of something ran through me. I felt completely out of place. Like that one sock that you can just never find the mate for, but you really, really hate to throw it away, because you know as soon as you do, the other one will turn up and you will regret throwing it away for the rest of your life. But if you hadn't thrown it away, the other one would never have turned up, because that's just the way things work, and . . .

"You're thinking again," Tate said, a half grin on his face.

"You always make that sound like a bad thing."

"There are a lot of ways to 'think,' and I can usually tell when you are in that mind-spinning, tongue-before-brain mode that gets you into trouble, so that's what I mean when I say that."

"Your life is awfully organized, neat, and comfortable," I blurted out.

"Exactly what I meant," he said, shaking his head slightly.

"Well, it is," I protested. "Look at this table. The only way something at my place would look like this was if I moved into a furniture store! Your house is always clean, your towels are always soft, your shower is always hot . . . I'm the lone sock here. I don't fit. You don't want to throw me away, because it's always possible the other one will turn up, but sooner or later you are going to realize you have no use for me, except maybe as a dust rag."

"Good God, Jenny." He grimaced, and walked over to me and pulled me into an embrace. "You are weird. I have nice things because I have money to buy nice things. You know that. My towels are soft because they cost a lot and my cleaning lady buys a great fabric softener, and the house is spotless because she gets paid a pretty penny to keep it that way. Yes, my life is very ordered. I like it that way. But I also like surprises, and spontaneity, and I like to laugh. I'm too tight and structured as it is. We've discussed this before. You *do* fit here, because I need you. I need you to keep things different."

"Different? What do you mean by different?" I wasn't sure that I was flattered by his explanation, so I pulled back and looked at him sharply, and he laughed, throwing back his head.

"That is exactly what I mean. Now can we eat?"

I gave him another look, but then my stomach smelled the spaghetti and garlic and warm yeasty bread, and told me that yes, we could eat. We could talk about different later. Maybe.

$\mathscr{F}$OUR

WHEN I WOKE UP THE NEXT MORNING, TATE was gone. That was normal. He was Superman. Who needed sleep? Me, that's who. And I must have had some wicked dreams, because the covers were off the bed, and I felt more tired than I had last night. Usually, I slept like a tree in Tate's bed, because it was so comfortable. Today, I felt as though I needed toothpicks to keep my eyes open. And I had dance to teach. In fact, I had solo lessons scheduled at . . . I sat up, my eyes wide. I turned to the alarm clock and gulped! It was almost noon. Tamara Freaking Williams would skin me alive if I missed one more solo lesson, and I'd promised her I'd be there on time. She was taking her daughter April out of school on her lunch hour to get this solo lesson in, and so time was limited. Tamara was already convinced I had it out for April, and favored Carly, Marlys's daughter, over her. The fact that Carly was a better dancer—and a nicer person—meant nothing to her.

I jumped out of the bed, hurriedly made it up—because I might have mentioned how orderly Tate's house and life are—and then ran into the bathroom where I quickly splashed water onto my face, ran my brush through my hair, pulled it into a ponytail to tame the curls, and changed into the spare dance clothes in my bag.

I brushed my teeth and then threw everything back in my bag, tucking it in the drawer Tate kept for me.

I raced into the kitchen, thinking I'd grab a bagel or English muffin, and stopped abruptly at the sight of a short, slender girl with black hair, pale skin, and eyes heavily ringed in black eyeliner. She was wearing a long black trench coat and black shoes. And she held a knife, too, a kitchen one. The big one, from the looks of it—you know, the kind that can easily carve up a side of beef. Or a small-ish dance teacher.

"What are you doing here?" she asked me, her voice low and dangerous.

"Uh, are you the housekeeper? I'm Tate's girl, uh, friend, Jenny Partridge. I'm sorry if I scared you, but I am really, really late for an appointment." Boy, if this was Tate's housekeeper, she had a pretty interesting, uh, manner.

"Tate doesn't have girlfriends. He has passing acquaintances and friends with benefits. So I'll ask again, who are you? Did you break in looking for something to steal?"

"Hello!" I said, more than a little offended. "Look who's dressed all in black and holding a carving knife."

Her deep frown got almost fierce, and I stepped back. She stepped forward.

"Maybe I should call the cops. Or maybe I should just take care of the problem myself." She jabbed the knife toward me.

"Don't you have toilets to clean or something?" I asked her, stepping back one more time. Boy, if Tate got this one from a cleaning service, he really needed to change. She was downright unpleasant. And dangerous.

"I don't clean toilets."

"Well, isn't that what he pays you for?"

"He doesn't pay me anything. Whatever I do for Tate, I do because I owe him."

"Owe him?" What sort of warped relationship was this?

"Yes, like when someone breaks into his house and tries to steal, I can take care of it."

"Steal? Do you see anything in these hands?" This girl was starting to annoy me, despite the large knife. "Oh wait, I used his toothpaste. I'll make sure and leave a dime on the counter to make up for the amount I took."

"I don't think I like you," she said, her eyes narrowed.

"I am pretty sure the feeling is mutual," I said, narrowing my eyes as much as I could without obscuring my vision. If she came closer with the knife, I wanted to know it so I could bolt. I gauged the distance between her and the front door. If she wasn't terribly fast, I could make it . . . Then the door opened. Tate walked through, shut it, and entered the kitchen. His eyes widened.

"Malece! What the hell are you doing here? And why are you holding a knife on Jenny?"

Tate's voice did not sound amused. Good. Neither was I.

"I caught her stealing."

"Stealing what?" I pointed out. "Nothing in the hands, Malece. Did you notice he used my name?" I turned to Tate. "You really need to do something about the housekeeping service you get your help from. She might do a good job cleaning, but she is definitely not very . . . wait. Malece?"

Malece. Tate's half sister. One of Mystery Man's family was standing in front of me, holding a knife, and still looking pretty dangerous. Wow.

"Yes. Malece, this is my girlfriend, Jenny Partridge. Jenny, this is my sister, Malece."

"Girlfriend?" Malece asked, looking very unhappy. "You don't have girlfriends."

"Well, I do have one now. And her name is Jenny. And you haven't answered my question. Why are you here?"

"And how did you get in?" I said, adding my own question.

"I'm his sister," she said, tilting her head, a cocky look on her face.

"And I'm his girlfriend," I replied, tilting my head right back, a warm feeling spreading through my stomach. *Girlfriend. Urp.* Girlfriend?

"I have a key."

"Me, too."

"All right you two, enough. Malece, put the knife down."

She stomped over to the kitchen counter and slammed the knife down, not putting it back in its holder. That was bound to make the *real* housekeeper unhappy, whenever she appeared. It appeared to anger Tate, too.

"Malece, you didn't answer me. What are you doing here?"

"I came to visit," she said, her voice a surly snarl.

"Good try, but not buying it. I haven't seen you in six weeks. So let's do this again. What are you doing here?"

"Ah, Gram got pissed because I was hanging out with my friends too much, and she wanted me to get a job. So she gave me an ultimatum. Grow up or get out. I got out."

Wow, Mystery Man's sister was a female Peter Pan. Interesting. Some chinks in the armor of his tidy life. Kinda like me.

"Great. You made Gram mad." Tate didn't look happy. Apparently, making Gram mad was against the cardinal rule of the Wilson clan, sort of like making my mother face the reality that her only child—me—was persona non grata. Or whatever that saying was.

"It's hard *not* to make her mad. She's wired pretty tightly."

"Actually, that's not true. She's one of the most easygoing people I've ever met. Making her mad requires supreme and concentrated effort. So fess up. What did you *really* do?"

"Nothing much, really. Just told her I was tired and going to bed, and then slipped out the window. I'm eighteen, after all. I'm an adult. I should just be able to walk out the front door, if I want."

"Then why didn't you?" Tate asked, his mouth a harsh line.

"Well, you know how she gets. She was already harping on me for hanging out and not working, and she said something about going to school—I just got out of school, thank you very much, and it was the worst twelve years of my life—and when I said that didn't interest me, she mentioned a friend of hers who was looking for a new person to train to work in their dental office. I mean, *ick.* Hello, people's mouths? Gross."

"So you are just planning on never working or holding down a job?"

"You sound just like *her,*" Malece said accusingly, glaring at her brother. Other than the black hair and dark blue eyes, they were very different. She had an almond-shaped cast to her eyes, and her nose was tinier. Everything about her was tiny, and Tate was a pretty imposing presence. I was short, but I probably had two inches on her. And she looked very thin, although I couldn't see much of her shape in the overcoat.

"Malece, it *is* time to grow up. You have to figure out what to do with your life. Gram is right. She's trying to help you."

"I'm not a nine-to-five kinda person," she said. Perhaps she and I had more in common than she did with her brother, although I was still a bit peeved at her over the whole knife incident. I certainly didn't want to go get coffee with her, but since I wasn't a "plays well with other adults" kinda girl, I could relate. Somewhat.

"Well, what kind of person are you? A 'let's collect a welfare check' kind of person?" Tate said ironically, his tone filled with disapproval. If I had a big brother, is this how he would have treated me? Undoubtedly. Probably even now. I could just see myself getting this lecture.

"I don't need welfare. At least I won't, once I get my trust fund."

"You're never going to be Paris Hilton, honey, so you can just put that out of your head. Until you show some responsibility, Dad will never let you have that money."

"He let you have yours!" she said accusingly.

"Yes, and I have a job, and a place to live, and lots of sound investments."

"And you're boring as hell, too," she shot back. "I thought you were cool when we first met, but now I see you're just like him."

Tate's face tightened, and I took a step back. It seemed they had both forgotten I was standing here, listening in on this conversation—and learning a whole lot about Mystery Man. I intended to stay quiet.

"I am nothing like him. Nothing. I would never walk out on my family and my responsibilities, which, by the way, he did to both of us."

"He didn't leave you," Malece said, anger simmering in her voice. "He never even acknowledged me until my mom died and he had no choice."

"There are other ways of leaving," Tate said, his expression harsh but his voice gentle. "And this is neither the time nor place to discuss this. I bet if you get a job, he'll increase your allowance and let you get an apartment. Maybe it's time you became a real adult."

"I have no idea what I would do," Malece said, her anger gone. "All the things I like to do don't pay money. At least not right now. Who wants a fashion designer who is eighteen and has never gone to school?"

Fashion designer? My ears perked up at that. "Fashion designer?" I asked.

They both started and looked at me like I had just fallen into the kitchen from another planet. Great, they really *had* forgotten I was here.

"Yes, fashion designer," Malece said, the snarky factor back in her tone. "I've designed and made my own clothes for years."

I ignored the snark.

"You sew, too?"

"Duh, I just said so. Did you think I used glue?"

It was getting harder to ignore, but I carried on.

"Have you ever made costumes, like, say, for dancers?"

"Dancers? God no."

"Well, if you were, say, paid to do it, would you?"

See, once Monica, my costume designer, fled Utah because of her troubles with the law, I was left with nothing to do but order dance costumes for my teams through catalogs. The other seamstresses around town were either too expensive or too conservative. A five-year-old's belly button is not an indecent sight, but sometimes you wouldn't know that living here in the land of morality. There was even a whole group of smart business owners who made money designing prom gowns and wedding gowns that showed no skin—at all.

So, I was always on the lookout for someone to help me with costumes.

"Why would I want to work with you? I don't know you, but I do know I don't like you."

"Ditto, girlfriend, but you have a problem and so do I. You need a paying job so you can get an apartment and live your life the way you want. I need costumes that won't terrify the judges. You don't make everything in black, do you?"

That was an important factor to know.

"No, I can use whatever colors or fabrics you want. I'm very good at what I do. And I don't come cheap."

"Well, if you're not interested . . ." I turned toward Tate. "So why did you come home, anyway?"

"I didn't say I wasn't interested. I just said I wasn't cheap," she protested.

"I came home to take you to your solo lesson. Remember, with your crazy friend Tamara Williams and her daughter April?"

Ack! I looked at the clock on the wall. Twenty after twelve. I was dead meat.

"Just for future reference, let me make it clear that psycho dance moms do not make good friends. She is just a paycheck. Now, come on, let's go. Malece, you come, too. We'll talk in the car," I said.

THE SILENCE IN THE CAR WAS PRETTY FROSTY. I searched my purse as Tate drove, looking for my cell phone. I wanted to check on Sal's condition, and after I fended off an angry Tamara Williams, I needed to go pay him a visit. I knew he was probably in a lot of pain, and I felt terrible. If I had some extra money, I would have bought him a stuffed animal or something. As it was, all I could offer was my presence. Good thing Sal liked me.

I finally found my phone, only to discover that it was dead. Just as dead as it had been the night before. I really needed to go home and get my charger. Actually, now that Malece was here, it was entirely possible I would just plain be going home. After all, Tate was not going to want me around, with his sister in the next room. Especially as it appeared he was trying to set some sort of example for her.

Good thing Sal now had his own apartment here in town and wasn't staying with Tate or me. It would be pretty darn crowded.

"So, have you checked on Sal?" I asked Tate. I knew

that even though the big Samoan man puzzled him, he actually liked him quite a bit. Tate was a thoughtful man. He would have called.

"He was sleeping peacefully when I called to check on him. The surgery went well, although he was pretty uncomfortable through the night. There's a steel rod in his leg, so that's going to take some getting used to, I imagine."

"Yikes. He's going to be down for a long, long time. I guess he won't be helping me jazz up my routines," I said glumly.

Malece sat in the back and sulked, although I could almost feel the curiosity bounding off her in waves.

Tate gave me a sharp look.

"Hey, I'm concerned about him. You know that. It's just that he was going to help me so I could win that big prize at the Ultimate Dance Championships. Now I'm not sure what to do."

"You have plenty of talent yourself, Jenny."

"I know, I know, but the thing is, sometimes you need to go to workshops, or classes, or work with other people to inspire you. You know? Or you just keep doing the same thing over and over again, and the same thing isn't going to cut it for this."

"Decent costumes would probably help," Malece said from the backseat. I tried not to smile. She was hooked, and I knew it. I remembered being eighteen, and my dad convincing me that "Really, Jenny, working at the sheriff's office will be fun. You'll be the first one to know whenever anything goes wrong." Right. Like I wanted to know that. People were nasty enough when I told them their children couldn't dance very well. Imagine telling them someone had been killed. Not a fun job.

But Malece was desperate. Tate was holding out an apple, in the form of independence, and she was the bunny rabbit. She wanted her own job, and she was good at designing things. I think. Based on her black attire, I couldn't be sure. Geez, I sure hope I hadn't jumped headfirst into yet another bad situation.

"So, just out of curiosity, what have you designed?" I tried to keep my voice mostly uninterested.

"Everything I wore to high school, and out with my friends," she said.

"Something like that?" I asked, pointing to her black overcoat, worn over black boots and black jeans.

"No, *not* like this. I put this on as a sign of my disgust at the repression of all the adults around me."

Great, a militant. I sure hoped she wasn't into burning bras or breaking into the zoo and freeing the monkeys. We had enough of those around here, in human form, of course. Thinking of monkeys made me think of the dead Gorilla-Gram guy, and I winced.

Tate sighed heavily at Malece's comment, since he couldn't know I was thinking about monkeys and all that. She was a bit over the top, I had to admit, and that was a lot coming from me. I dealt in "over the top" daily. I was a little bit that way myself.

"Look, do you want me to try or not?" Malece asked, her utter disgust at the fact I could still draw a breath obvious in every word she spoke. She wasn't being very grateful. Then again, it wouldn't be much different from working with Monica, my former costume designer, who had been fairly nice to my face but who had secretly named her costume dummy Jenny and maimed it on a regular basis. I sure hoped Malece didn't have warrants out for her arrest, but I figured Tate would know if she did.

"Yes, let's start simple. A solo costume for Carly Fulton. She's my best soloist, and she has a basic costume, but it needs to be jazzed up. I'll call Marlys and have her meet us at the studio after Carly gets out of school."

Malece sat back with a thump, and harrumphed.

"You could be a little bit grateful, Malece," Tate scolded her. I think I was grateful he wasn't *my* big brother.

"How much am I getting for this?" Grateful was not her last name.

"Well, it's a fix-up, so the base costume is already made. You just need to make it better. So, let's say thirty-five dollars plus any materials you need." I knew Marlys would pay, because she had been complaining about how plain the costume was and had even considered ordering a whole new costume, except we would never get it in time.

"And if I do a costume from scratch?"

"Team costumes, I have to put a cap on them at eighty-five dollars. Some parents won't pay more than that. So whatever you make after you buy materials is yours. But if you get some more soloists—and if you do a good job, you will, because these mothers are crazy and competitive—you can start at one hundred dollars, flat fee, and go up from there, depending on how much embellishing and sequins they want."

I could almost hear her ticking away the money.

"How many dancers do you have?" she asked, confirming my suspicions.

"I have about eighty-five right now."

"Do they all do solos?"

"Oh, heaven's no. I'd have to kill myself. Just the ones who are better dancers—and of course the ones who can't dance but have mothers who are completely nuts."

"Speaking of nuts . . ." Tate said dryly.

We had pulled into my parking lot, and at the top of the stairs stood a toe-tapping Tamara Williams and her daughter April. Both of them looked highly irritated with me.

"I have to get back to work," Tate said as I stepped out of the Taurus. "I'll send a guy with Bessie. He should be here in about thirty minutes. When you are done, call me. Go straight to the hospital, and call me when you get there. I have some things I need to take care of, and then I'll meet you there."

"Who's Bessie?" Malece asked.

"My dad's truck."

"Who names a truck Bessie?" she asked, scorn filling her voice.

"Don't be dissing my dad," I said, warning filling my voice.

"Malece," Tate said in a similar tone. This was bound to be a pleasant experience, working with Tate's sister. If the rest of his family turned out to be of the same disposition, I think I preferred him to stay a Mystery Man.

"I think I'll stay here with her," Malece said, jumping out. *Ack!* No! Tamara Williams and Malece in the same room. That had to be some bad juju.

"Okay, but be nice," he said. I wasn't sure if he meant me or her. I wasn't feeling nice.

I turned and pounded up the stairs.

"Well, Jenny, how nice of you to show up," Tamara said. "You knew, of course, that I pulled April out on her lunch, and now she is going to miss her math class, and she needs all the help she can get there."

"Maybe you should have left, then," I said. I was feeling mighty cranky.

"And not practiced her solo? With a competition little more than a week away? Are you kidding me?"

Malece was staring at Tamara with a puzzled look on her face.

I unlocked the door, and she grabbed the handle out of my hand and stormed through, April following.

"Is there something wrong with that lady?" Malece asked.

"That, Malece, is a psycho dance mom. Best get used to them. Welcome to my world."

FIVE

MALECE WATCHED THE SOLO LESSON WITH more interest and less disgust than I'd anticipated.

"Does she have a costume?" she asked when April was done. She indicated April, jabbing her pointer finger.

"Yes, I believe her mother ordered a costume from France."

"Jenny, you are such a kidder." Tamara was all smiles now that her little darling had gotten her required dose of dance-teacher attention. All was right with the dance world. Until tomorrow. Maybe sooner.

"Why do you ask?" Tamara said to Malece. *Uh-oh.* I should have given her a better debriefing in the ways that psycho dance moms work. I shook my head firmly, trying to warn her without words to stay quiet. If you played dead, sometimes the wild animals would leave you alone. She, of course, ignored me.

"Oh, because Jenny is trying me out as a costume designer, and she has me making a costume for . . . what's that girl's name, Jenny?"

She turned to me, a defiant glare in her eyes. She thought she was telling me how it was going to be. She had no idea what she had just done. Oh well. Everybody had to learn sometime, especially people who glared at me in such an unfriendly fashion. Even if that someone was my boyfriend's—boyfriend, *ulp*—sister.

So I just shrugged and said, "Carly."

"Carly Fulton?" Tamara's eyes narrowed.

"Well, she's the only Carly on our team."

"You have set up a special costume designer for Carly." This was not a question, but a statement. Flat, monotone, and I knew any second the steam was going to rush out of her ears and her head might even explode. Malece watched us both with a smug smile of satisfaction. It wouldn't last. I was a pro at this. She was nothing but a babe in the forest.

"Well, actually, Tamara, I've never seen what Malece can do. She only told me she can sew. She says she used to design and sew her own clothes, but she's not exactly dressed up now, so I'm not sure about it. I thought I'd do a trial run with Carly, since Marlys works with me, and see how it went. If she does a great job, I thought I would let her do more." Wow, it was all the truth, not one iota of fudging, and it was still working like a charm. I felt almost virtuous.

"Why Carly? Why not April?" Tamara's eyes were ice cold.

"Well, like I said, I don't know how it's going to turn out, and since Marlys will work with me, I thought I'd try it first with her."

"What do you mean you don't know how it's going to turn out?" Malece said angrily. "I *told* you I can design and sew. I've done it for years."

"You're eighteen," I pointed out. That got me another nasty glare. Sure was glad she had chosen to stay with me at the studio rather than go with her brother. "And I haven't seen any of your stuff, but because of my, uh, relationship with Tate, I'm willing to give you a shot. I just want to see it first, before I have you do a bunch of stuff." This truth stuff was kind of catching.

"I'm the best *you* could ever get," Malece said with disdain.

"Well, actually, I had a great costume designer, but she had a few legal and mental issues. And hey, I told you, I really need someone. So I'm glad to have you, but I wanted to do a trial run first and—"

"She's going to do a costume for April," Tamara said firmly. "That can be her trial run. How much does it cost?"

"A hundred and fifty," Malece quickly said, tacking fifty onto the price I had told her she could charge. "More if you require extra sequins and other embellishments."

"No problem. You're hired," Tamara said, a gloat spreading across her face. She had bested Marlys and won the totally unproved, untested, and possibly untalented costume designer. Marlys would be so . . . relieved?

"But . . ." I said weakly, not really trying to interfere.

"No, Jenny, this girl is going to work for me," Tamara said. She turned to Malece. "Now, let me tell you about my vision for her dance and costume. The song is 'Black Horse and the Cherry Tree' by KT Tunstall. I envision a costume that is maybe a mix between a horse and a tree, but not anything that will make her look ridiculous or strange."

Malece's eyes about popped out of her head. She turned to me with a frantic look and I just shrugged my shoulders. I'd tried to help. Oh yes I had. I'd tried to give her a very proper warning, one which she chose not to accept. Now, it was too late. She was doomed.

"And it can't be red, even though cherries are red, because everyone does red, and it's just too done. Green won't work, either, mostly because it won't emphasize her blue eyes. Maybe white and blue."

"A white and blue cherry tree with a horse head?" Malece squeaked.

"Horse head? Heavens no! No horse head, it just has to look, well, not horsey, but equine. Regal."

Malece turned to me again, her mouth agape, her almond-shaped eyes bigger than I'd have thought possible.

"Now, let's sit down and talk about fabric, and pick the color of the crystals—I'm paying for real crystals, not those cheap ones that don't shine when the light hits them. Oh no." She grabbed Malece's hand, and the other woman's face turned white and she gulped. I finally decided to take pity on her. A little bit.

"But didn't you need to get April back to school?"

"School? Oh yes, school." Tamara's glazed eyes cleared a bit. "You're right. School is important. But I need to set up an appointment with Malece here to discuss the costume in further detail, and maybe we can go to Salt Lake City to the dancewear store and pick out the fabric. I'll drive, of course. I'll even treat you to lunch." She smiled broadly and Malece gulped again.

"Call me later, Tamara, and we'll discuss it," I said. I figured I might as well tell her to call me, because even if I didn't, she would. Probably forty or fifty times.

After Tamara scooted April out the door, Malece turned to me and said, "What is wrong with that woman?"

"I tried to warn you. Psycho dance moms are a different breed. I really wanted to give you a chance to try a costume before you had to dive into a working relationship with someone like Tamara, but you weren't listening." I didn't get a chance to say "I told you so" very often. Usually, I was hearing it said to me, so I was going to milk this for all it was worth.

"But . . . but . . . but . . ."

"Look, she's a pain in the butt. And that's why I wanted you to work with Marlys first, because as long as she has caffeine, she's the most normal dance mom I have. But you dove in, and so April will get her solo costume first. If you ever finish it."

"But . . ."

And then she stopped talking, her head down, her face dejected. She realized, I knew, she'd gotten herself in over her head. She was young. Heck, I was still doing that, and I was nearing my late twenties. Okay, fine, early thirties.

The studio door opened and in came a police officer, holding the keys to Bessie. "Jenny Partridge? Detective Wilson asked me to deliver your truck and your keys. Here you go."

Right then, it hit me. I was going to have to drive the truck a dead man had been in. Not so long ago. Not long ago at all. A shiver ran up my spine. The policeman cocked his head and gave me a funny look, as I didn't reach out for the keys. I didn't want to touch them. I also never wanted to drive Bessie again.

"Ms. Partridge?" the policeman asked, an odd tone to his voice.

"Oh, thanks. I was just thinking about everything that happened. I appreciate you bringing the truck by. You can just set the keys down there," I said, motioning to the stereo, which was a lot farther away from him than I was. But he complied, walked over to put the keys down on the speaker, then looked at me with a sharp, quizzical expression. As if trying to figure out why I wouldn't touch the keys. Then he said good-bye and left.

"You want me to drive?" Malece asked, having somewhat recovered from her shock of dealing with Tamara Williams.

"No, I don't want to go anywhere near that truck." I shivered. She gave me a look like the one the cop had given me, so I felt the need to defend myself. "A guy died in there, you know. Dead guy. In the truck that my father calls Bessie. It's tainted now, and I don't know about you, but I've heard some pretty nasty things about what happens to a body after a person dies."

Malece blanched a little bit. "A guy died in it?"

"Well, I'm not sure he actually died *in* the truck, but that's where we found him. Now it's a Death Mobile."

"I think I'll walk," she said.

"Me, too."

"Do you think we can get a cab?" Malece asked.

I skirted around the keys sitting on the speaker, but something caught my eye. There was a bright yellow tag on the key chain, which had not been on my father's key chain. I stepped closer. It was the kind of tag that identified a car from a sales lot, not that I had a lot of experience with that. I'd gone with my mom when she bought her new Toyota Camry, though, so I had seen one or two of those tags before.

"Those aren't my keys," I told Malece, and I moved closer and picked them up. "My keys had a 'Teachers Rule' key chain on them, and there was also a key to my mom's house on there."

"Teachers rule?"

"They are my dad's keys, and he's a teacher."

She arched her eyebrows at me. "Technically, so are you."

"Yeah, well, anyway. These aren't my keys." I walked to the glass door that led out of my studio and stared into the parking lot. Parked in the middle was a dark green Jeep Liberty, a small SUV that looked brand new and impossibly expensive. Confusion ran through my mind. Either this cop had made one doozy of a mistake for which he would later pay, or I was dreaming.

"Is this really happening?" I asked Malece. "You aren't a dream, are you?"

"You are one weird chick," Malece said, glaring at me.

I decided that any dream with Malece in it would qualify as a nightmare, and since I was staring at a new car, this couldn't be one of those. So, I was awake. And the cop had made a big mistake.

Dang. I think. I sure would like to have a vehicle like that one.

"Well, this is really odd. There's a Jeep Liberty out there."

"Nice ride," Malece said after scooting up behind me and looking out the door.

I heard a pealing cell phone and automatically looked around, but of course, my phone was terminally dead, at least until I charged it. Malece fished her cell out of her pocket and answered it.

"'Lo? Okay. Okay." She handed it to me. "It's for you." Her eyebrows went up, and I had to admit I saw a little bit of Tate in her with that move, since he used his own brows to indicate all kinds of things—like amusement at the messes I managed to get myself into.

"Hello?"

"I'm guessing right about now you are pretty confused."

"Right about now, some other guy is really pissed off that his new Jeep Liberty is missing, and someone expects him to drive a 1963 truck."

Tate chuckled, that deep, throaty sound that made my knees quake just a little and arcs of electricity spike up my spine.

"This is a loaner. A friend of mine owns a lot, and owes me a lot of favors. I figured you wouldn't be wanting to ride in the truck any time soon, so I arranged for you to have another vehicle to use."

Tate's thoughtfulness and generosity left me speechless.

"Jenny? Are you there?"

There was a big lump in my throat. No one had ever done anything like this for me before. At least no "boyfriend" kind of person. I think I got a bottle of cheap perfume for Christmas once, and some disgustingly perverted underwear that ended the relationship. But nothing like this. Tate had also bailed me out last December, when I had hordes of angry psycho dance moms after me for refunds on their cookie dough and I had no money to give them. Of course, that had been a loan, and he'd gotten his money back from the owner of the cookie-dough company, but still . . .

Whenever I was in a bind, Tate was there. And an unfamiliar feeling ripped through my body like an electrical current. I was falling hopelessly in love with him, and that couldn't bode well. Things like that just did not happen in my life.

"Okay, either you answer me now, or I'll send an ambulance to check on you, because you are starting to—"

"I'm here. I'm sorry. I guess I'm just overwhelmed."

"Don't freak out, okay? Don't overthink this. Just accept the loan. Enjoy it."

"Okay," I said meekly, still trying to swallow normally.

"Take Malece with you, okay? You're headed to the hospital, right?"

"Yes."

"Okay, I'll meet you there in about an hour. And keep an eye out for silver Hummers. If you see one, call 911. Don't waste time. I don't care if you think it's a different one. Call first, worry about it later."

"Okay. And Tate? Thank you."

"You're welcome."

$\mathscr{S}$ IX

NO SILVER HUMMERS, OR ANY OTHER VEHI-
cles for that matter, dogged us on the way to the hospital,
and the Jeep drove like a dream. I still *felt* as if I were living in a dream. I kept pinching myself, trying to make sure
I was really awake. I quit after I noticed Malece giving me
odd looks. I didn't want her telling Tate I was one of those
masticators, or something like that.

We found Sal's room without too much trouble, and I
knocked lightly on the door. There was no answer. I knocked
a little louder. Still no answer.

I poked my head into the room and heard some loud
snoring. Apparently, Sal was out for the count.

"Sal?" I said softly. "Sal?"

"Jenny? Is that you?"

I recognized Marlys's voice, and I pushed open the door
and walked into the room, Malece trailing behind me.

"Hey, Marlys, what are you doing here?"

From the hospital bed came the loud snoring, and I
could see Sal's form, even though the room was darkened.

"Let's go talk out there," Marlys said, rising from the chair where she sat and walking out the door. Malece and I followed her.

We went into a visitors' room and sat down in the chairs. On the television screen, a soap opera played to an empty audience.

"I heard about the accident from Tate, so I came down to see if Sal was okay. He was in a lot of pain, so the doctors dosed him up with some medicine right before you came."

A twinge of guilt shot through my stomach as I considered poor Sal's sad state. I knew it had been an accident—I hadn't meant to send him flying down the metal staircase that led to my studio—but still, I felt pretty darn bad about it.

"So you were just sitting with him?" I asked, a little confused.

"Yeah, he was pretty lonely, telling me stories about his life, and then he dozed off, but before he did, he asked me to stay. He didn't want to be alone."

In some ways, Sal Tuatuola was just a big kid who didn't know what he wanted to be when he grew up, and Marlys was pretty motherly. If I didn't have my own mom—who wavered between wanting to tear her hair out and hide from the fact I wasn't a "conventional" daughter, and mothering me to death—I'd definitely want Marlys as a substitute.

"Sal's family was here earlier, and his mother cried so loud the doctor had to ask them to leave. There was about four million of them, roughly."

I laughed, and then noticed Marlys glancing at Malece, who had plunked down in a chair about four away from the one I'd chosen. She was watching the television with a scowl on her face.

"Marlys, this is Tate's sister, Malece . . . uh, Malece. I don't know your last name."

"Duh, it's Wilson," Malece said, not looking away from the television screen.

"I see she has the same wit and charm as Tate," Marlys said dryly.

"Hey, given the fact you weren't born . . . I mean . . . Never mind." I could not see this conversation ending well, so even though I had the desire to defend myself, it probably wasn't worth it.

"Why don't you just get on the PA system and announce to the entire hospital that I'm Tate Wilson's bastard sister," Malece said, her voice a surly growl.

"That is a word I do not use," I said primly, trying my best to look unbothered.

"Oh, quit the surly 'nobody knows the trouble I've seen' act, Malece," Marlys said sharply. "It's not unique or original, and teenagers have been using it since the beginning of time. Jenny is a nice person, even though she's a little eccentric, so get over whatever it is you have against her and stop acting like a spoiled two-year-old."

I stared at Marlys in disbelief. She was always a little bit to the point and matter-of-fact, but I'd never seen her this brusque with a total stranger.

"Still no caffeine?" I asked timidly, afraid of what was going to come out of her mouth next.

"No, I had coffee this morning," she said, then she sighed. "Sorry, Malece, but you are acting like a big brat."

Malece stared at us as though we had just fallen off the planet Crazy.

"Hey, what do you mean I'm eccentric?" I asked, her other words registering, finally.

"Are you going to deny it?" she asked.

I thought about it for a minute, then decided eccentric was better than weird. "No. But what the heck is going on with you, Marlys?"

"Nothing, just some things at home. I think I'll go now, since you are here. Don't leave Sal alone, okay?"

She stood up and walked away without saying good-bye or even looking back. Something was really wrong with my friend, and I didn't know what it was. And I was worried. More worried about her than the upcoming competition and lackluster routines, and even more worried than I was about the silver Hummer and dead Gorilla-Gram guy.

But maybe not more worried about her than Sal. I rose from the chair and walked back toward Sal's room; I knew Malece was following me, because I could feel her surly presence mere steps away.

I pushed through Sal's door and saw that the blinds had been opened. He was staring out the window at the Wasatch Mountains.

"Hey, buddy, how are you feeling?" I asked.

He turned to look at me and his face lit up, although his eyes had a slightly hazy focus.

"Oh, I'm so glad you are here, Jenny. I don't like being alone."

"Sal, I'm so sorry for what happened." I looked down at his leg, which was wrapped in bandages and encased in some kind of metal cage. It looked painful, and I winced.

"It was an accident. But now I can't help you with the routines," he said, sorrow in his less-than-focused eyes.

"You just need to get better," I said. "I don't care about those routines." And I mostly didn't. I was more worried about Sal, Marlys, and the sullen teenager who'd suddenly become my shadow.

"What happened?" asked the devil, er, I mean, the sullen teenager.

I turned to answer her but saw she was addressing Sal, and her face had lost its "angry goth" look and transformed into something quite beautiful. My mouth dropped open. Wow, I'd had no idea she was so pretty. Every time she looked at me she resembled a gargoyle. I guessed I didn't bring out the best in her.

"Well, there was this big hairy creature in Jenny's truck, and it scared me, so I took off running, and then I scared

Jenny and she turned, and I fell down the stairs and ended up here. Who are you?"

"I'm Malece Wilson, Tate's sister."

"You don't look like him. You're much prettier."

She giggled. I promise! *Giggled!* This was so not good. Somehow, I didn't think Tate would appreciate the fact that his sister and Sal—who had a history of running away from a Mormon mission to teach dance, among other things—were making goo-goo eyes at each other.

"So, how long do you think you'll have to stay? What did the doctors tell you?" I asked. I might as well have been on the moon, because they both ignored me—even Sal, who usually hung on my every word. Must have been the medication.

"Oh, it's nearly two. Time for my favorite soap opera," Sal said, pulling the white remote over to his hand and flipping on the television. "I can't miss *Passions*."

"*You* watch *Passions*?" Malece asked, an almost reverential tone in her voice. "I never miss an episode." I couldn't help it. I groaned. Didn't matter. I was Ms. Invisible.

Wait a minute. *Passions* was on television? It was 2 p.m.? Then what had Marlys been doing here? She had a noon bus run every day of the week, taking kindergartners home from school. Something was definitely up with her. And I needed to find out what. Especially since no one here knew I was even alive or breathing.

"I need to go take care of some things, Malece," I said, loudly, so they couldn't ignore me anymore. "Do you want to wait here for Tate?"

"Yes, I'll stay with Sal so he won't be alone. He doesn't like being alone," she said as though she had known Sal all her life.

"Oookay," I said, shaking my head. Tate's head was going to explode when he walked in on this scene. Nothing I could do about that, except perhaps warn him.

I left the hospital room, and no one said a word, of

course, because they were both entranced by the television set—and alternately each other. I found a pay phone in the hospital lobby and dug for a quarter in my sweatpants pocket. As usual, I found nothing but lint.

I rummaged through my purse, finding my dead cell phone and cursing it silently while I dug farther for a quarter. I finally came up with one, plopped it in the coin slot, and dialed Tate's cell phone number.

His voice mail picked up after a few rings, and I left a message. "I'm going to check on Marlys. For some reason, she isn't working, and something is up with her. I left your sister here at the hospital with Sal. They, uh, seem to be getting along really well. Be prepared."

I wasn't sure that was the best message I could have left, but I didn't really know what else to say. "Sal and Malece seem to have a thing going on" just didn't sound right. I didn't even know if that was what it was, although it was certainly possible. In my world, just about anything was possible.

I hurried out to the parking lot and found myself looking for Bessie. The sight of the green Jeep Liberty brought me back to earth. I really wished I could afford to keep this vehicle. It was pretty darn nice.

I got in and started it up and then headed toward Marlys's house. She was usually bailing me out of one problem or another. This time, I intended to be the kind of friend who returned the favor. Something was wrong, and I wanted to help her. What I could do was up in the air. But I intended to try.

When I got to the block where Marlys lived, I pulled into the driveway of her house and spotted her puttering around in her flower beds. It was spring in Utah, and even though it could still snow any day, because that's just the way Utah weather was, today was fairly mild, so apparently Marlys thought it would be a good day to weed. In the middle of the afternoon. When she was supposed to be driving the bus.

I parked and got out, and walked over to where Marlys was kneeling on the ground, pulling at weeds that she didn't seem to see. She didn't hear me come up, which really worried me. Normally, she knew everything that was going on everywhere at every time.

"Marlys?" I said.

She turned and looked at me, her eyes dull and unfocused. Slowly, she seemed to realize I was standing there, and she stood and brushed off her dirty hands on her jeans. "Oh, hi, Jenny. Why are you here?"

"A better question is why are *you* here? You should be on your bus run. I'm here because something is wrong with you, and I don't know what it is. I'm here because you're my friend, and I want to help. Why aren't you at work?"

"I took some time off. I needed to . . . think."

She was looking anywhere but at me, and I was puzzled by her demeanor. Marlys was never like this. What was going on? I'd been thinking lack of caffeine was the problem, but obviously it went much deeper than that.

"Marlys?"

"I think Roger's having an affair." She blurted the words out like they were poison, and I suppose, in a way, they were. Roger was Marlys's husband of sixteen years, and although I didn't know him very well, he'd always seemed to adore her and the kids; he was hardly the type to go looking for something else. At least, that was how it looked to me. Of course, appearances could be deceiving, but still. Roger? He was nearing forty, sporting the middle-age paunch, and I'd even seen him wear socks with sandals. Never a good look for a man. Definitely not a look for a man with a wild side.

"Why would you think that?"

"He's being secretive about something. At least twice a

week he says he's working late. Last time he told me that I drove by his office, but no one was there. He's never lied to me before. At least I don't think he has."

"Wow." Had to admit, that was a hard one to counter. I wasn't very good at this consolation business. "Well, there's probably a good explanation."

Marlys gave me a hard look.

"A reasonable explanation?"

Another glare.

"Something that we haven't thought of, but that will make perfect sense when you hear it?"

She just shook her head.

"Did you tell him that you drove by and you know he wasn't at work?"

"No, because he lied about being there. Maybe he's been lying for years. Maybe our whole marriage has been a lie."

"Are you *sure* you're getting enough caffeine?"

"Jenny, this is not about caffeine. My whole life is in a shambles, and I don't know what to do."

"Okay, okay, I'm sorry. Let's take this one step at a time. The first thing we have to do is determine where he is going. We'll follow him next time he tells you he is working late. After we know where, we can find out why."

"You sounded kinda like Tate there."

"Yeah, I kinda did, didn't I? Guess his copliness is rubbing off on me."

"Copliness?"

"It could be a word. Anyway, I can help with this. You call me, I'll pick you up, and we'll follow him."

"In that?" she said, pointing to the Liberty parked in front of her house. I didn't think she had noticed, but Marlys was pretty sharp, even when she thought her whole life was about to implode.

"Yeah, he's never seen it before, so he won't have any idea it's us. Once we figure out where he is going, then you'll have a better idea what you want to, well, do. I guess."

"I've never seen it before, either," Marlys said. "Where'd you get it? You rob a bank?"

"Yes, in my spare time I've taken up armed robbery and rolling drunks for cigarettes."

"Tate, huh?"

She knew me too well.

"It's a loan. From a friend of his. He figured out I wouldn't want to be driving a truck that recently hosted a dead body." He knew me too well, also.

Marlys put her hand to her forehead and rubbed, leaving behind a smear of dirt. "I never thought this would happen to me."

"You don't even know what *this* is," I said. "So let's find out what it is and go from there."

"You sound downright reasonable and logical. What's up with that?"

"Hmm, I don't know. Maybe my encounter with a dead body has given me a new perspective on life."

"Knock it off. You're freaking me out."

"Yeah, I have to admit, I'm kind of scaring myself, too. I'll try to stop." I wasn't entirely sure logic and reason were a good look for me. But I supposed I could try it on for size.

SEVEN

I LEFT MARLYS PULLING AT MORE WEEDS, BUT only after she promised to let me help her find out where Roger was going. I needed to go back to my place and charge my phone, so that when she called me, no matter what time, I could take off and go help her. Although, considering the fact that with Sal in the hospital I was now down one dance teacher, I really hoped she didn't call on a dance night. After all, we had only a little more than a week until our first competition. I decided to employ a little stealth, since I didn't want this vehicle—which did not even belong to me—blown up like the Pepto Mobile. My poor pink Volkswagen Bug had met with an untimely death thanks to an encounter with a particularly nasty woman, who, believe it or not, was not a psycho dance mom. Long story. Or possibly worse, suffering a death stain like poor, poor Bessie. My dad was never going to forgive me if his truck was haunted. And my mother? Wow, how was I going to break that one to her?

And where was Bessie? I was going to have to find out, before my dad asked.

I parked around the block from my apartment and headed toward the front of my building, cutting through some yards and staying close to places where there was cover, like big trees. Most of the houses in this part of Ogden were old, and so the trees were plentiful and tall.

I quickly made my way to the front of the building, and as far as I could tell, no one was following me. Nor was there a silver Hummer parked in front of my place. There was, however, something almost worse. Headed toward me, friendly waves and big smiles on their faces, were two Mormon missionaries.

Déjà vu!

Of course, I did not know these two, and quite obviously, they did not know me, or they would have been backing away and making the sign of the cross . . . Oh wait. Wrong religion. That was Grandma Gilly's reaction when she saw me.

"Hi, how are you doing today?" asked one of them, a young, handsome, dark-haired boy with a toothy grin and a dimple in one cheek. Some girl back home somewhere was crying every night over this boy being gone for two years. Maybe more than one girl.

"I'm great, but I'm in a really big hurry."

"Oh, okay, well, this will just take a minute. Are you a Mormon?"

I thought quick. If I said no, I was in their sights and they would keep hunting me down. "Yes, yes, I am. Very, very, faithful Mormon. Very faithful Mormon in a big, big hurry. I have to . . . I have an appointment with Church Leader Man . . . Wait. The bishop. That's right, I have an appointment with my bishop and he does not like me to be late, oh no. He's a stickler for timeliness."

The handsome boy looked confused. "You have an

appointment with your bishop in the middle of the day? Doesn't he have a job?"

"He's a . . . night janitor. So he makes all of his appointments during the day."

Bad move. Not my finest lie ever. Nope, because everyone knew that only the most successful businessmen ended up appointed as bishops, at least around here. Dentists, doctors, that sort of person. Janitors? Not really. At least as far as I knew. And as far as the missionary standing before me knew.

"A *janitor*?" the young man said with scorn. "What ward are *you* in?"

"Fine, you caught me. I'm not Mormon, but I don't really have time to deal with you, so it just seemed easier to go along and pretend."

"You lied to us?" asked the second missionary, who hadn't said much this far. He was a rather nerdy boy, with wire-rimmed glasses, remnants of acne, and a very thin upper lip. Still, it managed to quiver as he said the word "lie."

"Look," I said with a sigh, quickly scanning the area to make sure no silver Hummer had driven up while I was busy with the missionaries, and was now waiting to take me out. The coast was clear, if you didn't count the two members of God's Army standing in front of me. I wasn't getting away by lying, so I decided on the truth.

"Look, my good friend, a runaway missionary named Sal, is in the hospital with a compound fracture. I took my boyfriend's sister there with me, and now it appears they are hitting it off like gangbusters, and that is not going to make my boyfriend happy, because he thinks Sal is gay. I don't think he is, but you know how guys are. And I need to get in here and charge my phone so my friend Marlys can call me and we can follow her husband, because she thinks he's been having an affair. And on top of all that, this whack job in a silver Hummer is trying to kill me, and there was a dead guy that ended up in my dad's truck, wearing a gorilla suit . . ."

Both missionaries started backing up. The cute one put his hands up, aiming his missionary books at me, maybe to ward off the evil he suspected surrounded me. I know he would have been crossing himself had Mormons believed in that stuff.

"You're her, aren't you?" he asked accusingly, his eyes narrow.

I sighed. Yup, I was right. There was a list, and I was on top of it. Apparently not with a picture, though, or these two would never have gotten close.

A loud roar filled my ears and I turned to see a blur of silver.

"Hit the ground," I screamed.

These two missionaries were sorely lacking in survival skills, or just hadn't been hanging around me long enough, because the nerdy one took off running, and the other one just stood there, giving me the eye and holding his books up as though they were going to keep him safe in the event of an earthquake, a drive-by shooting, or an encounter with a redheaded dance teacher. The roar grew louder, and I knew I had no choice.

I ran as fast as I could toward him, his eyes growing wider as I neared, and I tackled him full on, both of us dropping to the ground just as a spray of bullets rang out, the sounds of smashing glass and pinging ricochets filling the air, along with an acrid smell.

The roar lessened, and the Hummer drove away.

I rolled off the missionary, whose eyes were wide with shock and fright. He didn't move.

"Are you okay?" I asked him.

I heard sharp screams from the apartment building, and fear filled my heart.

"Are you okay?" I asked again as I reached over to shake him. He didn't move. Just stared ahead and mouthed a prayer. People started coming outside, and I stood up and yelled at my neighbors, asking if anyone had been hurt.

Sirens pierced the air, and I rose from the ground and reached a hand out to the missionary. He still didn't move. Just his mouth.

I searched the road for the other missionary, because really he was in charge of this guy, not me, but he was nowhere to be found.

The first police cars pulled up, and officers jumped out, quickly securing the scene and checking for injuries. More cars, more sirens, an ambulance and paramedics, the fire department. Great. The news was probably on the way, too, and my picture would be plastered all over the Mormon-owned channel, with big red letters that said "Mormon Enemy Number One!"

"You had to pick my apartment building, today, didn't you?" I said accusingly to the prone missionary, who was obviously in some sort of shock or rigid mortis, or something.

"Ma'am, someone said you could tell us what is going on," said a tall, well-built blond officer with the words "Gang Unit" stenciled across his black jacket. He wore tight-fitting jeans, black hiking boots, and the usual gun holstered on his hip, along with some other cop tools.

"Sure, point out the crazy dance teacher as the one who caused it all," I said bitterly, the shock finally starting to hit me. I watched as paramedics administered to the cute missionary who had become a Popsicle the moment I landed on top of him. Or maybe it was just before that. Never mind that I *was* the one who—kinda—knew what was going on.

"Are you okay?" the gang-unit cop asked me gently. The compassion did it. Same tool—human tool—that Tate always got me with. The tears began to flow. "This has got to stop," I said. "It's just got to stop. I can't do this anymore. I just want my life to be normal, with no gunshots or fire-bombs or dead gorillas."

"Hey, you guys, I think this lady is in shock. Can you come check her out?" he hollered to two paramedics. I shook my head and waved them off, wiping at the tears. "I'm okay. I don't need medical attention."

"Are you sure?" His voice was gentle again. *Stop that!*

I fought back the tears. "Yes, I'm sure. The vehicle the gunshots came from was a silver Hummer. It's been dogging me for months. I don't know who is driving it, and it always happens so quick, I never get the plates or see who is in it. Oh, and the windows are tinted, too, I think."

"Let me get this straight. This drive-by shooting does not appear to be gang related?"

"Maybe if it's a gang of crazy psycho dance moms," I said and then sighed. This was going to take a while to explain.

TATE SHOWED UP JUST AS MY PRESENCE DOWN at police headquarters was requested. I'd been there a time or two before.

"Can I get my phone charger first?" I asked.

"I'll get it for you," Tate said, motioning me to stay put and in full sight of all the officers milling around.

"Do you need my keys?" He gave me that look, the one that usually set me aquiver, but I was pretty numb right now. Then he pointed to my door. The entire front of my building was shot up, including the door and the front window. He just walked up, put his hand through a large hole, and unlocked the door from the inside.

He came back with the charger a few minutes later.

"Is it bad?" I asked, tears on the back of my tongue, wanting to escape. I swallowed them down.

"It's kind of a mess, but the biggest problem is going to be keeping people out. I'll send some guys I know to board it up and move your stuff out."

"Move my stuff out? What do you mean?"

"Jenny, you can't really think you can live here anymore. Not only is it all shot up, but someone who seems very serious about killing you knows where it is. It just isn't safe anymore."

"And can you tell me where I will be safe?" I asked. "Because as far as I can tell, there is no safe place for me."

He stopped at that. I'd been attacked at my apartment, at my studio, and even at my mother's house.

"My place is safe," he said, his voice a low rumble.

"Oh yeah? A few hours ago, I had a knife held on me there, too. Didja forget that?"

"That was my sister, and the circumstances were different."

The gang-unit guy was giving us funny looks. I didn't blame him.

"I think I need to just get out of town for a while," I said. "But I can't. It's competition season, and next week I have the first one. And after that it's UDC, and if I win that one, I get a big money prize, and I could sure use that."

Tate's forehead wrinkled. "Competition season starts next week?"

"Uh, yeah? Where've you been? I've been moaning about it for two months now."

"The Gorilla-Gram said, 'Long time no see,' and 'I'm back to pick up your slack,' and to 'look out for me.'"

"Yes, I was there."

"I can't believe I'm saying this, but after having been around you for a while, I know it's possible. Maybe this is all related to your dance competition season. Maybe someone really doesn't want your teams competing and is willing to go to any lengths to stop you."

"Are you trying to say this is about *dance*?" the gang-unit officer asked, his voice incredulous. I couldn't blame him. He was used to working with surly teens who killed people to protect their turf—using real guns and bullets. In a way, the psycho dance mom wars were about turf, too.

The front-row-fifty, where every mother wanted her daughter to dance.

"I know it seems hard to believe, but some of these people are really nuts," Tate said.

"Is this Jenny T. Partridge?" the other officer asked, a slight smile quirking up the corner of his mouth.

"Yup, this is her."

"Hey, we have a vic in here!" came a shout from the apartment building. My heart dropped to my toes as Tate motioned me to stay back and they raced into the apartment next to mine.

It was home to Mr. Grundle. I didn't see him much. He was pretty old, and he used a walker, and sometimes he banged on the walls if I played my music too loud. I wouldn't say we were friends, or even really acquaintances. But I knew from his regular visitors that the local Mormon ward took care of him, which meant my ranking on "the list" just went up a whole lot. And someone totally innocent had died.

I sat down on the lawn, put my head in my hands, and cried.

$\mathcal{E}$IGHT

"Do you want the good news or the bad news?" Tate asked me a few hours later. Earlier, he'd picked me up off the lawn, put me in his car, and driven me to his apartment. Somehow, I'd gotten out of the station house visit. He'd tucked me into his bed, and I'd protested that I was not tired and would never sleep again. I was wrong. I'd drifted off immediately and awoke a few hours later feeling somewhat better. Must have been shock.

Now I dipped a grilled cheese sandwich into Campbell's tomato soup as Tate watched.

"Good news, I guess," I said between bites. Grilled cheese and tomato soup was comfort food, clear back from the days when my mother had made it for me on cold or gloomy days. Somehow, Tate instinctively knew that. Or maybe he was just a good guesser. I was going with instinct.

"Okay, Mr. Grundle didn't die from a gunshot wound."

"He's alive?"

"No, that's not the good news. He's definitely dead. And had apparently been dead for at least two days."

"Eww, and he was right next door to me?" I shivered.

Tate smiled. "The good news is that you can put away the guilt that made you collapse on the lawn. You had nothing to do with his death."

"And the bad news?" I stuck the last of the sandwich in the soup and then took a bite, savoring the tangy cheddar cheese coated in warm tomato soup.

"The bad news is, it looks like Albert Cunningham had no real enemies—or friends, either—and so it's most likely he was killed as a warning to you."

I sat up in the chair and shook my head. "But I didn't know him. I didn't know him at all, so why would it be a warning to me? When people send warnings, don't they kill friends or family members? Or chop their fingers off and send them to people in the mail?"

"You have got to stop watching so much television," Tate said, shaking his head.

"Hey, Mom and Dad gave me TiVo for Christmas. It's great. I never miss shows anymore."

Tate smiled at me, a quick grin, and then his face went sober again. "Well, the fact that he ended up in your truck is something we can't discount. He was killed somewhere else and then put in the truck. There's good news about that, too. Very little blood, and it was easy to clean up."

I winced. "How did he die?" I asked, my voice barely a squeak.

"He was shot, at close range. With the same caliber weapon that was used to shoot up your apartment building. Ballistics is doing a comparison right now."

"It just doesn't make any sense to me," I said. "Why has this person—whoever it is—been following me for months? They show up, then they go away. Then back they come. And now it's getting even worse. I just don't understand."

"Well, I was thinking about this while you were asleep. There is a pattern, you know. It's not as random as it seems."

"What do you mean?"

"The first time the Hummer showed up you were getting ready to put on your annual Christmas show, *The Nut-cracker*. The second time, your teams were getting ready to compete at the Hollywood StarMakers, where I believe your teams and soloists did really well, right? Now, it's competition season, and you're a week away from your first—"

"Someone is trying to stop me from . . . no, not stop me from dancing," I said as his words sunk in. "Whoever it is doesn't show up when I'm teaching dance, or dancing. Only when I'm doing something that other people will see. When other people will see my dancers."

"Yes. And that someone is trying to convince you that you aren't any good, as evidenced by the Gorilla-Gram, but the truth is, they must be trying to keep you from showing off your dancers. So can you think of anyone who has a reason to want your girls not to compete?"

"Every dance teacher up and down the Wasatch Front?" I said wryly. "Although they don't know that they aren't in trouble this year, because my routines just don't look that great. But they can't know that. There's a lot of jealousy in the dance world, and this past year about ten girls from other studios joined mine. It makes studio owners mad. But I didn't recruit them. They came to me because they wanted to dance like my girls. Parents always come up to me at competitions and ask if they can have studio infor-mation."

"Well, it makes sense. But the question now is who? It has to be someone who is really mad at you, really angry. I would think it would take more than losing just one dancer or losing one competition."

I thought about all the different studio owners and teach-ers I ran into on a regular basis, and while some were nice and some were not, none of them struck me as Hummer-driving, murdering psychos.

The ringing of my cell phone made me jump.

"I plugged it in to charge while you were sleeping," Tate said.

I rose from the kitchen chair and walked over to the phone, connected by the charger to an outlet above the kitchen counter. Next to it sat the keys to the Liberty, which had been in my purse. I figured Tate had fished them out and had the car delivered here. I saw James's number in the caller ID screen. I noticed the time right then, too, and I turned to Tate.

"You let me sleep through the first class. I'm supposed to be teaching dance. It's just a week to our first competition, and you let me sleep."

I answered the phone. "Hello?"

"Jennifer! I know you told Marlys I could handle this, but it's sheer chaos. I cannot do this. Where is Sal? Where are you? Where is Marlys, for that matter? She calls and tells me that I need to run dance, and now I can't even reach her!"

His voice was panic-stricken, and loud, but I understood why, because in the background I could hear the screams and yells of little girls who had obviously taken over the studio and were running roughshod over James—not an easy thing to do.

But with only one teacher, maintaining control wouldn't be easy—although he'd left me to do it more than once. Maybe I should just sit back and relax, and enjoy the evening with Tate . . .

"Jennifer!" James screamed into the phone. "I need help. No! No, girls, we do *not* make dresses out of toilet paper. Toilet paper is for wiping your . . . *Ack!* Kinley, put that tap shoe down! Those things are deadly weapons. Do *not* hit Maddie on the head."

"I'll be right there," I said and disconnected. "It's anarchy at the studio. Any minute they are going to tie James to the stake and light him on fire. Either that, or dance around him like he's a Maypole. Either way, I better get in there. So did you set Marlys up to this?"

"I thought you could use a break."

"It's a nice thought, Tate, really. But it's only seven days until our first competition, and I can't let whoever is doing this stop me from living my life. I briefly thought about running away, going out of town, but I can't. This is all I have."

"Then I'm going with you to the studio, and when I can't be there, I will have someone else covering you."

I started to protest, but then I remembered today's events. And decided not to complain.

I DIDN'T WANT TO WEAR THE CLOTHES I HAD slept in, so I asked him to take me by my apartment. Instead, he walked out of the kitchen and came back with a large duffel bag that contained dance clothing. I gave him a look. "You didn't really move me out of my apartment, did you?"

"The problem, Jenny, is that now that it's boarded up, it's a target for criminals. I wish it were different, but it's in the part of town that is located just a little too close to the criminal element. So I had two choices: get your stuff out of there, or leave it for the pickings. I chose to have it removed. It's in storage, all except for a few things I knew you would need, which are in my spare bedroom. After your apartment is fixed, and the danger is passed, if you choose to move back in, that's your call. But for now, you're staying with me."

I thought about the shots flying over my head, and dead Mr. Grundle next door. I shivered. Then I thought about some policeman or other guys Tate knew going through my bras and underwear, and that made me shiver, too. He must have read my mind. "Alissa took some time off to help me pack your things, okay? She was worried about you. I let her handle all the, uh, delicate items, and put some guys to work on the big stuff." Alissa was my longtime friend. We'd met while working for the sheriff's office. She was still there, working as a 911 dispatcher while attending the police academy.

I knew how busy Alissa was, so I appreciated the thought, but I still wasn't all that fond of the fact that he had packed up everything I owned and moved it into storage. I had to admit, his reasoning was sound—a boarded-up building in my neck of the forest practically screamed for someone to trespass, loot, and make mayhem.

But still . . . Since I had no idea how to react, I decided not to do anything just yet. Wow, Marlys was right. I really was acting logical.

"This will work for now. But what about Malece?" I asked him.

He sighed. "Apparently, Sal has offered her the use of his apartment while he is recuperating in the hospital."

"Sal and Malece. Yeah, I kinda tried to warn you about that, but I wasn't sure what to say that wouldn't make you pull out your gun and go down to the hospital and finish Sal off."

"It was a . . . surprise. I kinda thought he was gay."

"I guess you thought wrong. I'll go change."

TATE DROVE ME TO THE STUDIO AND FOL-lowed me inside, careful to scan the surroundings as we walked. He was alert and watchful, and I felt safe. The only problem was, I could hardly keep him by my side 24-7. What was I going to do?

I opened the studio door and walked into a zoo. "Girls!" I yelled, hands on my hips. No response.

I heard James yelling in the other room, and tried to pretend I didn't hear the words "matches" and "Doritos."

I put two fingers in my mouth and let out a piercing

whistle, the way my father had taught me back when he took me camping. Since I had a tendency to wander off, he'd wanted a way to be able to find me. I'd learned how to do the whistle really quickly, which was a good thing, because an outdoors woman I was not.

The whistle seemed to do the trick. The girls stopped what they were doing and stared at me in silence. The few in the other studio—who had apparently been working on their fire-starting skills—trailed into the room, their eyes wide. James came behind them, wiping his brow dramatically, a blue streak down the side of his face.

"What is going on here?" I yelled, startled at the remnants of food, clothing, and bags strung through the room. "You are supposed to be dancing and listening to James. I thought you girls wanted to dance. I thought you wanted trophies. You sure won't get them this way."

I was impressed. They were staying quiet and staring at me with fear in their eyes. Maybe I was finally getting control of everything in my life.

Then I remembered Tate was standing behind me. I turned, and sure enough, he had a hand on his hip, pushing aside his suit jacket, so that his gun was exposed. I certainly wouldn't condone any shooting in my studio, but they didn't have to know that. As long as it worked.

Quickly, I sent the Tots with James and kept the Minis in the first dance room with me. Finally, dance was under way, and there was a semblance of order. The routines still didn't look that great, though. I wasn't sure what to do about that. I'd been preoccupied for the past few months, and now it was time to compete them, and while they were good and clean, they just weren't . . . they just didn't have that oomph.

Tate watched the practice, and after I sent the girls home, he walked over to me and put his hand on my chin, tilting my face toward his. "What's wrong? You don't look happy."

James came cruising out of the other room, jacket on, bag packed. "That was crazy. Do not ever do that to me again, Jennifer," he said, wagging a finger.

"Uh, what's the blue streak on your face?"

He reached up and touched it, then the dawning of recognition filled his eyes. "Marker. Can you please tell me why children would bring crayons, markers, and coloring books to dance when the only breaks we give them are to get water and snacks?"

I just shook my head.

"I need to run home and shower, and then I'm meeting friends for drinks. This has been such a crazy night that I really need the alcohol. Since Trevor's in town, I figured . . ."

He stopped talking as I stared at him.

"Well, gotta go . . ."

"James?"

Tate was watching both of us closely.

"Yes, Jennifer?" He tried to look innocent.

"Trevor is in town? And you didn't tell me?"

"Oh, you've been so busy getting ready for competition season, I guess I forgot."

"Who's Trevor?" Tate asked.

"An old friend of mine," I said. "A friend who would have called the studio and asked for me. A friend who most decidedly would not arrange to meet James for drinks without me being present."

"I was going to tell you," James said quickly. "I just forgot, because of all the mess here and the chaos. Why did you and Sal bail on me, anyway? And where the heck is Marlys? She's always good at maintaining order, but I couldn't even get ahold of her."

"Good change of subject, James, but it won't fly. What's going on?" I needed to tell him about Sal, but that would have to wait. And I had no intention of sharing Marlys's business.

"Oh, fine. Trevor called, said he was in town visiting his relatives, and he really wanted to meet you for dinner or drinks. I promised him we would both be there at nine p.m., at the City Club. But you are busy with Mr. Hunky Policeman there, so I figured I'd just fill in for you."

"James, Trevor is straight. As straight as they come, and you will never get him to play for your team, so the time has come to stop trying. Give it a rest! If you show up there alone, he is going to bolt so fast your head will do fouettés without any help from your body! He knows you are interested in him, and he wants nothing to do with it."

"Hey, he's a dancer. Most male dancers have some sort of gay side to them. It's just a matter of helping them find it," James said.

"Glad I don't dance," Tate said.

James gave him a smile, and Tate shivered.

"James, Trevor is not interested. And you know that. And he's my friend, and you didn't even tell me he's in town." The daybreak of an idea started to form in my mind. I'd met Trevor at a dance-teacher convention a few years back, when he was teaching his incredible moves, and we were all learning—and ogling. He was a rarity in the dance world: a handsome, talented, sensual, and caring straight choreographer. The "straight" was the only real rarity in that whole equation, but that didn't really need explaining, did it?

Trevor Paulsen and I had danced around an attraction to each other, but the convention was short, and I wasn't a weekend-stand kinda girl, so we'd stayed friends, and when he was in town, he called and we met for drinks and light flirtation. It had never gone beyond that. He lived in Los Angeles, California, an awful long way from Ogden, Utah—in more than miles.

But Trevor was an incredible choreographer. The best. And he could help me come up with a routine that would knock the shoes off the judges—and maybe even fix the routines I already had.

"Feel like having a drink?" I asked Tate.

"I'm going where you're going," he said. But he didn't look terribly happy. I would have some 'splainin' to do.

NINE

THE CITY CLUB WAS CROWDED AND LOUD, even on a weeknight. It was located within walking distance of my studio on historic 25th Street, and it attracted a lot of Ogden's denizens, at least the ones who weren't active Mormons. I searched the tables for Trevor and finally spotted him in the back, with a bevy of beautiful women around him. Of course. He had that charisma.

We made our way through the throng toward the table where Trevor entertained. Heavy music pulsed and dozens of odors intermingled in the air, giving it a mysterious, nighttime vibe that I hadn't experienced in a long time. I wasn't much for bars, I didn't drink often, and I really didn't have money to waste. So I rarely came to this type of place.

"Jenny!" Trevor cooed after he looked up and spotted me. The bevy of beauties glared at me. I could sense Tate glaring, too, although he stood behind me and I couldn't actually see his face. Trevor jumped up, grabbed me, and

pulled me to him, placing his lips on mine in a friendly—
very, very friendly—kiss.

I pulled away.

"Trevor Paulsen, this is my, uh, friend Tate Wilson. And
you know James."

Oh, I'd muffed that up. I could see that from the thun-
derous look in Tate's eyes, and yet I wasn't secure enough
to call him my boyfriend—at least not in front of him. He
probably wouldn't understand that and would interpret it
the wrong way. And to tell the truth, Trevor's kiss made my
stomach do flip-flops. Just like it always did. I was in a
world of trouble. I hadn't thought this through very well.
What was new?

"Sit, sit," Trevor said.

"There's not room to sit," Tate said, icicles dripping
from his voice.

"Sorry, girls, I need to chat with my friends here. It was
nice meeting all of you." There were lots of disappointed
looks, and more than a few nasty stares sent my way.

"Will you be around later?" simpered one very pretty,
very slender, very young blonde. Was she even legal? Did
she use a fake ID to get in? Should I call the alcohol control people, who frowned on things like that, and report her
just because she was making me jealous? Probably not.

"One never knows," Trevor said. He'd picked up Tate's
vibe, I guess, because he kept darting worried looks his
way.

"So, Trevor, how are you?" James said, reaching forward to hug Trevor. The other man backed up a bit and
stuck out his hand. James had been trying to convert him
for quite a while, and it wasn't the Mormon Church he
wanted Trev to join. It was the Chapel of James.

James looked peeved but took a seat, as did I. Tate was
last, pulling out a chair and scowling at everyone within
scowl distance.

"So, Trevor, what brings you to town?" I asked.

"Just did some choreography for a hip-hop artist up in Park City. We were doing a music video. That place rocks, I'm telling you." Park City was a local ski resort town famous for its nightlife, celebrities, rich lifestyle, and of course, the Sundance Film Festival. Located just thirty miles or so from Salt Lake City, it was a popular destination for all types of celebs, skiers, and rich people. Naturally, I went there only once in a great while, as I was none of the above.

"And then you just happened to end up here in Ogden?" Tate asked, his voice calm and serene, but carrying an undercurrent of dangerous electricity.

"No, no happenstance. I always come to see Jenny whenever I'm in Utah."

"Oh, you do, do you?" The undercurrent started sparking.

"Oh, you don't just come to see her, do you? I'm so offended," James said in a faux hurt voice. "How could you forget about me?"

"Uh . . ."

"James," I said, warning in my voice. A waitress came over to our table and leaned down, asking for our drink order. She smiled broadly at Trevor and asked him if he wanted the same. He nodded and smiled. She turned to Tate, and her smile got broader. "Tate! How are you?"

The tall blond waitress leaned down and gave him a big hug, and he returned it warmly. What the heck was going on here? "Where have you been? You haven't called me for months. I thought you promised me a weekend in Wendover. Remember?"

"Wendover?" I asked, my voice rising slightly.

"Trevor?" Tate asked without looking over at me, still smiling into Blondie's eyes.

I'll see your blond waitress and raise you my hunky blast from the past! I scooted my chair closer to Trevor. "So, tell me all about your music-video experience."

Tate looked at me, ordered a glass of water, and pointed Blondie in my direction. "This is my girlfriend, Jenny Partridge. Jenny, this is my old friend, Karen Thompson."

At the word "girlfriend," three faces fell. Karen's, Trevor's, and mine. Mine mostly because he'd trumped me in the maturity department yet again. I was such an idiot.

I scooted away from Trevor and ordered a piña colada. I was all about froufrou drinks, because if you could taste the alcohol, then I wasn't having it.

"Helloooo," twittered an annoyed James, who absolutely despised not being the center of attention. Here, he was being flatly ignored. "I'd like a vodka collins, please."

A disappointed Karen left our table, and Trevor turned to face me and Tate. "So, you two are together?"

"Yes, we are. Matter of fact, we're pretty much living together right now, but that's only because Jenny's apartment had an unfortunate, uh, accident."

"Well, you have good taste, Tate. Jenny's the best."

Tate put his arm around me and pulled my chair—and me in it—closer to him. "Yes, she is. Life is never boring around Jenny."

Hmm, was that a compliment or a slap in the face?

Karen brought us our drinks, gave Tate a sad smile, and then left after Trevor told her to put the drinks on his tab. Now that the lines had been drawn, and everybody was safe in their own little cage, ownership of a certain dance teacher made clear—thank God we weren't dogs, and Tate didn't pee on me to mark his territory—the atmosphere relaxed a little.

Trevor started to talk about his last job up in Park City and how crazy the hip-hop scene was. He was a pretty laid-back guy, and it's not like we had a relationship or anything. We just enjoyed getting together, and flirting. I'm sure he wouldn't have minded taking it further, but I wasn't going there. Especially with Tate's arm around me. I already felt a blush rising in my chest and making its way toward my face. Thank goodness it was dark in the City Club.

Trevor and Tate were chatting about Park City, where, apparently, Tate's family had a second home—of course!—and James was sulking over his drink. I took a couple of sips of my piña colada, being careful to avoid the brain freeze I invariably got, and listened to the chatter around me.

"Hey, Jen, I have a week off, and I'm just going to chill here in Utah, I think. Do you think you want to do any master classes while I'm here?"

The lightbulb over my head went on so brightly I was surprised everyone in the entire club wasn't shielding their eyes. Trevor was the answer to my problems. This was one of those miracles that Grandma Gilly, my Catholic maternal grandma, was always nattering on about.

"I need your help," I said hurriedly, almost tripping over my tongue. "My routines need jazzing up, and Sal was going to help me with an audition Company routine, but then he fell down the stairs and broke his leg. Would you choreograph an audition routine for me?"

"Well, of course, Jen, but you know I'm not cheap."

"Yes, but I also know the psycho dance moms who inhabit my studio, and they will pay for both the audition and a choreography fee, especially if the girl who stands next to their daughter in line is already signed up. It's a fact of dance life."

Trevor chuckled and said, "Sure, let's start tomorrow."

Tate didn't say anything. I couldn't tell what he was thinking, but hey, he'd staked his claim, and Trevor had accepted it, and this was business. Strictly business. All business. Really.

"What do you mean Sal broke his leg? And when was anyone going to tell me about this?" James said, petulance spearing the words.

"Yeah, he kinda fell down the stairs, after he scared me and I grabbed my arm away."

"Is he okay? And who is going to take his classes, because I never intend to teach alone like that again. Those children are piranhas!"

"Trevor will be helping this week, and we'll just have to do the best we can. I'll call around and see if I can find someone else to come in and help."

"Well, I'm just telling you, I'm going to need more money if you expect me to put in double time, because—"

I gave James a look and he stopped talking. He owed me big-time, and he knew it. Every two months or so he got me into some sort of mess, whether it was with his Mormon mother thinking we were a couple, or alternately thinking I had turned lesbian, or siccing his married boyfriend's wife on me. It was always something. More money was *not* in the postcards!

We finished our drinks—or in my case, half of my drink—and then stood up. Trevor promised to meet me at my studio at 11 a.m. the next day so we could come up with some music and ideas.

"Where are you staying?" James asked Trevor. "Do you need a ride?"

"No, no, I just planned on staying in the Marriott tonight, because it's close. My folks live in Salt Lake City, so I'll be back and forth from there and here. And I have a rental car, too. I'm going to settle up the bill. Thanks for coming, you guys. Tate, pleasure to meet you. You have a great girl in Jenny. Uh, good-bye, James."

My sulky friend stomped off, and Tate took my elbow and guided me to the door. I turned to watch Karen lean down to Trevor, who had sat back down in his chair, and smile, her blond hair falling over her face, her cleavage right in his face.

A spear of jealousy spiked through me. Great. This

might be Utah, land of polygamy, but a girl didn't get to have two guys. And I had a great one in Tate. So why was I bothered by Trevor flirting with Karen?

I was a complicated girl. It had to be that.

TEN

TATE SPENT QUITE A WHILE, AFTER WE RE-turned to his place that night, staking his claim on me but I didn't mind a bit.

"So what is this Trevor guy to you?" he asked me just as I was slipping off to sleep.

"He's a friend. Never anything more. I promise." That was *so* not a lie.

The next morning, I got up to a note. I was used to that. I just hoped today there were no knife-bearing half sisters hanging out in the kitchen. I was in luck. I showered, sham-pooed, shaved my legs, and blew my hair dry, pulling it back into a sleek ponytail. That lasted about ten seconds, until the natural curl took over and waves began to form. It had grown out some since I'd let a psycho dance mom cut it—not real-izing how mentally unstable she was and how sensitive she was about her daughter's lack of dance talent—and I was fi-nally able to do some things with it.

I quickly dressed in dance clothes and then put on a light coat of makeup. Just some foundation, eyeliner, and mascara, because I was a redhead, and without it, my eyes disappeared into my head and I looked like I had no lashes.

I was very aware of the fact I never put makeup on when I was teaching dance, but I ignored all those guilty little feelings in the pit of my stomach. After all, Tate might come by later, and I'd want to look my best for him. *Liar!* Grandma Gilly's voice shouted in my brain. I tuned it out. I'd been tuning out Grandma Gilly for years. I was really good at it. Most of the time.

So why did I still feel so guilty? It was just makeup for Pete's sake! I hadn't put on my hoochie-mama clothes! I just wanted to look nice today. It put me in a good mood.

Straight to hell, Jennifer! Darn that Grandma Gilly.

I went back into the bathroom and scrubbed off the mascara and eyeliner. I couldn't get it all off, because I didn't have eye-makeup remover with me, and of course that was not something that Tate kept handy, so I ended up looking like a raccoon. I took some liquid hand soap, put it on a washcloth, and scrubbed away.

Some of the soap seeped into my eye, and it began to sting and burn. I quickly washed it out with cold water, but the damage had been done. Now, not only did I not have mascara and eyeliner on, but I also had a very red, half-opened eye. I'd seen plenty of cases of pinkeye, because I worked with kids, and I looked just like that. Great. Now I looked contagious.

I should have stuck with the mascara and eyeliner, and just planned on going straight to hell when I died. It would have been easier. Whenever I tried to do the right thing, it backfired. Well, maybe not every time. That truth-telling thing had been working pretty well for me the past few days.

After I made myself an English muffin with butter and jam, I grabbed my bag and headed out the side door that led to Tate's garage, which is where he had parked the Liberty after my unfortunate encounter with the Hummer and the gunshots.

Tate's house was pretty secure, and I felt safe as I got into the sporty little vehicle, but I still looked in the backseat and around the garage cautiously. When I didn't spot anything, I pulled the keys out of my purse and started it up. The only problem was, how did I get myself out of the garage? I spied a garage door opener sitting in a small compartment below the stereo, and smiled. Tate thought of everything.

I was glad I washed the mascara and eyeliner off, even if my eye still stung like crazy and I looked like I had pinkeye.

It was only 9:30 a.m., so I headed to McKay Dee Hospital to check on Sal. After I pulled into the street I noticed a police vehicle pull out from where it was parked and fall into line behind me. My police escort, I presumed. In the past few months, I'd had more encounters with policemen than any convicted felon would ever have. It had been eventful, to say the least.

I was meeting Trevor at eleven, so I had plenty of time. I parked in the hospital lot, which was currently under construction, so I had quite a ways to walk. The police car pulled into a spot near mine, and the officer behind the wheel gave me a small wave. I waved back, then scoured the area for a silver Hummer but didn't see one.

I quickly headed into the hospital and got into the elevator to go up to Sal's room. The policeman was following me, but not very closely. The elevator took off before he could get on it, since a slightly deranged-looking elderly man, wearing a hospital gown and robe, kept pushing the fourth-floor button over and over and over.

Before the doors shut, I spotted the policeman's worried look, and I stuck my arm out to stop the door, but the old man pulled me inside and the doors closed.

"Hey, what are you doing?" I said to him.

"I'm escaping, and you aren't going to stop me," he said, pointing an old arthritic finger at me. "They are not giving me one more enema. Not one!"

Hmm, can't say I blamed him for trying to escape. "You're going the wrong way."

"Huh?"

"You just got *on* the elevator on the ground floor, where all the exits are. Now you are headed up to the patient floors."

"Darnit," he said, pouting like a little child. "I get so confused." We stopped on four, and I started to get off. "Wait," he said. "You stay here. I'm holding you hostage until they let me out of here."

"I don't think so," I said. "Sorry about the enemas." He tried to hold on to my arm, but he didn't have a lot of strength. I bolted out and he yelled after me. A nurse walked toward me carrying a chart, and I said, "There's a confused old man on the elevator. I think he's trying to escape."

"Really?"

"Yeah, he was headed back down to the bottom floor, so you better hurry." She scurried off toward what I assumed were stairs.

As I passed a nurses' station, a woman looked up and alarm lit up her eyes. "Wait, wait, you can't go in there," she said, standing up and walking around the counter toward me.

"Why not?" I asked.

"You have conjunctivitis. Don't you know how contagious it is?" She stared at me like I had leprosy.

"What the heck is conjunctivitis?"

"Pinkeye," she said, a look of disdain on her face. She was middle-aged, with gray hair and tight lines around her lips and eyes—probably because she was the guard dog of the hospital—and she wore scrubs that had happy little pigs dancing all over. It was false advertisement, for I could tell her character was not one of happiness. She was slender and tall, so she obviously wasn't a pig, either. Maybe she should have worn scrubs with Dobermans chewing up mailmen on them, or something like that.

"I don't have pinkeye. I got some soap in my eye this morning, and now it hurts like crazy. But it's not pinkeye."

"Right."

She moved until she stood right in front of me, arms folded and toe tapping. Any minute now she was going to call the pinkeye police.

"Look, it's not pinkeye. I told you, I got soap in my eye this morning. I just want to visit my friend Sal and check on his progress, and then get to work."

"You can't go to work with pinkeye. You'll give it to everyone!" This woman had tagged me as some kind of dangerous health hazard. Any moment I was going to be quarantined.

"Please listen to me. This is *not* pinkeye."

"How do you know that?"

"Because, as I explained, my eyes were fine until I was washing some mascara off this morning, and I got soap in my eye!"

"You sleep in mascara? No wonder you have pinkeye."

If I had one of those knives, I'd probably commit Hare Krishna right now. Good thing I didn't carry sharp weapons with me.

"This. Is. Not. Pinkeye." There, couldn't make it much clearer than that.

"You a doctor?" she asked, her lips a snarl.

"No, but I know how my eye got red. Now, I'm going in to visit with my friend, Sal." I started to go around her, and she blocked my way.

"Not in my hospital, missy."

I stared at her and considered my chances. I didn't really want to get arrested for having pinkeye. That would be very hard to explain. I finally decided to give up. "Okay, look, will you just tell Sal Tuatuola that Jenny came by to see him, but you refused to let me in? And have him call me on my cell."

"Yes, I'll just run that message right to him," she said.

I sighed. I seemed to rub people wrong without even trying. I turned and headed back to the elevator, which reminded me about the crazy old man, and also my police escort. I hoped he wasn't going from floor to floor, trying to find me. The policeman, not the crazy old man, although I really didn't want him trying to find me, either.

When I got back down to the first floor, I stepped out into chaos. Security guards and hospital personnel were scurrying about, and someone was paging a "Code Purple" over the PA system.

"There he goes," someone shouted, and I spotted my police escort chasing after the same old man who had tried to hold me hostage in the elevator. He was pretty wily for an old guy, even though I knew from experience he wasn't strong.

I sighed and headed out to the parking lot. I didn't think I'd been followed by anyone anyway, and even if I had, the policeman following me, in a clearly marked car, would surely scare off the mysterious Hummer driver.

As I neared the Liberty, a loud roar filled my ears. I turned, panicked, to see the silver Hummer bearing down on me. I screamed and jumped to the side, lodging myself between two parked vehicles as it roared past. Right in the Hummer's path, another car was pulling out—an elderly woman driver in a large blue boat—and the Hummer was forced to stop.

I reacted without thinking, running up to the Hummer, which had made it only about twenty yards, and began pounding on the windows. "Just leave me alone, dammit, leave me alone."

The tinted window rolled down just a crack, and a raspy, androgynous voice said, "I have a gun. I've warned you off. Time to quit the dance business, Jenny Partridge. Better yet, leave Utah and start over somewhere else. This is your last warning."

"Who the heck are you?" I screamed. The window

rolled back up, and the Hummer driver put it into reverse and backed it out, tearing off. The old lady in the blue boat was still trying to maneuver out of her parking spot, without much success.

Quit the dance business? I couldn't quit the dance business. It was all I knew. Leave Utah? This *had* to be another crazy dance teacher who was threatened by my success. Okay, maybe not my success. I didn't make much money, but a lot of my dancers were really good, and my program was gaining a great reputation throughout the area.

That had to be what it was.

I dejectedly trudged toward the Liberty and got inside. I started up the car and then fished into my purse for my cell phone. Tate answered on the first ring, miracle of miracles. It usually went through to his voice mail.

"It's not my fault, but the policeman following me got caught up in chasing the old man who tried to hold me hostage in the elevator so he could escape."

"Old man? Elevator? Hostage?" His voice rose with each word.

"Yes, I went to the hospital to visit Sal, and this old guy was trying to escape because he didn't want any more enemas, but he was really confused and got on the elevator going up. He tried to hold me hostage, but he was pretty weak and he didn't have any weapons, anyway. Then when I tried to see Sal, the nurse wouldn't let me in because she thought I had pinkeye. When I went back downstairs, everybody was chasing the old guy, including the cop, and so I figured I would just go get in my car. And that's when the Hummer drove up."

"Whoa, whoa. First of all, are you okay?"

"Yes, I moved between two cars, so the Hummer couldn't get me."

"Do I need to send an ambulance?"

"I'm in the parking lot of the hospital," I explained patiently. Somewhat patiently. I was starting to shake pretty badly, as the latest encounter became reality. "I'm okay. But this old lady was backing her car out, and it was huge, and she couldn't really drive it very well, and so the Hummer was stuck. And I, uh, kinda ran up to it and started pounding on the windows and told whoever was driving to leave me alone."

"Jenny," he said sadly.

"Hey, I was freaked out. And the driver rolled down the window, just a little, and this voice warned me to quit teaching dance and to leave Utah, and said this was my final warning."

Now I was really shaking.

"Did you get the license plate?"

Darnit! First chance I had to actually see the plate, and I'd been too rattled to even look.

"Um, no."

He sighed. "Male or female?"

"Couldn't tell."

"Any glimpse at all of the driver?"

"Not really. Those Hummers are pretty high, and I'm pretty short."

"Where are you now?"

"In the parking lot of the hospital." That time I knew I wasn't patient.

"Okay, get in the Liberty and wait for me there. I'm about five minutes away."

MORE PAPERWORK, MORE INTERVIEWS, AND then Tate followed me to the studio. I was now about ten minutes late to my meeting with Trevor. He sat on the steps of my studio staircase, listening to an iPod and bobbing his head to the beat.

Tate watched me walk up the stairs, waved, and then waited. A few seconds later a police car pulled in, and I assumed a new escort was on duty. Unless my old one had not been fired after the escapade with the hospital escapee.

"Cops, huh? Why?" Trevor asked as I reached the top of the stairs. He pulled the iPod earphones out of his ears and tucked the unit into his shirt pocket. It was a warm spring day, and I hadn't even put on a jacket when I left Tate's. Which was a good thing, since I had no idea where my jackets were.

"Long story."

"Sure this boyfriend isn't a little overprotective?" he asked, his eyes serious and concerned.

"No, his concern is warranted, unfortunately. Someone has been threatening me, and the other night some guy was killed and put in my truck."

"That Jeep?" he asked, a look of distaste on his face.

"No, it was my father's old truck. That's why I'm driving the Jeep. No desire to sit next to death germs."

"Crazy stuff, Jenny. The mob after you?"

"Maybe a Mormon mob," I sighed.

"Oh, I don't think the Mormons do things like that anymore. Do they?" he asked.

"I was mostly kidding," I answered. "Let's go inside."

It would take a long time to explain how Mormon missionaries kept getting involved in some pretty life-threatening incidents every time they were around me. It would take even longer to explain about Sal. I had a routine to set.

I unlocked the studio door, and Trevor followed me in. I pulled my cell phone out of my purse, and he went directly to the stereo system in the main studio room.

I called Marlys and left her a message to call me ASAP. I wanted her to get the Pyscho Mom System, which we nicknamed PMS, started. It was really a phone tree, but we liked PMS better. Marlys would call four moms, and they would each call four moms, and so on and so on, like the old shampoo commercial.

It worked really well, except when they were gossiping about me. Oh well. Can't have everything.

"Uh, that's not pinkeye, is it?" Trevor asked, pointing to my obviously still red orb.

"No, it's soap. I washed my face this morning and got some in it. Burned like crazy. Still hurts." I wasn't about to explain the whole no mascara–mascara debate that had gone on in my head this morning.

"Okay, listen to this, and tell me what you think," Trevor said. He plugged his iPod into the stereo system jack, and soon the sounds of a fast rhythm, hip-hop beats, and a pounding cadence filled the studio.

"Wow, this is great. Who is it?"

"Friend of mine, record is set to break in two months. In other words, you have original music no one else will have." He smiled, the dimples on both sides of his cheeks making my heart flutter. Trevor had blond hair, sky blue eyes, and almost olive-colored skin, an odd combination. He resembled Brad Pitt, an asset that made it easy for him to morph into the world of celebrities, but dance was his calling and passion. He'd never had any desire to do anything else. He was medium height, sinewy lean, and dancer strong. And he knew how to dress. Probably why James was always trying to get him to play for his team.

"I really like this," I said, trying to get my mind off how dang hot he was.

"Do you have any girls who are en pointe?"

"Yes, there are four or five that are pretty good at it. They take lessons at my friend Coli's ballet school. She's just traditional ballet, and I like to jazz things up, but we get along great and send students to each other all the time."

"Cool. Listen to this part. It's perfect to incorporate both pointe and hip-hop, and do something totally unique."

He stopped talking as the music changed, morphing into an almost classical sound, and I could really envision what he was talking about.

"I was thinking maybe black tutus and red pointe shoes," he said when that part of the music was done.

"Yikes. Where the heck am I going to get red pointe shoes in a week?"

"You give me the pointe shoes, and I'll make them red," said a voice from the doorway.

We looked up to see Malece standing there, holding a small black CD case.

"Malece, what are you doing here?" I asked, trying my hardest not to sound hostile. After all, as long as Tate was in my life, I was stuck with her. I was also intrigued by her claim of being able to turn pink pointe shoes red. I mean, I could see Trevor's vision. If this worked, it would be like nothing else ever seen at a Utah competition. But the costumes would be a very big part of making it work.

"Sal wanted me to drop this music by for you. He had planned to mix it and combine it, but of course, he got pushed down the stairs, so that didn't happen. He says he doesn't blame you, though."

"I did *not* push him down the stairs! He came running up them, grabbed me, and scared the living night-lights out of me!"

"Night-lights?" Trevor asked.

"Whatever, you know what I mean."

"Anyway, you have a pair of those pointe shoes? Because I'll show you what I mean if you do."

I went into my office and came out with a pair of my old—very old—pointe shoes. They were my first pair, worn back when I was only twelve years old, and I treasured them. But I treasured my studio and reputation more. I would sacrifice them for the cause.

"These are kinda trashed," Malece said.

"Well, it's an experiment, right?" I asked. "If it turns out, we can get new shoes quick and you can do the rest of them."

"You think I can't do it?"

"Didn't say that. Just want to see it before I give you five pairs of eighty-five-dollar shoes. Plus, I have to have the girls sized and then buy the shoes, so it will take me a few days. And Trevor has to set the routine to see who is even going to be in it. This gives you time to turn these pointe shoes red. And do you think you can find black tutus?"

"I can make them," she said, no expression on her face.

"Are you sure?"

"I never say something I don't mean," she said, glaring at me.

"Fine, go make those pointe shoes red. Come back when you're done. We'll be here setting the routine."

"Who is he?" she asked, pointing at Trevor.

"This is my friend Trevor. He's a choreographer and dancer. He's helping me with a routine."

"Does Tate know you are all alone here working with this guy?"

"Yes, Tate knows. Did you see that police car out front? Put there by him. He's already met Trevor, and they hit it off quite well."

My cell phone rang and I picked up. "Hello?"

"Jenny, it's Marlys. I got your call." She still sounded strained, and very tired, and I knew her situation was not improving just by her voice.

"Anything new?" I asked.

"No."

"Okay, well, can you start the PMS? Tell everyone we are having an audition routine this afternoon, at four p.m. Girls eight and up only. Everyone can come audition, but no one is guaranteed a spot. An outside choreographer is picking the dancers and placing them, and there will be an eighty-five-dollar fee to be in the routine, plus twenty dollars to audition, as well as costume and competition fees. Tell the girls who are en pointe to bring their shoes."

"Who's the choreographer?"

"Trevor Paulsen."

"He's the best."

"Yes, he is."

"Okay, I'm on it."

I hung up the phone and looked at Malece, who was watching me with something akin to consternation on her face.

"What?" I asked her.

"You aren't going to get anyone to come do this, on short notice, for that kind of money. How much money will this one routine cost them by the time they are done?"

"Probably around five hundred dollars."

Her mouth dropped open even farther. "And these are all just young girls, right?"

"Yep."

"There's no way. No way."

"You just work on those pointe shoes and come back around five. You'll see."

"I don't understand."

"Remember Tamara Williams?"

She blanched as she remembered the costume she had signed up to design, and nodded.

"Well, I have a whole lot more like her, although maybe not as extreme. And then there are the girls who actually dance because they love it and not because their mothers have delusions of grand mal."

"Huh?"

"Just come back. You'll see."

She turned and left without saying good-bye.

"Who is that?" Trevor asked. "Friend or foe, because she sure doesn't act very friendly. At least to you."

"She's Tate's sister, and she doesn't much like me. And yet, she can't seem to stay away from me. Like all the rest of the crazies I have to deal with."

Trevor just nodded, then went back into his own little world, listening to the music and moving with it, choreographing step by step, starting and stopping the music. I sat down on the floor to watch him, fascinated by the process. I usually worked the same way, but it was interesting to see it from a bystander's point of view.

I watched him for two hours, without even realizing the time had passed. He was fluid and strong, and I felt something stir in my stomach. His love for dance matched mine. Our hearts had a shared passion.

Tate thought I was funny and eccentric. I was something weird in his rigid and structured life. I broke up the routine. Was that enough to make a relationship work?

Trevor stopped dancing, wiped the sweat from his forehead, and grabbed a bottled water from the small fridge I kept stocked for teachers. Okay, fine, Marlys kept it stocked, but I asked her to do it!

"So, you like the music, you like the moves. You think it's going to work?" he asked me. He'd taken off his long-sleeved shirt an hour before and was wearing a wife-beater T-shirt, one that showed off his long, lean musculature. He also wore baggy UFO sweatpants that allowed him to move easily. "You think we can make this happen?"

"I think it's going to work." The routine, I meant. Nothing else was going to happen. Nothing.

ELEVEN

AT 3:45 P.M. DANCERS AND MOMS BEGAN pouring through the door. Many of the girls had fancy curls or new hair accessories, and many were wearing obviously new dance clothes. The key here was to stand out. I always stressed that the way to stand out was to be a "standout" dancer, but I understood that looking nice was also a part of the package.

Several of the older girls ran up to Trevor and gave him hugs, and chattered at him excitedly. He'd been to my studio before, for master classes, and he also taught at some of the dance conventions that came to town.

By four, I had around fifty dancers ready to audition.

"All right, girls, let's get this jam going," Trevor said, and he flipped on the music, loud, and started them through a warm-up routine. I stood in the back and stretched along with the girls. Obviously, I would have to know the routine, too, since Trevor wouldn't be here past next week. All the cleaning and practice after he left would be up to me. And to get it up to snuff in a week's time meant there would be *a lot* of practices required.

After the warm-up, Trevor started the music and let the girls listen to it one time through. I could tell which ones were feeling the music, which ones were listening to the beat, and which ones were just waiting for him to teach them the moves. The ones who felt it would do much better.

"Okay, you all ready?"

The girls all shouted, "Yes!"

"Let's go!"

Trevor taught the first half of the routine in about an hour's time. The little girls were struggling, although a few picked it up. Some of the older girls had the moves but not the passion, and some just plain couldn't do anything. It would be easy to cut the first round.

Malece walked in during the routine and looked around at all the dancers and moms. She was carrying a pair of bright red pointe shoes in a shoe box without a lid.

"Wow," Trevor said, stopping the routine. "Those are exactly what I wanted. That is perfect!"

"Don't touch them, they're still wet."

"How did you do it?" I asked, admiring the bright red shoes.

"Trade secret. Are you convinced?"

"Yes, I'm convinced. As soon as we know who is doing the pointe part, we will arrange for a fitting, and I'll get the shoes to you. But can you stick around now and measure the girls who make the routine, and then sit down and discuss costumes with Trev and me? Also, watching the routine might give you some ideas."

"Well, Sal is expecting me back at the hospital. He doesn't like being alone."

"I know, I know, but you want to be out on your own, right? This is going to be a good job, if you can pull it off."

"Fine, I'll stay. I'll go visit Sal after we discuss what

you want for costumes. And there are no ifs about it. I will pull it off. Didn't this convince you?" Malece thrust the box toward me.

I took it from her. "Yes, I'm impressed. But these are shoes. Let's see how the rest goes."

She gave a snort and flipped her hair, then walked to the back of the room. She was still in black, apparently still protesting, although today she was wearing pencil thin black jeans with a black T-shirt that said "Born to Be Bad" on the front, and on the back was a very beautiful face of a woman, done in glitter and sequins. It caught my eye and I couldn't look away. She turned and looked at me, and smiled—a very rare occurrence.

"Yes, I did it."

Hmm. I was beginning to think this would be a beautiful . . . no, no, not beautiful, but at least wonderful . . . no, not that, either. Maybe together we would make good artistic partners who wouldn't kill each other. I couldn't think of another way to say it.

The hard-driving music shut off, and Trevor walked over to me.

"Okay, I'm ready to set spots. Jenny, can you come here?"

The girls started twittering nervously. We walked into the other room, and he told me, "You have some really good dancers here, but some of them will never pick this up in time to perfect it. What I want to do now is pick about a dozen girls, most of them older, although you have a few young ones that picked it up fast. I pretty much know who I want, but I'm going to have them run it one more time and then pick them. Then I want to work with them, setting the choreography and places. Will their parents freak if we do another three hours?"

"Not if they want their daughter in the routine, they won't."

"Okay, let's do it. Anybody I should steer clear of?"

I thought for a minute, then said, "No. I'm gonna let you just go with this. I trust you."

"Cool."

We went back into the main studio room, and the girls instantly hushed and stared at us with expectant eyes. The moms were quiet, too.

"All right, girls, we're going to run this one time, and then I'm going to pick spots. You all did a great job, and unfortunately, I can't pick all of you. But keep coming to my classes. I hope Jenny will do this again, and you guys just keep working hard, and give it your heart and soul, and if you don't make it this time, maybe next time it will be your turn.

"Now, everybody, one time through. Give it everything you have." He turned on the music and returned to where I stood at the front of the group.

We watched as the girls went through the moves of the routine. Trevor had one hand on his chin and the other cupping his right elbow as he watched the girls dance. Some were clearly out of their league with the difficult choreography, but others had gotten the steps down. A few were making the movements fine but not getting into the beat or "feeling the music."

Trevor and I stood at the front of the group and watched. When the music was done, he told them to get a drink and turned to me.

"So, I see maybe fourteen that could pull this off in the amount of time we have."

I chuckled, even though he didn't surprise me. Trevor was a professional choreographer, and he was going to move quickly, and most girls were not at a professional level yet. "That many?" I asked.

"It's not going to be an easy routine, Jen. And they have to learn and perfect it fast. Thing is, I hope the girls I've picked are your girls who are en pointe, or I'm not sure it will work."

"I'm pretty sure they are," I said. "Coli only takes girls by referral, and so only my best dancers work with her."

The girls gathered back around, and Trevor asked them to stand up.

One by one, he pointed out the girls he had picked, and I called them by name. When he finished, he told all the other girls to give themselves a big hand for their hard work and to make sure and come to the next audition. He was really planning on coming back to help me again, which I didn't quite know how to interpret. I was thrilled to have the opportunity but scared to death because he caused me to have some feelings that I just didn't feel comfortable, safe, or honest with.

The girls who made the routine all jumped around excitedly and hugged each other, while some others left dejectedly. April Williams looked angry, and when she threw her dance bag at her mother, narrowly missing her, I knew I had interpreted her reaction correctly. Even worse, Tamara was glowering at both Trevor and me, giving me a major case of heartburn. The Williams duo stomped out the door—and if I was lucky, right to another studio. A few girls left with tears streaming down their faces.

Rejection was never easy. I understood that. And it was, of course, another reason I was hesitant to do this type of thing, but I needed something special, and the butterflies in my stomach told me this was going to be good.

Malece had been watching in the background, and she came forward. "I got a pretty good idea, and I think I can go with this. Black and red theme, and what about maybe some black-and-white-striped socks for the hip-hop dancers, and black mesh tights for your girls in pointe shoes. The black tutus only on the pointe girls, of course, and some really thrashy-looking tops, with lots of mesh. Mesh gloves, too."

"She's got it," Trevor said, smiling at Malece. She

returned his infectious grin and then sobered up when she turned to me.

"Remember I need the rest of the shoes. The sooner the better. Now, I need to measure these girls and write down their sizes. Who is using the pointe shoes, and who is hip-hop?"

"She even knows the different parts," Trevor said admiringly. "You are really good, girl."

"Thanks!" she said girlishly, flashing him another smile.

I just shook my head. "Okay, girls, raise your hand so Trev knows who can dance en pointe."

After we determined which girl would be dancing which part, Malece pulled a tape measure out of her pocket and set to work.

"Do you always carry a tape measure?" I asked her.

"Of course. You never know when you might need it."

"Uh, okay."

I left her to her work and went to talk to the parents who were still hanging around, waiting for instructions on when to come back to pick up their daughters.

They were all excited and chattering, and none of them were the least bit bothered that I was now asking them to shell out eighty-five dollars apiece for choreography and would soon be asking for competition and costume fees. On top of those they had already paid. Dance parents were an interesting breed. There were always those who complained and whined, but when it came right down to it, when I told them that it was all optional and their daughter certainly didn't *have* to dance, boy, did they back down.

I collected checks and handed them over to Marlys, who had walked in a few minutes before. She had apparently dropped Carly off earlier, and left, because her daughter was—of course—one of the girls who Trevor picked to be in the routine.

After the other parents filtered out, Marlys turned to me.

She was morose and sad, her eyes filled with the burden of things she didn't, and couldn't, understand. "He did it again. Said he had to work late. So I dropped Carly off, took the boys to my mom's, and went to his work." In addition to Maribel and Carly, Marlys also had two boys, Max and R.J., short for Roger Jeffrey. I didn't see them much, obviously, as they were soccer fiends. Marlys kept pretty busy between dance and soccer games.

"Marlys, I told you to wait for me!"

"I knew you were busy with this."

"So, what happened?"

"I saw him leaving. Right at five p.m. And he was dressed in Levi's and a casual shirt. He works in a suit. It's all a lie, Jenny."

"Marlys, you don't know that. Did you follow him?"

"Yes, although I lost him. He was downtown, and he pulled into a side street, but I was so far back that when I got there, he was long gone. Maybe he saw me."

"If he saw you, he would have called you and tried to cover his tracks. That is, *if* he is doing something wrong."

"How can he not be doing something wrong? He's leaving work when he says he's staying to work late. He's dressed casually. And he's not being honest."

"What does he do, anyway?"

"He sells insurance."

"I can't believe I've known you all this time, and I didn't know what he did. I mean, I am closer to you than just about anyone else."

"You're a little caught up in the drama of the dance world and all the weird things that happen to you," Marlys said, without censure. I looked at her closely. She'd just had her thirty-seventh birthday, but she looked like she was twenty-eight. Her face had some lines, but they were character lines, brought on by humor and experience. She had beautiful blue eyes, long brown hair without any hint of gray, and she was medium build, not thin, not fat. In my eyes, just right.

And all the time we had been working together, I had never asked her what her husband did for a living.

"I'm not a very good friend, am I?"

"You provide the comic relief in my life. That is priceless. I couldn't ask for more."

"Yeah, well, you are always having to get me out of messes, and rescue me from psycho dance moms, and what do I do for you in return?"

"You have taught my daughter Carly to be an incredible dancer and helped her realize her dreams. You've given her self-esteem and purpose, and you keep her busy when other girls her age are getting in trouble with friends, and God forbid, some even with boys. You taught her that it's possible to reach your dreams, even when they seem so far out there they can't be touched. And you've taught me that sticking with something is worth it. That's what you've done for me."

I blinked back the unexpected tears in my eyes and gazed at her. "Wow. Well, I want to do more. I want to be the kind of friend you confide in."

"I don't do that, Jenny. It's not my way."

"Yeah, but you did tell me about this, and that means you need my help. Now, let's go find him."

"But you need to stay here with Trevor."

"I need to come back, that's for sure, but he needs some time alone with the girls. Just enough time for you and me to go looking for Roger."

"Jenny . . ."

"No arguments, let's go. And I can grab some dinner for us on the way back."

TWELVE

THERE WAS A SMALL PROBLEM WITH MY PLAN.
Okay, my whole life was filled with small problems that
turned into large problems. Why did my life never go like
it did on television or in the movies?

See, there was my boyfriend Tate, a silver Hummer, and
a man in a police car that had been assigned to guard me.

So how was I supposed to go try to find Marlys's husband
with a cop tailing me? That just sort of took all the steam out
of espionage. But there he was, large as life, sitting in the
parking lot, looking totally bored, probably wondering what
he had done wrong to deserve this assignment. He got out of
the car when we walked down the stairs.

He was definitely not the same cop that had gotten involved in the madman chase at the hospital. This guy was
much younger, pretty handsome, and when Marlys and I
headed toward the Jeep, he waved.

I waved back.

"This is not going to be easy."

"His job is to follow you, right?"

"Yup, and so I guess we are going to have to lose him."

"Lose him? Are you nuts? Jenny, I swear, sometimes . . ."

"Well, we can't exactly go looking for your husband with a cop tailing us."

"Why not? It's not like I think Rog is dealing drugs or doing something illegal. Just immoral." Her face dropped, and I put my arm around her.

"Okay, you never know when having a cop around might be handy."

We got into the Jeep and headed toward the last place Marlys had seen Roger, just off Washington Boulevard. Our escort followed close behind us. When we got to the side street where Marlys had last seen her husband's car, we turned in and I drove slowly down the street.

Only the rear entrances of businesses lined the street, but at the end there was a parking garage. "Do you think he went in there?" I asked Marlys.

"I thought about it, but I didn't dare go inside, because it would be too easy for him to spot me."

"Well, let's try it."

I turned into the garage, taking care to turn on my right signal, very conscious I was being followed by a cop.

"Do you think he'd give me a traffic ticket if I did something wrong?" I asked. "That would really suck."

"I imagine he would."

"I don't think I'm liking this police escort business very much."

No sooner had I made that comment than his lights went on behind me, complete with a very loud siren. Obnoxiously loud. Possibly the most obnoxious siren in the history of police vehicles, going off when I was trying to be inconspicuous. "What the . . ."

I pulled into a parking space, and he pulled into another one alongside me. He got out and walked around his car and over to my window, tapping on it. I rolled it down. "Do you mind turning off those lights and sirens? We're trying to be inconspicuous here," I said crossly.

"Why?" he asked. His badge said his name was Officer Kinard.

"Because, we are, uh, we're trying to find someone."

"Who?"

I sighed with exasperation. "Why are your lights on? Why did you pull me over in a parking terrace?"

"Well, first you ran that red light back there, and then you didn't turn on your blinker in the appropriate amount of time."

"I didn't run a red light!"

"It was yellow," Marlys protested.

"That's not what I saw," he said, a grim look on his face.

"Are you going to give me a ticket?" I asked him, finding it hard to believe this was happening.

"No, not today. I just wanted to meet you in person. The infamous Jenny T. Partridge. Oh, and I have a message from Detective Wilson. He wants to know what you are up to now."

"I knew I should have tried to lose you," I muttered.

"Tsk, tsk," he said, chuckling, his grim look from a moment before totally gone. "So, what do I tell Detective Wilson?"

"Tell him that we are looking for a tattoo parlor. Marlys and I are going to get matching tattoos declaring our undying love for each other."

"I don't think he'll buy that."

"Fine, tell him we are looking for Marlys's husband, and leave it at that. And turn off the lights and that obnoxious siren!"

I turned my head and saw that to the right of my car, a small crowd had gathered, lured by the flashing red and blue lights and obnoxious siren. Smack dab in the middle of the crowd was Roger, standing next to a lithe, tall young woman with close-cropped black hair.

"Get down," I hissed to Marlys. "There's Roger."

"What? What is he doing?" she whispered as she ducked down.

"He's standing there staring at the cop car, and at the Jeep." I didn't mention the woman. After all, that could be mere coincidence. Never mind that the others standing there were also seemingly matched off. Three men and three women. All the men were older, two heavyset—one of whom was Roger, of course—and one quite gaunt. The women were young and tall and lovely. Almost exotic looking. What the heck was going on here? It didn't look good.

After the police lights went off and the siren faded away, the crowd wandered away, and I watched in the rearview mirror as the three couples—and it was obvious they were couples—crossed the street and went through the back door of a building.

"Okay, coast is clear," I said, and Marlys sat up.

"Where did he go?"

"In there," I said, pointing to the door.

"What is it?" she asked.

"I don't know. We'd need to go around front to find out."

"Then he might come out the back, and we'd miss him."

"Okay, I'll walk around front and see what kind of place it is. You stay in the car and wait to make sure he doesn't come out this way. Call me on my cell if he leaves through the back, and I'll jet back here."

I got out and made my way to the exit of the parking garage, crossing the small street. I examined the door through which the couples had entered, but I didn't see any sign indicating what type of place it was.

"Taking a stroll?"

"Yikes!" I yelped, jumping about two feet. It was Officer Kinard.

"Just what is it you are up to, anyway?"

"What makes you think I am up to anything?" I asked crossly.

"Because you are being sneaky, evasive, and furtive. Usually signs of someone committing a crime."

I started walking. "Maybe in your business, but not in mine."

He kept stride with me. "Teaching dance requires you to drive down side streets, slowly, enter parking garages, and peer through doors of buildings?"

"Look, Officer Kinard, I'm helping a friend out here. Her husband is the one being sneaky, furtive, and what the heck other noun you used, and so we're trying to figure out what he is up to, not that that is any of your business."

"Adjective."

"Huh?"

" 'Sneaky,' 'evasive,' and 'furtive' are adjectives, used to describe the actions of a noun."

"What are you, a moonlighting English teacher?"

"Nah, I just paid attention in school."

"Obviously, I did not. Now will you just let me do this alone?"

"No can do. You're my assignment."

We reached the block that ran in front of the building, and I turned and walked north, Officer Kinard right with me.

"You are not making this easy," I said.

"Didn't know I was supposed to," he answered, a smile hiding in the corner of his mouth. He was enjoying this! That would explain the siren.

I stopped when I reached the building that lined up with the back entrance. There were no business names on the door, just a big number: 806.

"Well, this is no help. Guess I'll have to go inside."

"And do what? Ask them where your friend's cheating husband is hiding?"

"No, I can tell them I'm looking for an insurance agency or something, and then ask them what businesses are located in this building."

"That would work."

"Except you have to stay here."

"Nope."

"Come on," I groaned. "Don't you think that is going to look awfully suspicious?"

"It doesn't matter. My instructions are not to let you out of my sight."

"You are becoming a gigantic pain in my butt," I said. He just smiled, and my heart did a little pitty-pat. I was such a wanton hussy, but the man was cute. Grandma Gilly was turning over in her grave, except of course she wasn't dead yet. I'm sure she believed that when it happened, it would be my fault. But I couldn't help myself. What was it about police work that it attracted such hot men?

"Well, how the heck am I supposed to find out what is in here?"

"You could just ask me."

"You know?"

"No, but I can find out."

"And can you tell me why you did not share this information with me before?"

"Too much fun watching you."

Great. Yet another person that I provided entertainment for. Good thing I was in the entertainment industry, or I might start to get a complex.

He pulled a handheld radio from his belt and called into dispatch, asking to confirm what businesses were located in 806 24th Street. A few minutes later, the dispatcher came back with three businesses: APlus Massage, Twinkle Toes, and Fern's Travel Connection.

"Yikes. Massage. Not good. Aren't those usually a front for prostitution?"

"Not generally in Ogden," he said dryly.

"Still, massage . . . And what the heck is Twinkle Toes?"

I heard a quick honk before he could answer, and saw

that Marlys had driven the Jeep around to the front of the building.

"Well, there's my ride. Thanks for the help!"

I ran and jumped into the passenger side of the Jeep and Marlys shot off.

"Looks like we finally lost our escort," I said, staring back at him as he took off running around the block to get his police car. When he caught up with us, he was going to be steamed.

"There he is," Marlys said, pointing to a blue sedan up ahead of us. Roger's car.

"Um, what happened to not trying to lose the cop?" I asked her. "When I suggested it, you acted like I should be locked up just for thinking about the idea."

"I wasn't trying to lose him. I was trying to catch up to Roger," she explained.

"Well, then that makes *everything* better. I'm sure he'll understand."

Lord, somehow, we had switched roles again. This was not good. In fact, it was downright scary.

We followed Roger until he pulled back into his work building parking lot, and watched from the street as he parked and got out of his car, heading quickly into the building.

"Well, that was fun. Let's do it again," I said.

"What did you find out?" Marlys asked me, without tearing her eyes away from the building.

"Um, well, there's three businesses in that building." I still hadn't mentioned that it appeared that Roger and the others had been paired off, and all the women were young and attractive. Was he getting a massage? Who was I trying to kid?

"What are they?"

"Something called Twinkle Toes, and a travel place, and one other . . ."

"Twinkle Toes? Wonder what that is. And a travel

place . . . Hmm. Could he be planning a surprise for us? A vacation? Or is he planning to leave the country and start a new life? Is he in trouble, so he has to disappear?"

"Okay, this is getting ridiculous. This is not you. You are acting like me, and I don't like it one bit! Let's go back to the studio and research these places on the Internet."

Marlys's cell phone rang, and she pulled it out of her purse and looked at the caller ID. "It's him," she said.

She answered it, and after her greeting, listened. "Okay, I'll see you at home. Oh, I'm at the studio with Jenny. She has a special choreographer in town, and he auditioned a routine. Yes, Carly made it. She's really excited. What? Okay, takeout would be nice. I'll be home in about an hour. The kids wanted to go visit my mom. Okay. Bye."

She hung up the phone, and big tears welled out of her eyes and rolled down her cheeks.

"That did not sound like the kind of conversation that makes a person cry," I commented, reaching out to put my hand on her shoulder.

"He's acting so normal. Like nothing is wrong. Like he's not lying through his scum-sucking teeth to me."

I could see Marlys was in no shape to drive, so I made her switch places with me. Then I started up the Liberty and headed downtown toward my studio. So far, I had gotten away with not mentioning the third business in the building. I figured that one thing would send her right over the edge, especially since she already had Roger planning to leave town and take up residence in Tahiti.

She continued to cry as I drove, and I started feeling like I wanted to punch Roger in his scum-sucking teeth, because he was hurting my friend.

We pulled into the parking lot of my building and spotted a very angry cop standing by his police car, arms crossed, glare directed right at me.

Marlys wiped her eyes and asked me to give her a moment. I got out of the vehicle and walked over to Officer

Kinard. "Look, it wasn't my fault. Marlys was driving, and she took off after her husband, and there was nothing I could do."

"No worries," he said, through clenched teeth. "I put out an APB and a BOLO, though, so be prepared to get stopped by every cop who sees your vehicle for, say, the next two weeks."

I'd spent a short—very short—amount of time working in the sheriff's office as a 911 dispatcher, so I knew what APB and BOLO stood for—All Points Bulletin and Be on the Lookout For. This was not good.

"You did not."

"You just go ahead and think that. Every time you pass a cop, though, you'll be wondering, won't you?"

"*You* have a mean streak, Officer Kinard."

"*You* are making it awfully hard to do my job."

"What did you do to get assigned this duty, anyway? Botch a shoot-out?"

"Are you kidding? This is a popular duty. Everybody wants to be assigned this detail. You're famous down at the station."

I sighed. Marlys stepped out of the car and joined us, now fully composed.

"Well, we'll be going inside now. We promise not to lose you again," I said. "You didn't really put out an APB and a BOLO, did you?"

He just smiled.

THIRTEEN

INSIDE THE STUDIO THE GIRLS WERE WORK-
ing hard, with Trevor in front of them, demonstrating the
moves. He didn't even acknowledge our return. That was
common. When he got into the zone, like me, the outside
world went away. While this had been a regular dance
night, he was working with the elite girls from the teams,
and the others had gone home. I had a few more moments
to help Marlys, so we went into the office and booted up
the computer. It was an older model, and we had only a
dial-up connection, something that Alissa assured me was
practically archaic. I didn't care. I'd just figured out how to
turn a computer on. I knew how to click the AOL thingie
and how to read mail. Oh, and I'd even figured out how to
use a map program, so I figured I was set.

Marlys, on the other hand, was good at just about everything, so as soon as we got online, she called up Google
and typed in "Twinkle Toes Ogden Utah." A bunch of en-
tries came up, and I leaned over her shoulder and watched
as she scanned them. One of them was a link to a Web site,

and she clicked there. "Twinkle Toes, Utah's Premier Dance Studio."

"What the heck? I've never heard of a Twinkle Toes. How could it be one of Utah's premier studios when I've never even heard of them? That's fake advertising, that's what that is."

"False advertising," Marlys said.

"Whatever. Have you ever heard of them?"

"Nope, never."

We scanned down farther and read a section of the site that told us what they offered. "The finest instruction in ballroom, Latin, line, and swing dancing. For adults." Farther below that was a picture of a lovely woman dancing with a handsome man. "Husbands, want to make your wife happy? Learn to dance. She will fall in love with you all over again."

"Well, no wonder. That explains a lot."

"A lot about Roger?"

"No, a lot about why I've never heard of them."

She rolled her eyes.

"Has Roger ever expressed interest in learning to dance?"

"No. He won't even come to dance competitions. He says he doesn't understand it, and it bores him, and can't Carly and Maribel take up soccer?"

"So that's probably not it. Maybe he is planning a surprise for you. Taking you on a trip."

"What was the name of the travel place?"

"Fern's Travel Connection."

She typed it in and came up with some information from an online phone book, but no Web site.

"What was the third place? I don't think you ever told me."

Dang! Why hadn't I just said there were two businesses? Why couldn't I think fast enough to get myself out of these types of situations? "Uh, I don't remember."

That was believable! Not!

"Jenny?"

"What, I'm sorry. I have a short memory."

"You aren't being honest. You have a weird look on your face. I know when you're lying, and you are lying now."

"I am *not* lying."

"What is it you don't want me to know?"

"Nothing!"

"Jenny!"

"Okay, fine. The third business was called APlus Massage, but I do not want you jumping to conclusions. He could be going to the travel place, or maybe he suddenly had a desire to dance. Look at Sal. He ditched his mission so he could dance. You can't stop the music when the music starts to talk to you."

"Roger is not Sal." She had a look in her eye I did not like. Not at all. "And you wouldn't go to a travel place twice a week, plus they usually close at five p.m. So, the only logical choice is the massage place."

"You know, Officer Kinard assures me that all the massage businesses in Ogden are legitimate. They aren't fronts for prostitution like you see on television." Hmm. Maybe I shouldn't have mentioned that.

"Why would he need a massage? Twice a week? What, his life is so stressful he needs a massage twice a week? He goes to work, comes home, sits in front of the television, picks up his fork to eat the dinner I prepare, and then back to the television. I run the kids around, drive a bus, deal with other people's kids all day long, clean up poop and puke and all kinds of other icky bodily fluids, and pay all our bills. I schedule dentist and doctor appointments, make sure the kids get there, drive to and from dance and soccer games and . . ."

"Marlys?"

"Yes?" She sounded surprisingly calm.

"Don't you think you should just ask him? Confront

him with what you know, and ask him what he's up to?" I was so not going to tell her I saw Roger standing next to a sleek young woman who looked more like an actress than a massage therapist.

"So he can lie some more? No, next time, we are following him in."

Great. *We*. I sighed. Oh well, I owed it to her. She had gotten me out of more than one mess, including rescuing me from the basement of the funeral home that time I was trying to get away from Tate. Long story.

She shut down AOL and stood up, gathering up her purse and the light jacket she'd been carrying over her arm, since it was a pretty warm day. "I'll see you tomorrow, for dance," she said. She walked out the door, and then turned and came back in.

"Jenny?"

"Yeah?"

"Thanks for being a friend. I appreciate it."

She didn't wait for a response, and while I wished she wasn't in this situation, I was glad that I could finally do something for her. My cell phone rang, and I pulled it out of my purse. I saw from the ID that it was Tate, and pondered whether or not I should pick up. After all, Officer Kinard had probably tattled on me—I didn't really believe he'd put out an APB and a BOLO. But I was pretty sure he'd reported my escapade with Marlys to Tate.

I pondered long enough that Tate's call went to voice mail. Well, wasn't that convenient.

I walked back out into the main room and watched as Trevor worked with the girls, running them through the first half of the routine. I was thrilled to see they were all catching on quickly. He'd made good choices. The same ones I would have, and I didn't even have to take the flack from the psycho dance moms about the girls who weren't chosen. He stopped the music and moved their spots around until he had them in a formation that pleased his artistic senses. He told them to take a drink break and then turned to me and smiled. "So, what do you think?"

"I think it's going to be great," I said. "Like nobody else has seen or done around here. I can't wait to compete with it."

"Well, I kind of need to finish it first. Girls, let's get back to it."

By 9 p.m., the piece was set and the girls were really starting to look good. We called it a night and let the girls go home, arranging another practice for the next day. As usual, we had to wait a bit for some of the parents to pick up their daughters. Carly got a ride home with her neighbor Emily, so I didn't see Marlys. I hoped she was talking to her husband so I could give up my role as a private detective. I wasn't dumb enough to think it was something I did well.

Finally, after the last dancer left, Trevor said, "Well, I'd invite you to come have a drink with me, but I think your boyfriend would frown on that."

"I agree," I said.

He smiled and said, "Should I wait and walk you to your car?"

"No, I'm sure my own personal bodyguard is waiting out there."

"Wonder how your boyfriend got them to approve that detail."

I thought about it for a minute. "I don't know. I guess because I've been shot at and threatened."

"Hmm," Trevor said. I didn't like it when people said "hmm." It always made me think. How *did* Tate get this approved? I guess I'd have to ask him. *Tate!* He'd called me hours before, and I hadn't returned the call. I was surprised he wasn't in the studio right now, giving me that look. The one that spoke of huge disappointment in my lack of common sense and disregard for social skills, all relayed without words.

The front door opened, and the look walked through the door. Attached to Tate's face and body, of course.

"Catch you tomorrow, Jenny," Trevor said, hurrying out the door. "Nice to see you again, Tate."

"So now you aren't even returning my phone calls?" Tate asked me.

"I forgot," I said. "I've been really busy putting this routine together with Trevor, and I totally forgot . . ." The look worsened. Perhaps "I forgot" was not the best thing to say, especially combined with the name Trevor.

"Tate, I'm really sorry. I meant to call you. I just got caught up in dance. You know how close it is to competition season and how important it is to me."

"I'm not sure I like this competition season thing."

"Well, it's who I am. I never complain when you disappear in the middle of the night."

"Touché," he said.

Wow! A point for me. This was rare.

"Now, would you like to explain what you and Marlys were doing when you very unwisely lost your police protection?"

Lost that point already. Wasn't that always the way.

"It was an accident. Marlys was driving, and she was following Roger."

"Roger?"

"Her husband. She thinks he's having an affair."

"And you two are trying to catch him at it? I don't see this as a good idea."

"Me, either, but I'm all she's got."

He groaned. "All right. I know a guy. I'll give him a call tonight."

"You sure know a lot of guys."

He just smiled, and his eyes twinkled, and I got all warm and fuzzy inside. The man was seriously hot, even when he was peeved at me.

"Let's go home."

I liked the way that sounded, even though it scared the living heck right out of me.

We locked up the office and headed down the stairs. There was no sign of Officer Kinard, but I assumed Tate had dismissed him. As we reached the bottom of the stairs, a loud roar filled my ears—a familiar roar. The sound of a motor. A Hummer motor. Tate heard it, too, and I watched as he drew his gun and pushed me behind him. The vehicle pulled into the parking lot and stopped. Tate nudged me backward and up onto the staircase, although I figured if that Hummer decided to ram us, my metal staircase probably wouldn't survive.

My heart pounded and I could taste fear and apprehension. Tate was taut and alert, ready to shoot and kill to protect me. The driver's side door opened and out jumped Tamara Williams, psycho dance mom extraordinaire.

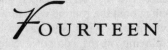OURTEEN

TATE LOWERED HIS GUN BUT DIDN'T PUT IT away. Tamara advanced on us, and Tate told her to stop, using his left hand, since his right one was busy with the gun. She stopped, a confused look on her face.

"Jenny, what is going on here?"

"Why are you here, Tamara? And how long have you been driving a Hummer?"

"What? Oh, the Hummer? It's my husband's. My Suburban is in the shop, so I had to take his car."

I watched as Tate put his gun back in the holster. Tamara watched him, too.

"Were you going to *shoot* me?" she asked, her voice high-pitched. "Isn't that a little drastic? I just wanted to talk to you about the audition, Jenny."

I groaned. "I didn't pick them, Tamara. Trevor picked the dancers he wanted. I had nothing to do with it." So much for not being held responsible for the girls who didn't make it.

"Well, April is home, crying into her pillow. She's been

doing it all night. She's just devastated. Can't you just talk to Trevor and tell him she's one of your best dancers and ask him to reconsider?"

I was still sort of hung up on the fact that Tamara Williams had access to a silver Hummer, and so I had a hard time thinking about the routine we had just set. Plus I doubted April was home crying. She was probably texting her friends or playing on the computer. She didn't love dance half as much as her mother thought.

"How often do you drive this Hummer?" Tate asked, nonchalantly.

"Oh, maybe every couple of months," she said. "My husband is pretty selfish with it."

Couple of months? I tried to get Tate's attention, but he was zoned in on Tamara.

"Can you tell me where you were on Wednesday?"

"Why are you asking me all these questions?" she asked, a serious frown on her face. She wanted to talk to me about her daughter, not be questioned about her activities by a police detective. In Tamara's world, nothing was as important as April's dance. Which would give her a good reason to threaten me. The first time I was threatened by the Hummer was in December, and Tamara had been upset because April didn't get the role of the Sugar Plum Fairy in my annual production of *The Nutcracker*. Then I was run off the road right after I had declined to take April's solo to the Hollywood StarMakers competition.

And now? Well, Tamara could not have known that April would not make Trevor's routine, although if she had bothered to ask me, I certainly would have told her. Despite her mother's fervent belief, April was not one of my best dancers. She was passable, mostly because her mother had her practice for hours and hours.

But she would never have the heart, soul, and desire that it required to be really good. Oh, and the fact that she had flat feet didn't help, either.

If Tamara was the Hummer Bandit, maybe her purpose was to get me upset so I would be easy to bully and manipulate.

"So, can you tell me where you were on Wednesday?" Tate asked her again.

"Why do you keep asking me that? I was where I always am. Taking care of my children."

"You're not exactly being cooperative," Tate said.

"I didn't come down here to talk to *you*," she said. "I need to talk to Jenny."

"You're wasting your time, Tamara," I said. "I told you before, I didn't pick the girls, and I'm not going to ask Trevor to add anyone. And they learned the whole dance tonight, so it's too late."

"April learns fast, and she is—"

"Tamara. Please. She is not in the routine. I'm sorry." I was tired and cranky, and I did not want to talk about this anymore. She was standing between me and Tate's warm comfy bed—and Tate himself, of course—and I didn't like it one darn bit. And the fact that the most psycho of the psycho dance moms had access to a silver Hummer did not make me feel the least bit comfortable.

"Fine. Fine. You'll regret it. You'll be sorry."

She turned around and stomped off, getting into the silver Hummer and roaring off.

"I thought about stopping her, but she was getting really irritating, and it's late," Tate said. "However, considering her behavior, I'd say it's entirely possible that we may have just found out who has been dogging you in the Hummer."

He pulled out his cell phone and dialed a number. After a moment, he identified himself and gave the particulars on the Hummer and the license plate number—which I had not noticed, yet again—to someone in dispatch.

After he was done, he hung up, put his arm around me, and guided me toward the Liberty. "I'll question her tomorrow, when you aren't around to distract her."

"But you don't really think it's her."

"Why do you say that?"

"You just let her drive off. If you thought it was her, you'd have her at the station and be questioning her."

"True. But it could be her. So I'm going to follow up."

"She had motivation, at least for the first two attacks. I didn't give April the role of Sugar Plum Fairy, then I didn't take her to Hollywood StarMakers to do her solo. But this last one . . . Well, I can't figure out why she would want me to quit. Then April would never get into my routines. And the shooting occurred before I even decided to do this routine."

"You don't think it's her, either."

"Well, let's just say I'm not entirely comfortable with this development."

"Let's go home," he said again. And again I got those tickles of excitement in my stomach . . . followed by sickly fear.

I was definitely a freak.

AFTER WE GOT BACK TO HIS HOUSE, TATE made me forget all about Hummers, and psycho dance moms, and even food. That wasn't easy to do, considering I had totally forgotten to eat, and even worse, forgotten to offer to get Trevor anything, either!

I realized that when I woke up the next morning to a growling stomach, and as usual, an empty bed. I don't know what it was about Tate and his bed, but I slept like a rock whenever I was here. I never even heard him leave.

Likewise, I wouldn't hear someone enter, which made me sit up and listen carefully, just to make sure there were no knife-wielding half sisters waiting for me today. It was going to take me a while to get over that.

I didn't hear a sound, so I got out of bed and faced the day. I'd be busy with teaching class today, while Trevor worked with the girls in his routine. I suspected James would be absolutely no help and would spend all his time ogling Trevor.

And I had to try and sneak into the hospital to see Sal before I got busy. Most people didn't have to sneak into hospitals. But I really didn't want to face Attila the Nurse again. My eye had cleared up well; there wasn't a sign of red in it. Maybe if I wore a hat, I could sneak past her. A hat and sunglasses. And maybe a mask.

I sighed. My life was definitely not boring.

After I showered and attempted to do something with my hair, I ate an English muffin with jam, brushed my teeth, and headed out the door. The Liberty was parked in the garage, right where I had put it last night. No firebombs. No gunshots. I could get used to this life.

As I backed out I waved at Officer Kinard, who was on duty in front of Tate's condo. He returned the wave.

He followed me to the hospital, parked next to me, and got out to walk in with me.

I almost belted out, "Me and my shadow," and did a few dance steps, but someone might think that was odd. That wouldn't do.

"So, did you have a good night?"

"It was pretty boring actually, especially after spending a few hours with you," he said, a quirk on the left side of his mouth. "I could hardly wait to get up and come to work today."

"Well, good, because I'm all about providing the Ogden Police Department with entertainment."

Attila the Nurse was on duty when we got off the elevator, but she eyed the police officer I was with and decided not to make a fuss. Plus, my "pinkeye" was miraculously cured, and so she had no real reason to hassle me. I'm sure that was causing her pain.

Sal was propped up in his hospital bed, watching television while Malece sat in a chair on the side of the bed, sewing on some black tutus. She glared at me. The girl was anything but grateful.

"Jenny," Sal said with delight. "I'm so glad you're here. Guess what?"

"What?"

"I get to go home today."

"Wow, that's great news, Sal."

"No thanks to you," Malece muttered.

I ignored her.

"Malece, it wasn't Jenny's fault. I've explained it to you several times."

"Sorry," she said without remorse.

"Are you going to be okay at home? Without help?"

"Oh, Malece is going to stay with me and help me out."

Yikes! I saw storm clouds on the horizon when Tate heard this news. I didn't want to be the one to tell him.

"And then I'm going to help her with costumes, since I'll be laid up for a while."

"Help her with costumes?"

"Yes, I'm really good with a needle and thread. Give me a Serger, and I can decorate your whole house."

"You can sew?" I asked Sal in amazement.

"I come from a family of ten boys. My mother always wanted a girl, so some of us had to appease her. I was always really good at it. I made my brother's wife's wedding dress."

Officer Kinard was staring at Sal with something akin to amazement. I imagined my face looked the same, although maybe not quite as perplexed, since I was getting used to Sal.

"Amazing," I said.

"So, how is everything at dance? I'm so sorry I can't help you. I feel terrible."

"Well, Trevor, my friend from Los Angeles, is in town, and he did an audition piece like we were talking about doing. And he's going to help with teams, too. So I think it will work out."

"Yes, Malece told me about him," Sal said. He looked slightly peeved, so I guessed maybe he was a little jealous. Or something. I didn't know if it was because Trevor was working with me in the studio or because Malece had said nice things about him. From the way she had smiled at Trevor, I imagined that was probably the case. Unless she just did it to irk me. Who knew?

The nurse came in to check Sal's vitals, and I told him I'd check in on him in the next day or so. After we left, Officer Kinard said, "That guy is a little strange."

"He's very interesting."

"That's one way of putting it," he said.

We headed down to the first floor on the elevator, and as the door opened I caught a glimpse of a man in a hospital gown leading some security guards and nurses on a merry chase.

"What the heck is that about?"

"Too many enemas. He doesn't like them."

"Can't say I blame him."

There were no Hummers waiting to attack me in the parking lot, and I made it to my studio without further incident.

I walked over to where Officer Kinard had parked his car, and he rolled down the window. "If you need to use the bathroom, there's one in the studio," I said.

"Thanks."

"I have bottled water in there, too."

"Appreciate it," he said.

"Have a good day, Officer Kinard."

"Jenny?"

"Yeah?"

"You can call me Aaron."

"Right. Officer Aaron."

He grimaced and I laughed.

Officer Aaron kind of rolled off the tongue nicely. I suspected he was stuck with that moniker, at least as long as he was stuck with me.

Poor guy.

FIFTEEN

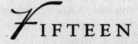

I'D CALLED A SATURDAY PRACTICE, USING OUR PMS system, because I was so stressed out about the upcoming competition, and the girls in the new routine needed all the practice they could get, as they had just learned the routine. I was at the studio early, so I went through and did some cleaning. Girls always left food wrappers and drink bottles, bobby pins, hairnets, ponytail holders, and all sorts of other things. I had a lost-and-found for the clothing and big items, and the rest went into the garbage.

After I swept the wood floors and cleaned the bathroom, I went into the office and sat down at my desk. The cordless phone was back in its base, having mysteriously reappeared. The message light was flashing, of course. It always was. Usually, the majority of calls were from Tamara Williams.

My cell phone rang, and I fished it out of my purse. It was a call from my mother's cell phone, which was unusual. She didn't go out much, and she used her cell phone rarely, mostly because the only way she could effectively

talk on the phone was while she was stirring a pot of something on the stove. The two went hand in hand with her. I
wasn't sure why. I had a sudden premonition that it wasn't
a call I wanted to take. But it wouldn't work out well for me
to put it off.

"Hello?"

"Jennifer, are you alive? Are you okay?" My mother's
voice sounded full of concern.

"Of course I'm okay, Mom."

"I'm here at your apartment, Jennifer. I came over to
bring you some chicken and mashed potatoes, and a nice
banana nut bread. And there appears to have been some
kind of problem here. It's all boarded up, the windows and
the doors covered. Someone has spray painted nasty words
on the boards, too. Did you make someone mad?"

Her voice was surprisingly calm, considering this was
my mother. She lived in an entirely different world than the
rest of us, and her world's name was denial. When I was a
child, she had driven me from dance class to dance class,
secure in the knowledge that she was furthering my mar-
ketability as a bride, or perhaps even for a life on the stage.
I sincerely doubted her intention had been to prepare me
for a future as a dance teacher who seemed to have a target
on her back.

"Uh, the police think it was a random drive-by shooting,
Mom."

"Drive-by shooting, Jennifer?"

My mother's tone was an entire pitch higher than it had
been before.

"Drive by? Drive by?" That was my father. He freaked
out fairly easily but then calmed down and handled every
situation. My mother, on the other hand, acted as though
she was very, very calm, when in reality, at any moment she
was going to hold up a drugstore and take all their valium.
Or go home and cater a four-hundred-person wedding.
Probably the second one.

I heard a thunk and some scrambling noises, and then my father's voice came on the line. "Jennifer, what in tarnation do you mean, drive-by shooting? Do you know how upset your mother is going to be?"

"Uh, Dad, isn't she sitting right there beside you?"

"What's your point?"

"My point is, you just asked me . . . Never mind. So, how upset is she?"

"She's shaking."

I heard my mother say, "Take me home, Larry. I think I'll make some bread."

"Would you stop that stupid cross stuff. You're making me feel like a werewolf."

I didn't even respond. I knew my father was talking to my mother, and not me, because that is what she did when she was upset. That sign of the cross thing. I'd even tried it myself a time or two, although I probably didn't get it right. I hadn't spent enough time in a Catholic church to get it right, since my mother was a mostly lapsed Catholic. My father, a lapsed Mormon, understood the cross stuff even less than I did. Mormons did not like crosses, for reasons I could not even try to explain. But see, as both my parents were "lapsed," I was raised "lapsed." Didn't know much about either religion.

At least my mother was talking about baking. All the drugstores were safe for tonight. I was kinda kidding about that whole drugstore robbery thing. My mom was anything but criminal. But she certainly might benefit from some pharmaceuticals. Either that, or she needed to eat more potato salad.

That stuff was like crack to me. Maybe heroin. I wasn't sure, because I'd never done either. I was a little boring that way. I figured I was "colorful" enough without drugs.

"Jenny, what is really going on? This can't possibly be random."

"Why not, Dad? Random things happen all the time. Life is really random."

"Jennifer T. Partridge . . ."

My dad had some kind of crap-o-meter built in. It probably came from years of teaching kids, but he always knew when I was dishing it out. Even when I felt it was to his benefit *not* to hear the real story.

"Look, Dad, remember the silver Hummer?"

"You mean the bus incident, and the time you almost killed Bessie?" Great. I'd been injured when I crashed Bessie, and the truck barely had a scratch, but did my father remember that? No, just that I'd hurt his beloved truck. He was going to be seriously peeved when he found out about the dead guy who'd shown up in her.

"Yeah, Dad, and if Mom hears this she is going to freak out. But it's back, and Tate is trying to figure everything out, and I have police protection."

"So if you aren't staying in your apartment, where are you staying?"

I hesitated. "That's the part that you might not want to hear. Although it's very, very safe."

"Tate?"

"Yes."

I heard my mother's voice in the background. "Tate? What about Tate? She's not staying with Tate, is she?"

I had no idea whether my father nodded or she already knew the answer to her own question. Whatever it was, she commenced praying, "Holy Mary, Mother of God, pray for us sinners now, and at the hour of our death. Amen."

Now, I'm sorry, but if you are lapsed from something like, say, the Catholic Church, I would think there would be some sort of sin attached to using the prayers. I could ask Grandma Gilly, but that would require actually speaking to her, and since I was not her favorite person, I wasn't going there.

"Dad, tell Mom to knock it off."

"Yeah, like she's going to listen to me."

"Please."

"Carol, knock it off. At least she's safe. And at least she's straight. You were worried after that whole lesbian thing . . ."

I groaned. "I have to go, Dad. Tell Mom I'm fine, and I'll call you guys later this week."

I disconnected and put my head in my hands.

Could life get any worse?

The front door swung open and in came Tamara Williams. Yup, it definitely could.

$\mathcal{S}$IXTEEN

I'D GOTTEN RID OF TAMARA BY PROMISING TO work with April on her solo on Monday. I wanted Tate to have more time to investigate her before I was alone with her for any length of time. I was somewhat uncomfortable around her now, since she'd driven up in the big old Hummer of my nightmares.

Dance passed in a blur; I was busy running classes, while James was busy ogling Trevor as he worked with the Company team. Trevor completely ignored my soon-to-be ex-friend, who was about to find himself in need of a new job.

"James, get busy! You are supposed to be cleaning the Petites routine."

"Jennifer, it is not exactly easy to do when you have pulled the three best dancers out of the formation."

"James, they are working with Trevor right now. Just pretend they are there."

James groaned and skulked off, and a minute later I heard him yelling at the Petites in the other room.

The studio phone rang, and I ran into the office to snatch

it off the base. Marlys had been preoccupied with her situation, so she hadn't been spending as much time at the studio, and I really missed her. And needed her.

"Hello?"

"Jenny, this is Marlys." Chills ran down my spine as I listened to her voice. Maybe I had that extra-sensitivity perception or something. "He called again. It's getting pretty regular. I need you to come with me."

Since Tate hadn't come through with his "guy" yet, and I had promised, I knew she really did need me. But I had only six days until our first competition, and I needed to be in the studio.

Still I had promised, so I told her I'd be there in a few minutes, and then I had to listen to James's moans as I put him in charge of all the groups who weren't dancing with Trevor.

As I drove to Marlys's house, Officer Aaron following closely behind me, I thought about my ESP experience and Marlys's call just as I was thinking about how much I missed her. After considering all the times in my life when I'd been blindsided—either by a psycho dance mom or just an everyday psycho—I decided I could not possibly have ESP, and the only reason I was thinking about Marlys was because, well, because she was having trouble and I wanted to help.

She came out just as I pulled up, and got into the car. Her eyes were blank and she had large brown circles under them. She wore no makeup, and her hair was brushed back into a simple ponytail.

I drove to Roger's work, and we waited for him to come out. It was about 5:10 when he exited his building, again wearing casual clothes, and not the suit coat and slacks he would have worn to conduct business.

"Does he normally work on Saturdays?" I asked.

"No." She didn't say anything more.

Was he behind at work and trying to catch up, because

he had been leaving during the weekdays? We followed him down to the same building where I had spotted him before. He pulled into the parking terrace, and I stayed back, parking at a meter at the far end of the street, Officer Aaron right behind me. As Roger left the parking garage, he looked down the street and saw my Jeep and the police car, but didn't seem to have any reaction to either.

He walked inside through the building's back entrance, and I turned to Marlys, who seemed to visibly collapse as she watched her husband's shifty behavior.

"Okay, here's the deal," I told Marlys. "I'm going to go in there and look around. You are going to stay here."

"He's at the massage place. I just know it."

"You don't know it. I'll find out. That's where I'll start."

"What are you going to do?" Marlys asked.

"I'll go in, and inquire about rates and all that, and try to get a look around."

"Okay."

Usually when I was contemplating doing something stupid—and I really felt this could be stupid, especially given my current status as the target of a monkey-killer—Marlys would be the first one to stop me. The fact that she was willing to let me walk into possible danger told me just how bad this situation had gotten for her. I knew I had to do this for my friend. Besides, how dangerous could a massage parlor be? Never mind.

I got out of the Jeep and heard a car door open and shut behind me. I turned and watched Officer Aaron as he took long, even strides until he reached me.

"Not a smart idea," he said.

"You have a better suggestion?"

"We're trying to find her husband, right?"

"No, I'm trying to find out what her—her name is Marlys, by the way—husband is doing. *You* are following me."

"Which means we both have a common goal, because I am not letting you out of my sight."

"You can't go in here. You're wearing a uniform. You'll stand out like a punk rocker at a Mormon Tabernacle Choir concert." I considered my words. "You know, it might work better if you thought of this as an undercover job. You know, wear jeans and that kind of stuff, like they do on television."

He grinned, the dimples in his cheeks pronounced. I knew there were cops in Ogden that weren't hot and built, but it seemed like I always ended up with the ones who were all that—aggressive, hot, very male, and, well, hot.

"I think Tate wants me in uniform, driving a squad car. There's a reason for that. It makes it very obvious that you have protection."

"It also makes it very hard to go into a building and find out what my friend's husband is up to!"

"Well, I'm not getting myself in trouble with Tate. I'm up for promotion, and he wields a lot of power in the office. I want off patrol and into the D-squad, so I'm not letting you out of my sight."

I filed away the fact that Tate "wielded power," hoping to be able to use that information at a different time, and considered my options. If I walked into a possibly illegal massage parlor with a uniformed cop, I had no doubt that chaos would ensue.

But I'd been assured that all the city's massage businesses were on the up-and-up. I sighed heavily. "Fine, but they never have to deal with stuff like this on television."

He followed me into the building, and I climbed a narrow staircase to the second floor. I could tell that many of the offices were empty and that some recent upgrading and refurbishing had gone on. I suspected a new owner had recently taken over a previously failing office building and was now attempting to lease out office space.

My footsteps squeaked softly on the floor, while Officer Aaron's brown work shoes made a heavier tap-tap sound. We passed the door of Fern's Travel Connection, and it was closed up tight, with no visible activity or light.

I could hear the tinkling sounds of music coming from down the hallway, and I quickly walked about halfway down the corridor, to a door that said, "Twinkle Toes. Instruction in ballroom, Latin, swing, salsa, and line dancing." Below that was a picture of ballet shoes, which had very little to do with ballroom, Latin, swing, salsa, *or* line dancing, so it was a little bit confusing. At least to me, but maybe not to the ordinary person.

"You think he's taken up dance?"

"Well, no. Marlys said he has absolutely no interest in dance. But I would rather think he is dancing in there than getting a massage from a, er, lady of the evening."

"You know, massage is a perfectly respectable way to earn a living. It's rarely a front for something seedy, except in the movies and on television."

I gave him a look. "Look, a man who is getting a massage twice a week, and hiding it from his wife, is not someone who is innocent."

Officer Aaron just shrugged. "I think we should check in here first."

"Fine. Let's check here." I pushed the door open and stepped inside. Immediately I saw a beautiful wood floor that I would kill for—well, maybe not kill. But I sure wish I had that kind of money to spend. Whoever was dancing must have been in another room, because there was no one in sight. I heard the soft tap of heels and saw one of the tall, young, lithe women I had seen yesterday checking out the police commotion in the parking garage. She hadn't been the one standing next to Roger, but I definitely recognized her. She spotted us and came over, her round, dark eyes checking out Officer Aaron from top to bottom.

"You vould like dance lesson?" she asked him, ignoring me. Her tone was seductive, her accent Russian or something close to that.

"No, no, we're just looking for someone," Officer Aaron said.

"Someone in trouble vith police? Ve run respectable establishment here. No one in trouble."

"I'm looking for Roger Fulton," I said, butting in despite the fact she had barely spared me a glance.

"Oh, you vant Roger?"

She knew him.

"He is in middle of lesson. Forty minutes. You can vait there." She pointed to an uncomfortable-looking chair pushed against a wall, even though there was a comfortable couch in the waiting area. She turned back to Officer Aaron. "You sure you don't vant lesson? Don't vant to fox-trot? Maybe rumba?" She made it sound slightly obscene.

"Uh, no thanks."

"We'll come back," I said, and turned and walked out of the dance studio, followed by the policeman. When the door shut behind us, I turned to him. "Didn't you find that really weird?"

"What?"

"That she totally ignored me and focused only on you."

"I'm a good-looking guy." I could hear the humor in his voice, or I might have had to slap him.

"Think about it. A dance studio should cater to all adults. This one seems to be catering only to men. There is something wrong with that."

"I think you're jumping to conclusions."

"I think you're a . . . never mind."

"Look, Jenny, it's a dance studio for adults. She's a female instructor, so of course she zeroed in on me. I'm sure they have male instructors, too, and you would have been the target there."

"I don't know. Something just doesn't seem right here."

He just shook his head. "Let's go tell your friend Marlys

to relax. Her husband is taking dance lessons, probably to surprise her."

It still didn't feel right to me, but I couldn't think what was wrong, short of leaping to really ridiculous assumptions, so I followed him out and walked to the Jeep. Marlys looked at me as I got in.

"So?"

"Well, believe it or not, your husband is at Twinkle Toes, apparently learning to dance. Probably to surprise you."

She gasped. "You saw him?"

"Well, no, but the lady told me he was having his lesson and he would be out in about forty minutes. She also said I could wait for him. So it must be on the up-and-up."

"Hmm. That's weird. So unlike Roger."

"People change."

"I guess so," she said, a puzzled look on her face.

"Look, this is good news, right? I mean, dance lessons? That's a whole lot better than him getting massages twice a week. And a lot easier to explain, too."

"Yeah," she said, "so why doesn't he just tell me?"

"Like I said, it's probably a surprise."

Finally, relief flooded her face. "I guess you're right. I'll just wait until he tells me about it. Thanks, Jenny. I really appreciate you doing this for me."

"Good. You're welcome, and now will you please come back to the studio? I miss you there."

"Sure, let's go now."

We drove back to the studio with Officer Aaron following behind. He watched as Marlys and I went into the deli next to the studio to grab some sandwiches. He was still sitting in his car when we came back out, not moving, faithful to his assignment.

Tate had picked well.

SEVENTEEN

WHEN WE GOT BACK TO THE STUDIO, JAMES was working with both the Petites and the Smalls. Things were relatively calm, for once, and Trevor had the Company team looking awesome. I knew the girls he had picked could pull it off quickly, and I'd been right. If Malece came through with the costumes, this routine was sure to be a winner.

James sidled up to me. "You know, if you paid me the outrageous amount I know you are forking out for him, I could have done the same thing. Maybe even better." I guessed he wasn't thrilled with Trevor anymore, since he kept getting ignored. "And I wouldn't even leave in the middle of class."

"What do you mean, James? It's pretty obvious from the way the girls are dancing he's been here the whole time."

"Sure he was. Except for that hour he was gone, when he said he had to get some Starbucks to up his energy. And didn't even offer to grab me one, too, mind you."

"Well, he's been working pretty hard. I think he probably

deserved a Starbucks break. And knowing you and your exaggeration skills the way I do, I'm sure it wasn't an hour."

"Well, maybe closer to a half hour. But the girls were just sitting around while he was gone."

"Well, they look great now."

James just harrumphed and sashayed away, but not before giving Trevor—who had just walked up to us—another sultry look. He still couldn't give up. I sighed.

"Monday, can you help me with some of the other routines?" I said to Trevor. "Just make suggestions to jazz them up?"

"Sure. I won't charge you for that one. I'd love to help out my favorite dance teacher." He gave me the sweet smile that melted me, and I gasped just a little. I hoped he hadn't heard, but his smile turned slightly wicked, and I knew that he had.

We finished up class, and Trevor asked me out for a drink. This time he didn't say anything about my boyfriend. And I realized that I had gone the entire day and not heard one thing from Tate. I picked up my purse and pulled out my phone. Lots of missed calls from Tamara Wilson, but not one from Tate. That was weird. It was time to go home, and right now my "home" was *also* his home. Maybe one drink, while I waited to hear from him, wasn't such a bad idea. I felt really awkward just showing up at Tate's house, even though I had a key and a lot of my stuff was there.

"Okay, one drink. But just one. I'm a lightweight."

"Fine. Just one."

He led me out of the studio, watched as I locked up the door, and then we walked down the metal staircase and into the parking lot of the Marriott. He beeped a key at something in the lot, and I saw that his car—the one he was leading me to—was a very large, very noticeable silver Hummer.

My heart jumped into my throat and refused to move from there. I stopped walking.

"Jenny? What's the matter?"

I couldn't speak for a minute. Trevor? That made no sense. He didn't even live in Utah, and I doubted he had driven here. I strained my eyes to see the license plate, but I couldn't tell what it was in the dusky night.

"Jenny?"

"Is that your car?"

"No, it's a rental. I like to travel in style."

"You know what, I think I just remembered something. I promised Tate I would get back and, uh, water the plants." Talk about a lame excuse. "I was supposed to do it earlier, but I totally forgot, and apparently there is one of them that has to be watered daily or it will die." He stared at me with skepticism. I couldn't blame him. "It's a really expensive plant, you know, and so I really can't let it die. Maybe to-morrow night, okay?"

"Jenny, are you okay? Look, I know you have a boyfriend, and I don't have any intention of trying to take advantage of you or make you do anything you'd regret."

That gave me an out. "Look, Trevor, it just doesn't feel right, okay? I think I need to keep this strictly business between us."

"Okay, I'll walk you back to your Jeep."

"No, no, not necessary." Officer Kinard's car had been sitting in the studio parking lot when we'd exited, and al-though he hadn't started it up yet, I figured he was waiting for us to get into a car before he followed. "Monday at four, okay?"

He looked as if he wanted to say something else, but finally he just shook his head and said, "Four sounds good. See you then." He turned and walked to the Hummer and got inside, and I jogged back to the Jeep Liberty. I waved at Officer Aaron, who didn't wave back. That wasn't very friendly.

He must be peeved that I had been about to get into a ve-hicle with another man, since he liked Tate and wanted a promotion as well. My driving off with another man might not help him, in his eyes. I walked over to the car to smooth things over.

I knocked on the window, but he was looking down and didn't turn, and prickles of fear suddenly ran through my stomach and up and down my spine. I knocked harder. Still nothing. Then I heard a click and a metallic poke in my back, and I turned to see what the heck was going on. Bad move. Whoever was there did not want me to see them; I felt a sharp prick and then the world started to get kind of blurry and I slid down the side of the police car to the ground.

It wasn't a very comfortable place for a nap, but I really, really needed to close my eyes, just for a minute, and then I'd feel better. Just a short rest . . .

I WOKE UP IN A HOSPITAL BED, WITH A MOUTH full of cotton and an IV in my arm.

Tate sat in the chair, watching me anxiously. My mother and father were hovering nearby, and I could swear I heard the grating sound of Auntie Vi's voice out in the hallway. It was probably what woke me up.

"What happened?" I croaked.

Tate stood up and brought me a glass with some water and ice in it, holding the cup before me so I could sip through the straw.

My throat burned as the cool liquid went down, and I didn't know whether to laugh or cry.

"Someone shot you full of morphine," Tate said grimly. "A whole lot more morphine than someone your size should be given. You've been pretty out of it for more than six hours."

I tried to sit up as the events of the past night came back to me. Officer Aaron, in a car . . . not moving.

My head pounded, and I groaned and put my head back down on the pillow. "Officer Aaron?"

Tate quirked an eyebrow. "Officer Aaron?"

"You know," I said, not wanting to explain my quirks. Not with this pounding headache and very dry, sore throat.

"He was drugged, too. A woman walked over to his car, and he got out to talk to her. He remembers she was looking for directions, and then a prick, and nothing. He's here in the hospital, too."

"Did he give you a description?"

"Yes, she was tall, blond hair, pretty. He didn't see her in a car or anything like that."

"Why?" I asked. "Why would someone do this?"

"There was a note."

"A note?"

"Yes. It said, 'Roses are red, violets are blue, the games are all over, and soon you'll be through.' "

My mother softly cried, her hand over her mouth. My father looked strained and old, and I watched both of them, standing at the foot of my bed.

"I can't understand this. I can't leave here. This is all I know how to do. I've lived here all my life. And it's almost competition season. This whole thing is just crazy."

"Well, it's happening, so we have to address it. First we need to write a list of anyone in the dance world you have had a problem with in the last five years. We should pay particular attention to anyone with a penchant for bad poetry."

Although I didn't know anyone who tended to write bad poems, the list would be a long one. Dance teachers and dancers were artistic and eccentric, and often fiery. Fights between studio directors were commonplace. Egos were thin and easily bruised. We all thought we were the best. Some of us just didn't like having that thought challenged.

But who could I have possibly challenged in a way that led to this?

"Whoever this was is deadly serious, Jenny. She attacked a police officer, and that comes with some pretty ugly penalties, not to mention a whole slew of people who take that kind of thing very seriously."

I tried to wrap my mind around the events of the night, but my thoughts were still muddled and confused. One stood out above all others. I'd had a policeman standing watch over me, and it hadn't been enough. He'd been hurt himself. Did I have any choice but to stop teaching dance and leave town?

Tears poured unbidden down my face, and I wanted to be calm, to be controlled, but I couldn't. I had no idea how to fix this, and it looked as though she—whoever she was—was going to win. I was not a quitter. Well, sometimes I was a quitter, when it came to things like keeping a regular job and staying on diets, but when it came to dance, I didn't quit. My teams would be at the competitions, and I would be there with them.

Tate looked at my face and just shook his head.

"Do you think you could teach me to shoot a gun?" I asked him. I wasn't really serious. I hated guns, and I also knew my shortcomings, and even though I'd never been faced with handling a firearm, I had a feeling it was the last thing I should do. Right next to trying to play private detective. Still, desperate times called for desperate methods.

"Jenny!" my mother gasped.

"No, I am not teaching you to shoot a gun."

I was relieved. "That's probably a good choice. It was just a thought."

"Well, maybe a gun wouldn't be such a bad idea," my father said.

"Larry!" my mother gasped.

"No guns," Tate said. "I've hired some serious muscle for Jenny. The police didn't scare this person off, so I am going to have her guarded 24-7 by some guys I know. Former cops who went into security work in Salt Lake."

"I can't afford that," I said. I knew I was wasting my time protesting, but I had to at least pretend to maintain my independence. Still, I was tired of getting shot at—and being given shots—so I wasn't going to fight too hard.

"I can." Tate didn't offer anything more.

Auntie Vi came into the room emitting loud exclamations of terror and ranting against whoever had done this to her poor little niece. She was a bit of a drama queen, and the whole thing would make a great story to tell to everyone in Ogden. She had to be on hand to get the scoop straight from the cow's mouth.

"Oh, Jenny, are you okay? Are you going to be fine? Will there be brain damage from the drugs?"

"Vi!" my father said. Tate snorted.

"Well, we all know the dangers of drugs and drug abuse."

I groaned. "First of all, Auntie Vi, I'm not abusing drugs. Someone gave them to me without my consent."

"Oh, yes, I hear that happens a lot. Were you at one of those rage parties?"

"Rage parties?"

"I think she means rave," Tate said. "I wonder if that's where you got it?"

"Got what?" I asked, scowling at him as much as I could without hurting my head.

"Nothing."

"No, I was not at a party. I was leaving my studio, and someone came up behind me and the next thing I knew—"

"Well, that's not very exciting," Auntie Vi said. "How about we tell people that you were trying to save that young runaway missionary from his headlong descent into disaster, and that you went to a rave party to try and get him back on the straight and narrow path? That will probably undo any damage done by the fact that you helped him escape from his mission."

"Vi!" my father and mother said in unison.

"Well, I'm only thinking of Jenny and her reputation," she said with a huff.

"Maybe you should all leave and let Jenny get some rest," Tate suggested. My mother gave him a sharp glare. It spoke volumes, probably with the first chapter titled, "You Slept with My Daughter and Turned Her into a Wanton Hussy."

Tate recoiled a bit from the glare. He'd never been subjected to it before. I was very familiar with it, as she had inherited it from my Grandma Gilly, and I'd seen various versions of it all my life.

"I think that's a good idea. Let's go," my father said. He hadn't had as hard a time accepting that I was a grown woman as my mother had. It was times like these I wished I had a brother or sister, a real screwup, someone who could keep my parents busy while I lived my life.

After everyone left, I asked Tate if I had to stay in the hospital overnight. Right as that question came out of my mouth, Attila the Nurse came into my room, and I almost jumped from the bed and ran as fast as I could. Except I was pretty sure I could barely walk, and running was probably out of the question.

She gave me that disapproving look, and asked, "Why does this not surprise me?"

"I don't know, why?" Tate answered. She turned to look at him, and her face softened and she blushed. Tate smiled, and she turned a darker shade of red.

The beast was charming the beauty. Or was it the other way around?

"Jenny is wondering if she can go home," Tate said. Attila simpered. I swear! She simpered.

"Well, the doctor's note said as soon as her vitals were stabilized, she could be released, as long as she has someone watching her closely."

"She will. How are the vitals?"

She smiled winningly. I felt nauseated. Wasn't there a puke pan here somewhere?

She turned to me and the smile went away. She roughly took my blood pressure, checked my beeping monitors, and then pronounced me well enough to leave.

"You didn't tell my parents about me leaving," I said as I pulled back the hospital room covers and swung my legs to the ground, trying to stand. I reeled as the room suddenly swam in all kinds of directions.

"Slowly," Tate instructed, and Attila took one arm, and Tate, the other. I was wearing one of those stupid hospital gowns, and I just wanted to put my own clothes on and leave this place. "I figured you had probably had enough family for one evening."

My hero. I'd have kissed him, but it would have required figuring out which head actually belonged to him, out of the four or five I could see, and that was just too much work.

They walked me over to a chair and sat me in it. The nurse got into the room's closet and pulled out a plastic bag. "You want me to help her get dressed?" she asked Tate.

"No, I can handle it."

At that, she backed up a bit. She looked at his ring finger and then over at me, and shook her head. His charms probably wouldn't work on her anymore. She harrumphed and left the room.

"What was that about?" he asked, as he pulled my leggings, long T-shirt, and bra and underwear from the bag.

"I'm sure in Attila's eyes I lured you away with my wanton ways, and now you are intimately involved with me, outside the holy bonds of sacred matrimony."

Tate gave me a funny look. "First of all, how do you know her name is Attila? And why are you talking like that? Did you hit your head when you got drugged? Should I have the doctors check you out some more?"

Since I believed people generally got dumber when they

injured their brains, his questions made me cranky. I gave him a glare and he chuckled.

"Let's get you home."

AFTER HE HAD ME TUCKED IN HIS BED, HE brought me some chicken noodle soup, toast, and hot tea. He served them on a nice bed tray, like the kind I'd always imagined rich people had in their homes. It made me stop to consider just how many other women Tate had entertained in his home, using this tray. That made my head hurt, so I chose to block out that unwelcome thought and concentrate on the softness of the bed, the flavor of the soup, and the fact that I was still alive.

"You know, there's something about all this that is bothering me," Tate said, as he watched me eat.

"What?"

"Well, the poetry with this note was different than what the Gorilla-Gram guy sang to you. More like a nursery rhyme."

"Neither one was great. Someone is just whacked-out crazy."

"Well, something else is bothering me, too. In the past, the Hummer has stayed far away from the police—or at least whenever it was possible. Whoever this is, she was brazen enough to attack a police officer. It really makes me wonder."

I finished the soup, leaned back against a fluffy pillow, and closed my eyes. I tried to open them back up, but they didn't want to obey my command. I couldn't fight the sleep, but I vaguely remembered Tate moving the tray and then a bit later sliding into bed next to me, and holding me tight. Maybe I could just stay here forever. Nothing bad had ever happened to me in this bed.

I really, really liked it here.

EIGHTEEN

I AWOKE TO REALIZE TATE WAS STILL SLEEP-ing beside me, something that rarely happened. Since I was mostly a night person and he was a morning person, he was almost always up and gone long before I had even managed to rouse myself from bed.

I snuggled in closer to him, wanting to savor the moment and the safety I felt here.

"Morning," he said sleepily, his voice scratchy and low. "How do you feel?"

"A little bit of a headache, but mostly okay."

"Good."

He pulled me close to him and started tickling the sides of my neck with feathery kisses.

Fireworks shot off in my stomach, and I rubbed my hand across his cheek and chin, the overnight stubble pricking lightly at my fingers and heightening the senses that told me he was all man, and all mine—at least right now.

I trailed my hand down his chest and to his stomach, stopping as I got to the top of the boxers he wore to bed.

My hand shook a little as I considered the incredible sensations I felt when I was with Tate. I was in over my head. "Scared?" he whispered.

"Of you? Terrified," I whispered back.

"Not me. I mean this whole situation. I promise I won't let anyone hurt you again. If I have to chain you to me, no one is even going to get close." I was frightened of all the events that had happened recently, but I was also terrified of all these feelings I had for him, and the fact that I didn't really know how he felt in return. Although he seemed to like me. He moved in closer. Right now, he seemed to really, really like me. I closed my eyes and dove into the sensation.

WHEN I WOKE UP AGAIN, HE WAS GONE FROM the bed, but I could hear noises in the kitchen. I stretched, then winced a bit as a dull throb made its way through my head. I got up out of the bed and looked down at my naked self. Memories of the time we'd spent not too long ago came to me and I felt color rise in my face. I quickly covered myself in the large T-shirt I'd worn to bed and pulled on my thong panties, which were, oddly enough, thrown over the top of a lampshade.

I padded into the kitchen to see a shirtless and boxer-clad Tate making breakfast. I walked up behind him and cuddled up against him as he stirred scrambled eggs in a pan.

"Morning," I said, kissing his back.

"Afternoon," he replied.

"Afternoon?"

"Yes, it's nearly three. You are still sleeping off the effects of the morphine, I guess."

I pulled away from him and stared. "It's nearly three, and you haven't left for work, and you are wearing boxers. There is something very wrong going on here."

He just laughed. "The guys I hired for you had to finish

up a gig today. And Sunday is my day off, so I decided just to hang out and take care of you today. I'd really appreciate if you would consider just staying here and resting today."

I pretended to be considering, although in reality, I knew I wasn't going anywhere. I needed to feel safe and not worry about assault and threats and silver Hummers— even if just for a few hours.

"Okay, fine," I finally answered. "It will be a relief to hang out and not worry about anything. I'm telling you, once I saw that silver Hummer in the Marriott parking lot, I just about lost my mind."

"Whoa, silver Hummer? When? When did you see it? Why didn't you tell me? Did you see it before you got attacked?"

"I . . . well . . . it was Trevor's. I mean not his, but a rental. He said he liked to drive in style, and whenever he rented a car, he got a Hummer."

"And you saw it when?"

"Last night. He asked me to get a drink, and I hadn't heard from you, and I felt silly coming here because I don't really live here, so I said yes. But then I saw his car, and I freaked out. I'm going to suffer from silver Hummeraphobia for the rest of my life."

"First of all," he said, as he pulled me into him, "you had better not feel silly coming here. You are a part of my life, and I really like having you here. I wouldn't care if you never left."

I gulped a little. It wasn't a declaration of love, but it was close.

"Now tell me more about this Hummer he was driving. Same color as the one that keeps showing up?"

"Yes, that is what freaked me out so much. I mean, it was getting close to dark, but still, I can tell that color anywhere."

Tate pulled away from me and picked up his cell phone off the counter. He dialed a number and waited. I listened as he told someone on the other end to start digging into the whereabouts and behavior of one Trevor Paulsen, paying particular attention to any rental-car contracts in the months of December, February, and March. They were looking for a silver Hummer.

After he hung up, he asked me a few more questions. Did I know Trevor's address in California? Nope. Had I ever been there? Nope again.

"Why does Trevor come to Utah?"

"He was born and raised here. In Salt Lake City. He comes to visit his family, and sometimes he comes with different dance tours that come through."

"Dance tours?"

"Yeah, you know, like Hollywood StarMakers? They hire teachers to do the tours, and Trevor is sought by all of them. He used to do more, but he doesn't do many anymore, because he is so busy choreographing movies and music videos in L.A."

"Did he contact you in December or February?"

"Nope, I haven't seem him since last September, when he was here for Utah Dance Teachers Camp. That's one that all the best choreos come to, so I always save my money and attend it. I can only afford to do one a year."

Tate went back to the scrambled eggs and gave them a quick stir, then turned the gas burner off. He dished them onto two plates sitting on the table and then motioned me to sit down. A plate of toast was already on the table, and he pulled a carton of orange juice out of the fridge and filled two large glasses to the rim.

"So, as far as you know, he wasn't here in December or February?"

"Well, his family is here, so it would make sense if he came in December, because that's Christmastime, but I didn't hear from him. And not in February, either."

"Okay. Well, I'm adding him to the list of suspects, with Tamara Williams."

"What possible reason could he have to want to hurt me, or chase me out of town?" I asked.

"Did you turn him down? Say no to him?"

"Well, yeah, kinda. I mean, he was pretty, uh, amorous with me one night at the dance camp, and I told him I wasn't a one-night-stand kind of girl, and he backed right off. Was a perfect gentleman after that."

"Was that September the first time you met him?"

"No. He's been coming to UDTC for years, as an instructor, and I told you, I always save my money to go."

"How many years?"

"Probably six."

"And whenever he comes to town, he calls you?"

"Well, I don't know that for sure, but he has called me six or seven times in the past few years."

"And you get together for drinks, but never anything else."

"No, I told you, I've never been involved with him." He was questioning me like the cop he was, and even though I knew he was doing it to try to figure out why I was being threatened, I didn't like feeling that I was being interrogated.

"And this time he got 'amorous,' was that recently or at the beginning?"

I bit back a smart-mouth reply. "It was last year, in September, at the camp. We'd been hanging out there for years, but this was the first time he ever tried anything."

"So, being rejected would give him motive," Tate said.

"It wasn't that big of a deal. He took it really well."

"Maybe you only thought he did."

I sighed heavily. "It can't be Trevor. It just can't. He hasn't acted like a stalker or anything. I don't even see him very often. Besides, what is the point of scaring me to death?"

"Well, he drives a silver Hummer, rented or not. Maybe he thinks you'll turn to him. If you have to leave and go somewhere, why not L.A.? And his arms?"

"That's just crazy. He's never even pursued me like that. Surely it would take more than one gentle no to create a stalker."

Tate just shrugged. "Until I rule him out, he's a suspect."

"It seems more likely that it would be Tamara Williams than Trevor. Not that I think it's her, but please. Trevor?"

"All I know is that you are going to change the way you look at these two, and proceed with caution. You have to."

"This whole thing is making me cranky."

"You just need to eat."

"Eating isn't going to solve this problem."

"No, but it will make you less cranky."

The man knew me too well. I ate.

After our late-afternoon breakfast, I called Trevor at Tate's request and asked him how long he planned to be in town.

"Hold on, just one sec. Let me check my calendar." It was quiet for a moment, and I thought how weird that was. Check his calendar? Didn't he know how long he was staying?

After a moment, he came back on the line. "Hey, Jen, sorry. I had to see if I had anything pressing in L.A., but I don't. So I can stay for another week, if you need me." Ah, that explained it.

"Wonderful," I said. "I'll see you tomorrow at four p.m."

"I'll be there. Oh hey, I have a question. Did you ever get a chance to read that screenplay I gave you?"

Ulp. Yeah, I remembered the screenplay. He gave it to me last time he was in town, said he really wanted to know what I thought of it. Thought it could be a really good movie. I promised I would read it, but I, uh, hadn't gotten around to it yet. And now, with all my stuff in storage, I had no idea where it was. It was called *Big Talent and Big . . .* something. I couldn't remember.

"Uh, I'm about halfway through, actually. Loving it. When I finish, I'll tell you more."

"Okay, cool. See you tomorrow."

I hung up and turned to Tate, who was sitting next to me on his comfy sofa. I told him Trevor was going to stay another week, but I couldn't tell how that made Tate feel. On one hand, it gave him time to investigate Trevor, but on the other hand, I would be working with the man every day.

"You're about halfway through with what?"

"Well, he gave me this screenplay to read last time he was in town."

"Let me guess. He wants to know how you liked it. You haven't even started it, and in fact, don't even know where it is."

"You know me too well." I smiled.

Tate didn't smile back. I knew he was worried about Trevor, but even though seeing Trev in the Hummer had freaked me out, I still didn't think he was capable of anything.

"So, why did you tell him you'd see him Monday? Wouldn't it make sense to not put yourself into possible danger until we have ruled him out as a suspect?"

"I asked him how long he was staying, and he said he could be here for a week. I need him. He choreographed the routine, and he wants to work with the girls. Like I'm going to turn him down?"

"He could, very possibly, be trying to kill you. And you are worried about competition routines?"

"Did you forget that the person that drugged Officer Aaron and me was female? Trevor can in no way pass for a girl. And look, yes, it made me uncomfortable seeing the Hummer. But I don't believe he is behind this. I just don't."

"Trevor could have an accomplice. And you don't think Tamara Williams could be responsible, either. You would rather just close your eyes and make this whole thing go away."

"Hey, you agreed with me about Tamara. And I am not a head-in-the-dirt kind of girl. I'm just trying to be sensible.

And if Trevor does have an accomplice, that destroys your whole stalker theory. Stalkers don't really work in pairs, do they?"

"This is your idea of sensible? I like the old Jenny better. And I agreed that Tamara seems an unlikely suspect. I didn't rule her out."

"And pairs of stalkers?"

He glared at me with his cop stare. I wasn't falling for it. "Fine," he said. "No, they don't work in pairs. But maybe his motive isn't stalking. We just don't know what it is yet."

"Well, don't you have bodyguards lined up for me?"

"Yes."

"Then nothing is going to happen."

Tate pulled me onto his lap. "Your logic frightens me."

"It frightens me sometimes, too."

"Well, for now, I'm going to keep you safe. Preferably in my bed."

My heart raced. My mind raced. And then other parts of my body joined in. Tate was magic that way. He could make me forget about everything with just a touch—of course, where he was touching me was the key.

I liked that touch.

NINETEEN

MONDAY MORNING CAME AND I AWOKE ONCE again to find Tate lying next to me in bed. I turned and looked at the alarm clock. It was 7 a.m., and this was highly unusual. Tate was usually long gone by now.

He stirred and then opened his eyes. He blinked a few times and then noticed me staring at him. "What?"

"You're still here. You're never still here when I wake up on a weekday morning. I'm confused."

He yawned and sat up. "Well, you wore me out this weekend." He gave me a wicked grin, and I felt myself blushing. "And the guys I hired will be here at eight a.m., so I wasn't willing to leave you alone until I've turned you over to them."

"I feel like a prisoner."

"If it keeps you safe, feel free to consider yourself one."

"Gee, thanks."

"Look, Jenny, it's important that you don't lose these guys and never go anywhere without them."

"I understand, warden."

"Ha ha."

He rose from the bed and told me he was going to shower. He invited me to join him, but I was already a little sore from our recent activities, and I declined. After I heard the water running, I made my way to the kitchen and thought about making him breakfast for a change. I found some eggs in the fridge, and I cracked four of them into a bowl, except the fourth one kind of shattered and then shells went all over into the egg, and no matter how many times I tried to get the shell out, the slippery egg meant I couldn't keep hold of them. I considered pretending I just didn't notice the shells, but the thought of eating crunchy scrambled eggs made me slightly nauseated, so I poured them down the sink.

I settled for toasted English muffins with jam and peanut butter.

When Tate came whistling into the kitchen, dressed in his suit coat and slacks, he stopped and considered the English muffins on the plate on the table.

"Breakfast? For me?"

"Yeah, I tried eggs, but those things are slippery."

He looked around as though he expected to find his nice clean kitchen floor covered with egg. He sat down, picked up an English muffin, and bit into it. After chewing for a minute, he said, "I don't think I've had peanut butter since I was a kid."

"Then why was it in your cupboard?"

"I had my housekeeper stock up so I had things you would like. I told her you were a mac-and-cheese, ramen-noodle kind of girl, and she went from there."

"I like other things. I just can't afford them."

He smiled. "You might want to get dressed. The body-guards will be here any time."

I showered and did my beauty routine, which never helped much, and decided to allow my naturally curly hair to just do its thing, since I didn't really have time to blow-dry my hair.

It was a mass of red curls as I headed back into the kitchen, where Tate sat at the table with two big, beefy-looking men.

One was dark haired, broad chested, and hard looking, with a slash of scar across his cheek. The other was bald and portly, with a Fu Manchu mustache and thin lips. Neither looked friendly or law-abiding, and I found myself questioning Tate's statement that these two were former cops. They looked as though they had Mob connections, not that I had any real experience with the Mob. I'd had a student who turned out to be in the Witness Protection Program, but they'd taken her away and I had no idea where she was now. I always hoped she was safe. And dancing her heart out.

"Jenny, this is Arlo Child and Stanley Parks." The bald guy was Arlo, and the dark thug was Stanley. It didn't fit. Maybe he'd turned tough just because of the name.

The two men nodded but didn't speak. I was suddenly desperately wishing that Officer Aaron was back, and making himself annoying.

"What happened to Officer Aaron?" I asked Tate. "Is he okay?"

"Yes, but he's sworn off protecting you. He also asked to be reassigned to traffic."

"What? But he wanted to be a detective!"

"I guess you cured him of that."

Great. Now I was responsible for turning people away from their lifelong dreams.

"These two guys are going to scare the tar out of the little girls at dance."

"Now, that's not nice," Arlo said. "I have two daughters, and they aren't afraid of me."

Probably because they were used to him. Stanley Parks didn't comment, just glowered at me.

"I don't want to do this," I said to Tate.

"It will be okay. You need the best, and these two are the best."

To me, Tate's faith seemed a bit misplaced. But I wasn't always the best judge of character. Still, these two looked like hardened criminals, not security experts.

Tate watched me, and I finally shrugged and accepted I was going to have to travel with the two thugs.

He kissed me good-bye, and I told the thugs, er, bodyguards that I needed to go visit Malece and Sal. Much as I hated to do it, I had to check on how costumes for the new routine were coming along.

I discovered quickly that things were going to change drastically. I grabbed my purse and keys, then checked for my cell phone. When I determined it was in my bag, I headed for the garage door. Arlo shook his head at me and pushed me toward the front door.

He opened it and Stanley pushed his way through, looking cautiously right and left. As soon as he determined it was safe, he nodded to Arlo, who promptly took my arm and hustled me out to a large black expensive-looking car.

They hustled me inside, and Arlo sat next to me. Stanley was apparently the designated driver. I felt as though I were being kidnapped.

"Is this really necessary?" I asked, trying to keep a whine out of my voice.

"*This* is what we are being paid for," Arlo said.

I gave Stanley the address to Sal's apartment, and he navigated the streets of Ogden without asking me for directions. I noticed, however, that he had put the address into some thingie located on the front dash that told him when and where to turn.

"That's a pretty handy gadget," I said by way of conversation, because neither of these guys were talking to me. "What do you call it?"

"GPS," Stanley said. I waited for more. There wasn't any.

"Oh, yeah, I've seen that on television. Never in real life though. Sure would make life easier for people."

"Yes," Stanley said.

Arlo was staring out the window, scanning the scenery—or watching for Silver Hummer Bandit—and he did not join in on the, uh, well, conversation.

We pulled up at Sal's apartment building, and I went to get out on my side. Arlo grabbed my arm. "Ouch, you're hurting me."

"Sorry," he said, and released the grip a bit. "You get out after me. After I've checked the perimeter for threats."

Perimeter? Threats? I'd fallen asleep and awakened in a scene from a Steven Seagal movie. That had to be it.

Arlo exited the car, looked around, sniffed the air (I swear!), and then pulled me out of the car. None too gently I might add.

They followed me closely as I headed up the walk to Sal's apartment. He'd found a small studio on the bottom level of an old house that had been turned into individual units.

The house, a two-story white faux colonial, was old but well maintained. Sal's place was the size of my office, but he was as happy as a very large pea in a very small pod. I suspected after growing up with ten brothers, having his own apartment was glorious—no matter the size. I was, however, worried about his ability to pay rent now that he was unable to work for me. Not that I had been paying him enough to pay rent, anyway. Hmm.

I pushed that thought aside and rang the doorbell. Malece opened the door, frowned and glared at me, checked out the two goons behind me, opened her eyes wide, and then stepped away from the door.

Arlo and Stanley followed me inside, making Sal's already tiny apartment seem miniscule. There was a large recliner in the middle of the room, and that is where Sal had taken up residence. He had pillows tucked in around him and a blanket over his lap, and he was reclining back while hand-sewing beads on a black camisole. Arlo and Stanley gave Sal a hard look and took a step back.

"How are you feeling, Sal?" I asked.

"Sore, and bored, and antsy. But okay. Luckily, Malece is keeping me busy sewing these costumes, so I have something to keep me occupied."

He lifted up the camisole and displayed it for us, and I said, "Wow," when I saw the intricate design.

"You like?" he asked.

"Oh yeah. How is the rest coming?" I turned to Malece to ask this question. She frowned at me, then pulled a box of tutus out from behind the couch and showed me them.

"All done. You'll need black fishnets for all the girls in the routine. The red pointe shoes are drying. You didn't show up for that fitting, by the way, and I had to do it myself. I know nothing about pointe shoes."

Dang! The pointe shoe fitting. I'd called Malece and given her the time of the fitting, then promptly forgotten about it myself. I hoped this wouldn't set her off, seeing as she was not entirely balanced—at least not in my eyes.

"I'm sorry, Malece," I said. "So much has gone on in the past few days that I completely forgot. I'm really glad you were there to help out. Thank you so much."

She gave me a suspicious glare, then said, "You're welcome."

I knew, of course, that Clarissa Pace, who owned the ballet store and personally supervised all pointe shoe fittings, had been perfectly capable of doing it without me, but still . . . Malece had gone. She seemed to take this very seriously. And the costumes looked like they were going to be stunning.

I told Sal and Malece to keep up the good work, and turned to leave.

"Who are these guys?" Malece asked, suspicion tingeing her voice.

"Meet Arlo and Stanley, hired by your brother to protect me."

Both men nodded but didn't speak. Sal and Malece stared at them with wide eyes as I waved good-bye.

I was glad I wasn't the only one who found the two a little, well, intimidating.

As had happened before, Stanley pushed ahead, and Arlo used an arm to keep me back until the first man gave what I assumed was an all-clear signal.

After they loaded me into the car, I sighed heavily. Neither man reacted. This was going to be one long day.

TWENTY

AT THE STUDIO, THE TWO MEN STOOD GUARD while I did some filing and paperwork. You never knew when an invoice for dance shoes was going to upset the balance of world peace. After I was done with paperwork, I went out into the studio and made sure the place was tidy. It was not. I suspected garbage fairies came into the building at night to leave messes, because I didn't know how little girls could be this bad. Arlo and Stanley followed me from place to place.

I was heading into the other room of the studio, my bodyguards on my heels, when I turned around and put my hand out. "Stop. I need to work on some choreography, and I cannot do it with you two dogging my every move. There is no other entrance to this room. I'll be perfectly safe."

"Window?" Arlo asked.

"Yes, there are a few windows."

"Wait here."

Stanley went into the other studio and did his thing,

then came back and nodded at me. *Sheesh*. What would happen when I needed to use the bathroom?

I spent an hour or two refining some choreography for two solos I had not yet taught—the girls were little and would compete only once or twice at competitions down the road.

As I walked back into the other studio, Marlys came through the door. It was a little before noon. She stopped short as both men gave her a once-over, each with a hand tucked inside suit jacket to get whatever weapon they deemed suitable to stop her.

"Relax, boys, this is Marlys, and she works with me. And just so you know, in a few hours, there are going to be streams of girls coming through those doors, so you might want to temper that reflex a bit. It wouldn't be good for business if you shoot one of my students."

"Who are these two?" Marlys asked as she handed me a skinny caramel latte and a blueberry muffin.

"Marlys Fulton, meet Arlo and Stanley. Apparently, Officer Aaron didn't like his duty anymore, so he went back to traffic. And Tate hired these two go—er, guys."

"They're gonna scare the kids," she said.

"Hey," Arlo protested.

Marlys ignored him. "I just stopped by to say thanks again and see how you are doing. It appears you are in very, uh, zealous hands."

"I'm doing much better now you brought me these," I said, sniffing the sweet aroma of the drink. "Are you back to work?"

"Yes, I went back today. Just waiting for Roger to fess up to his big secret, so I'm still a little bugged by that, but I don't want to let him know I was snooping."

She looked mostly back to herself, so I kept the fact that something seemed wrong at Twinkle Toes to myself. I would have to do some more snooping. That was not going to be easy with Goon One and Goon Two on my tail.

There was an uncomfortable moment while the two bodyguards stared at us, and then Marlys said, "Well, I think I'll go now."

"Will you be back tonight? We need to do notes for Friday's competition and hand out all the wristbands."

"Yes, I'll be here. Will *they* be here?"

"We go where she goes," Arlo said.

"Right," Marlys said. "Okay, until later."

I realized I had to use the restroom, and headed in that direction. The two men dogged my footsteps again. "Hello, I have to use the ladies' room. You can stay here."

"Window?" Stanley asked.

I sighed. "Yes. Go ahead."

I sure hoped the Hummer Bandit decided to show his- or herself soon, so I could lose the bodyguards.

AT 2 P.M., MY YOUNGEST TEAM, THE TOTS, began to arrive. A few of them took one look at Arlo and Stanley and, as Marlys and I had predicted, started to cry. A few others—the type who were undaunted by anything—started peppering them with questions.

"Hey, are you here to dance?"

"Do you like Jolly Ranchers?"

"Have you ever seen a leprechaun?"

The two men looked in my direction, dark scowls on their faces. The little girls were pretty persistent and didn't intend to leave until their questions were answered.

If I didn't have a competition coming up so soon, I might have let them continue asking questions, but Friday was only a few days away, and I needed to work their routines. In reality, of course, the team competitions were on Saturdays, and solos on Friday night, but since I had to be there for my soloists, and, in fact, most of my best dancers also soloed, Friday was a lost day.

I lined up all the girls and turned on the music. Soon the

sounds of "Cooties," from the *Hairspray* sound track, floated through the room, and the "cute factor" was out in full force. I watched smiles quirk on the faces of Arlo and Stanley as they watched the Tots wiggle their little behinds and shimmy.

They looked at each other, caught the smiles, and turned away abruptly, then started shuffling around, clearly embarrassed. And determined to look anywhere *but* at me and the Tots. Hmm, maybe I should travel with a flock of Tots. Perhaps that idea had some merit.

Carnie Jones chose that moment to pee her pants, and I changed my mind. But it had been fun while it lasted.

TREVOR CAME IN AT CLOSE TO 4 P.M., AROUND the same time Marlys walked back through the door. He eyed the goon squad, then looked at me and raised his eyebrows.

"Bodyguards," I said.

"Interesting," he responded.

He unloaded his things and then asked me where I wanted him to start. Arlo and Stanley were sitting in chairs, one facing the door, one facing the room. They'd given up standing after the first few hours. Both were still trying not to look in the direction of the dancers.

Trevor spent the next few hours helping me add some pizzazz to each routine, and I felt a lot happier when we were done. Happy and hungry.

The girls filed out, Arlo and Stanley stood up, and I waved them back down. I walked around the room picking up things the girls had left. Trevor appeared to be considering asking me something, but he glanced over at my protective pals, and must have changed his mind. He waved good-bye, and for the first time all day, I was grateful.

When I was done in the studio, I gathered up my things, shut off the light, and we repeated the routine of Stanley out first, surveying the area. This time, there was a change. Arlo made me wait until Stanley drove the car up to the base of the stairs and then led me down them to the car.

It was getting dark as we headed toward Tate's apartment, and I pulled my cell phone out and checked for messages. There was a text message from Tate. I wasn't sure how to read it, so I asked Arlo for help. He gave me a funny look, hit a button, and the message came up.

"Hi, Hon, busy day. Didn't get a chance to call you, but know you are safe with the guys. See you at home around nine thirty. Love ya, Tate."

I got a warm and kinda squishy feeling in my stomach. Love ya? Did that mean "I love you"? Or was it just like signing "sincerely"? Did I "love ya" him back? This was complicated.

I was looking out the window, pondering my questions and wondering how the hell he learned how to text, when I saw something that made me scream, "Stop this car!" Stanley hit the breaks and pulled over. On the side of the road, just off 25th Street, stood Marlys's husband Roger and the tall, dark-haired woman I had seen him with days before. Definitely not in the studio and definitely not having a dance lesson.

He handed her an envelope, and she peeked inside, then gave him a big smile. She hugged him, then turned and walked away. He dejectedly headed in another direction, and I tried to get past Arlo and out onto the street so I could question Roger, but the big man was having none of it.

"It's not safe."

"Then you go get him. Go get Roger."

I pointed to the back of Marlys's husband, and Arlo exited the car and caught up with Roger quicker than a jackelope.

He grabbed him by the arm and pulled him back toward the car. Roger tried to fight him, looking around for help, but it was a futile effort. A few people walked by, but they mostly ignored his situation. All kinds of strange things happened on 25th Street.

Opening the car door, Arlo directed Roger to get in, and Roger squeezed in next to me, Arlo on the other side of him. He was trapped in the middle of us.

"Why are you doing this?" he asked, fear in his voice. "I paid her the money, just like you said. I did exactly what I was supposed to do. So why am I here?"

He didn't seem to notice me sitting next to him. His eyes were on Arlo and Stanley.

"Ask her," Arlo said, pointing a thumb toward me.

He turned to look at me and his eyes widened.

"Don't try anything," Arlo warned. "I'm armed, and I guarantee I'm a lot quicker than you are."

"Jenny, what is going on? Why are you having me kidnapped? Are you in cahoots with those Russians?"

"Russians? You mean the Twinkle Toes people?"

"You *are* in cahoots with them!"

He looked totally panicked now, glancing first right, then left, searching for a way to escape. Arlo squeezed his arm, and he stopped struggling, but the panicked expression didn't leave his face.

This was kind of cool. I was like some kind of Mafia princess, and now I could totally find out what Marlys's husband was up to, with the help of my bodyguards. Perhaps the situation wasn't as annoying as I had thought.

"What were you doing with that woman, Roger?"

He gave me a perplexed look. "If you are in cahoots with them, why are you asking me that? And what have you gotten my wife mixed up in? Do you send them people's names, as targets? Huh? Turn your own friend Marlys in to them?"

"What is this idiot yammering about?" Arlo asked me.

I just shrugged my shoulders and turned back to Roger. "What are you yammering about?"

"I . . . I . . ." He had turned pale, and his face was covered in sweat. I decided that my Mafia-princess routine was wearing thin.

"Look, Marlys knows you are up to something, so you might as well come clean. We followed you to the dance studio, and she knows you are going in there. She knows what you are up to." I said that last sentence with a stern look, because I had pretty much convinced Marlys that Roger was trying to surprise her by learning how to dance.

He didn't need to know that. And since I had just seen him hand an envelope to the woman who was "teaching him" dance, I knew I'd been right in my feeling that something was wrong with Twinkle Toes.

"She knows? I just wanted to surprise her. I just wanted to learn to dance, because she is getting tired of me not supporting what the kids like, and what she likes, and I thought learning to dance and taking her dancing might make her love me again."

"She does love you, you idiot." Oops. The Mafia princess hadn't quite worn off.

"We've been married a long time, Jenny, and the spark has kind of gone out. You know, in the bedroom."

Ack! I did not want to hear this.

"Look, Roger, Marlys loves you. She thought you were having an affair, and it about drove her crazy."

"It did?" A look of relief spread across his face. "She cares?"

"Yes, she cares. You, on the other hand, I'm not so sure about. So tell me why you were giving that woman money."

He sighed and leaned back against the seat.

"It all started out innocently enough, but then one night, I went to my lesson and told them I was done. I felt like I knew enough. And Svetlana told me that no, I was not done. And then she produced these pictures of us dancing. Close-ups, that if you see them you can really get the wrong idea. And she told me that I would keep coming, and that I would pay even more for my lessons, and if I didn't, these pictures would go to my wife."

"I told you!" I said triumphantly to Arlo.

"Told me what?"

"Never mind, it wasn't you, it was another cop. But I was right."

"These guys are cops?" Roger asked, panic on his face. "Oh, please don't tell my wife. Please don't arrest me. Please don't—"

"Chill," Arlo said to Roger.

"A dance shakedown?" Stanley said from the front seat. "That's crazy."

"Welcome to my world," I said. "Look, Roger, if you are telling the truth you have nothing to fear. You need to talk to the police and tell them what happened."

"No, no police. They threatened my family, my kids, and to give the pictures to Marlys if I told the police."

"Roger, these people are extorting you! And they are dancers. They can't be that violen— well, never mind that, but you need to tell Tate. We'll go there now."

"No, I can't. I am not going to the police station. Besides, it was all going to be over after tonight. I made a deal with Svetlana. I paid her a lot of money, and she said I didn't have to come back."

"How much did you pay her?"

"A lot."

"Roger!"

"Fine, it was ten thousand dollars, okay?"

"How the heck did you get that kind of money?" I asked him, fearing what he was going to tell me.

"I had to borrow it from the kids' college fund. I plan to pay it back, before Marlys knows anything about it."

"Hello! This is Marlys we are talking about. She will notice tomorrow."

Roger's whole body sagged with despair. "I know. Who was I kidding? But I was desperate. I didn't want her to leave me."

I decided not to point out that plundering the college accounts of his children was bound to make her more angry than taking dance lessons. "Look, we need to take this to the police."

"No, I told you, not the police station. They threatened me. What if they are following us?"

"They aren't following us," Stanley said.

"No one is following us, because we aren't moving," I pointed out.

"Look, I can't go to the police station. They are going to send me the pictures and negatives as soon as they determine whether or not I contacted the authorities."

"Fine, let's go to Tate's. It's not the same as the police station. Home, James," I said to Stanley. He was not amused.

TWENTY-ONE

"So let me get this straight. You think this establishment, Twinkle Toes, is a front for the Russian Mob, because they are attempting to shake down Marlys's husband."

"Something like that," I said.

"Interesting," Tate said. "You are aware that the Russian Mob is virtually nonexistent in Utah?"

"Well, her name was Svetlana. That's not your typical Utah name."

"True, but again, generally, I don't think the Russian Mob runs dance studios for adults. Generally, they are involved in drug and weapons trafficking."

I gave him an exasperated sigh. "Svetlana!"

"Svetlana is not enough to get us a search warrant."

"Then send someone in there undercover. I'd go, but they don't appear to like women. Plus they've seen me. Not that they paid me any notice."

"Jenny—"

"Tate, they took ten thousand dollars of the money intended to send Marlys's kids to college!"

"I agree this needs to be investigated, but Roger is going to have to file a report."

Sitting on Tate's sofa with his head resting in both hands, Roger moaned. "No police, they said. Said they'd hurt the family. Hurt my kids."

"Is he okay?" Tate asked me quietly.

"I'm pretty sure he's not."

"You believe his story?"

"Well, he's always been a pretty stand-up husband, as far as I know. Marlys doesn't complain much. They've been married a lot of years."

Tate walked over to Roger and put a hand on his shoulder. The other man looked up. "Roger, the only way we are going to make this end, or go away, is to put these guys away. They won't stop now that you've come up with money. They'll just keep asking for more and more." Roger went back to his head-in-hands pose.

Tate continued. "Look, buddy, here's the deal. You file the complaint and we'll send an undercover officer in to check it out. These people are doing this to other men, too." At that point, Tate's grip must have gotten a little firmer, because Roger jerked his head up in alarm.

"And you better be telling the truth, because anyone who hurts a friend of Jenny's will answer to me."

"It's the truth," Roger said, unshed tears sparkling in his eyes. "I just wanted to surprise my wife. And look what came out of it. What a huge mess."

Tate shrugged at me. I guessed he believed Roger's story, for the most part, and would quickly find out if it wasn't true.

My cell phone rang in my purse, so I fished it out and looked at the caller ID. Marlys! I couldn't answer. What was I supposed to say? "Yeah, Marlys, he's here. He just gave some Russians your kids' college money, but he was only trying to learn to dance—I hope."

I chose not to answer. It went to voice mail, and then immediately rang again. I picked it up. Marlys! Cripes, what was she doing, taking lessons from Tamara Williams?

"Aren't you going to answer that?" Tate asked.

"Marlys."

"Oh my God, no, no, don't answer," Roger said. "Please don't tell her about this. Please."

"Okay, Roger, I'll just let her think you're out having an affair with another woman. That's certainly a better story."

He looked at me and gulped, his Adam's apple bobbing up and down in his throat. "Um, maybe you better answer and tell her what happened."

The phone rang for the third time, and I picked up. "You're persistent."

"What's going on? Why aren't you answering?" Marlys said.

"I never answer my phone. Half the time I can't even find it."

"You always answer when I call, and this time you didn't. And it's important. Roger is late again. This time, really late. And I'm starting to think there's more to this story."

"There is. Better have Carly watch the kids, and head over to Tate's."

"Oh no. Something's wrong, isn't it? Roger's dead, isn't he?"

"Marlys! If Roger were dead, would I tell you to get in your car and drive to Tate's house? Even I'm not that stupid. But Roger's here, and you need to come over."

There was silence on the other end of the line. "Roger's there?"

"Yes."

More silence. "He's having an affair, isn't he? I was right. I was *right*! Wait. Roger is there with *you*?"

"Oh, for Pete's sake. If you keep this up I'm going to have to put you in the psycho dance mom hall of fame. No, he's not having an affair, and he is especially not having an affair with *me*. Did I mention we are at Tate's house? You remember Tate? My boyfriend, who is also here at his house?"

"Sorry. Temporary lapse of sanity. I know you wouldn't lie to me."

It was my turn to gulp. I sure hoped Roger's story was true. "But there is something going on that we need to talk about."

"I'll be right over," she finally said, her voice calm and collected. I hoped that Marlys was back and that her psycho phase was over. I could hardly run my studio without her, and she wouldn't be a lot of help from the loony bin.

TWENTY-TWO

MARLYS TOOK THE NEWS FAIRLY WELL, I thought, considering her husband had given some Russians ten thousand dollars of her kids' money. Tate assured her that they would get to the bottom of it and hopefully recover the money. He admitted to me he wasn't too optimistic about that last part.

After Roger and Marlys left, he shook his head and gave me one of those "I cannot believe you" looks. I couldn't believe me, either.

"Hey, I told you something was wrong with that place."

"You did?"

"Wait. That was Officer Aaron."

"Now you can't keep me straight from other cops?"

"Oh, give me a break."

He advanced toward me. "I know how to make sure I'm the only one you think about."

He was right.

* * *

THREE DAYS UNTIL OUR FIRST COMPETITION, and I was a nervous wreck. The Hummer Bandit was being awfully quiet, and there had been no parking lot assaults, no drive-by shootings, and no Gorilla-Grams. The dancers were getting used to Stanley and Arlo at their stations, guarding me and my studio. Marlys was back to normal, too. Everything was moving smoothly except for the fact that at any moment my life might be in danger. That tended to put a damper on my enthusiasm.

The girls started to pile into the studio for practice. Today and tomorrow would be dress rehearsals for the Friday competition. Thursday night the girls would spend with their families and hopefully getting some good rest. Friday would be solos, starting at 4 p.m. with awards around 10 p.m., and the Saturday competition would run all day long with awards given around 6 p.m.

I personally considered this week's competition to be a practice run for the UDC competition the following week—where they gave away the big money prize. Money that I really wanted to win. Money that could change my life.

My life needed some serious changing.

James came in, and I'll be darned if he didn't have that little rat Winkie under his arm.

"James! You have got to be kidding me. Three days until competition and you show up at the studio with the rodent."

As I knew would happen, the girls began screaming and gathering around James, all of them anxious to ooh and aah over the ugly little Chihuahua. No offense to owners of that breed of dog intended, but the mutt was ugly.

And it was also not kindly natured. It peed on my floor all the time.

"James!" I said again. "Please get that animal out of here. We need these girls to focus today. No dogs!"

"I had no choice. You know I gave him to Mother, but

she's visiting her sister in Provo this week, so I have to take care of him."

I sighed heavily. What else was going to happen? *Ack! No, please tell me I did not just think that. I take it back. I take it back.* Too late.

I saw Jordan Stewart zero in on Trevor, who had come through the door just a few minutes before. She was one of my favorite Minis, mostly because she said whatever the heck was on her mind, and dang the consequences. That was Jordan. One day, in the middle of a routine, she blurted out, "I like cheese."

Okay, that one was mild. Last week she had come in regaling us with the story of walking in on her father using the bathroom. I was still trying to recover from that one.

"Hi," Jordan said to Trevor. I moved close and grabbed her by the shoulder.

"Hi back, cutie," Trevor said.

"Hey, Jordan, time to line up." She ignored me.

"Are you gay?" Jordan asked, her eight-year-old voice filled with curiosity, her eyes round and wide with wonder.

"Uh . . . ," Trevor's eyes narrowed, and he looked at me, a little frantic, then back at Jordan. "No, I'm not gay."

"Jordan," I chided, "you aren't supposed to ask people questions like that!" I was a little relieved she didn't share with him the "ginormous" proportions of her father's . . . well, never mind.

"Well, I just wondered, because my dad said that James is gay, and he says that any guy who would dance for a living has to be light in the loafers. I asked him what that meant, and then my mom shushed him and she said it meant that someone was very graceful. But I'm not that dumb."

I sighed heavily.

"Go get in line," I said, and pushed her away.

"Well, I guess that's not the first time that someone has wondered that," Trevor said with a chuckle. "Comes with the territory."

"Sorry about that. She just says whatever comes to her mind. She's kind of bad that way."

"No big deal. But if you're curious yourself, I could prove to you, beyond any shadow of a doubt, that I am one hundred percent heterosexual." He moved a little closer to me, and alarm signals went off in my head.

"Uh, well, honestly, there really hasn't ever been any doubt in my mind," I said. "So we probably better get going on rehearsal."

Trevor leaned in closer and kissed me on the cheek. "Always running, Jenny. You should have been a marathoner instead of a dance teacher, because you never stay still long enough for me to tell you how I really feel."

Feel? He wanted to tell me how he "felt"? I was in deep trouble. "Uh . . ."

Jordan, who in a roundabout way had gotten me into this situation, took that moment to run back over and rescue me.

"Jenny, Marcy says she can make herself puke whenever she wants. Can I watch?"

"Marcy, quit it," I said, heading in the direction of the little girl who had a crowd gathered around her, and possibly a career in the circus in her future.

Secretly, I was relieved that I'd been saved from a "feeling" moment with Trevor, because the truth was my feelings were all tied up with Tate, and I knew it. I might look at other men, but as long as he was in my life, there wasn't going to be any other man touching me. Emotionally or physically.

The girls in Trevor's routine gathered around him, so we didn't have an opportunity to talk more. Thank goodness.

James was talking to the Petites, with Winkie tucked under his arm like some sort of demented handbag. Every time I got near them the dang thing growled. That was the demented part. *Growl away, rat dog, I don't like you any more than you like me.* At least the Petites were old enough not to be distracted by the little dog.

We spent the next three hours running routines, including walk-ons and walk-offs. To someone who didn't understand dance, that might have sounded silly, but a bad entrance could set a tone that would ruin a routine. And a bad exit was the same way.

Trevor stopped routines from time to time to make seemingly small suggestions that made a huge difference in the overall dance. When the practice was finished, I felt a lot better about my chances at the competition. The Company routine was stunning. Malece was bringing final costumes tomorrow, and I really believed that her work was going to put us in the number-one spot. I was a lot more optimistic about next week's UDC and my prospects of winning the money.

As we finished up the rehearsal, Malece breezed in carrying a single costume bag. I figured it must be April's solo costume. The dreaded horse costume. I couldn't wait to see it.

I dismissed the girls, and as they slowly trickled out, I watched as Tamara Williams walked over to Malece. She was still peeved that April wasn't in the Company routine, so she had spent the better part of an hour—she had come into the studio to watch, despite the fact I said no parents— glaring at the girls who did make the routine. Especially Carly. Good thing Tamara didn't have laser-beam eyes, or more than a few of my best dancers would have been smoking and disintegrated by now. Tamara clapped her hands and jumped up and down like a little girl as she waited for Malece to pull out the costume.

I walked over to where they stood, and watched the unveiling. Malece looked nervous as all get out. I felt a tickle of apprehension in my stomach and realized that I was nervous for her.

She pulled out a costume in a beautiful shade of blue-green, covered with intricate beadwork and crystals that sparkled every time the light hit them.

"Wow," I said. "That's gorgeous."

"I love it," April gasped.

"But there's nothing about it that says black horse," Tamara said, disappointment in her voice. "Or cherry tree."

"That's what you told her to make," I said to Tamara. "You even specified color."

"No, no, this was not what I asked for at all!" Tamara protested.

"Yes it is," Malece said. "You even helped me pick out the fabric."

"Yes, but I told you that it needed to say regal, and equine. There is none of that here."

"I'll buy it," Marlys said. She'd come over to check out the commotion, and she stared at the beautiful costume. "April and Carly are almost the same size, and it will go great with her solo. I wasn't too thrilled with the costume I bought, anyway."

Of course, that was all it took. I was pretty sure Marlys knew that when she made the offer. She was one smart potato chip.

"Well, of course you can't buy it," Tamara said, her chin high and haughty. "This is April's solo costume. Now that I look at it, I see that it's exactly what I wanted. It just took me a few minutes to get used to it, but it's wonderful. It will be great. How much do I owe you?"

Malece glared at me, as though I was responsible for how darned crazy this particular psycho dance mom was. Hey, I'd tried to warn her.

"It was two hundred fifty dollars with labor. The crystals were really expensive, and that's why it's so much. Plus the hand-beading."

"I'd pay two hundred fifty dollars for it," Marlys said before Tamara Williams could protest.

Tamara quickly got out her checkbook and started writing. April grabbed the costume with a squeal and headed to the bathroom to try it on.

Tamara handed the check over to Malece, who took it with big eyes. I suspected she had highly inflated the price just because Tamara was such a pain in the keister to work with. She undoubtedly was surprised when the woman paid her asking price.

April came out and danced around in her costume, which was truly beautiful. Malece really had a gift. Now if only she didn't hate me. It would be easier to work with someone who wasn't poking pins into a voodoo doll she'd named Jenny, like my last costume designer.

"Beautiful job, Malece," I said. "I can't wait to see the costumes for the Company team."

"Thanks," she said gruffly. "I'll have them here tomorrow."

"I would love your help making Carly's costume look better," Marlys told her. "It's already sewn, but it needs to be jazzed up."

Several other moms crowded in around Malece, some asking her to make costumes from scratch and some asking her for help in fixing up costumes they already had. We hadn't had a decent seamstress since Monica split for parts unknown, trying to evade the police. Malece looked a little shell-shocked, but she wrote each order down, and got the phone numbers and names of all the moms and their daughters.

After the crowd dissipated, and everyone had left but me, Malece, and Marlys—and of course, Arlo and Stanley—I turned to Tate's sister. "Just remember, team costumes first. Then you can do whatever you want, but your first priority has to be my studio."

"I'm not stupid, Jenny," she said with a grimace.

"I know you aren't stupid. In fact, you're a downright genius. I'm so impressed with your work. I just knew you hadn't done this before, so I was trying to help."

She considered for a moment, then gave me a half smile. "Thank you."

Phew. Maybe she'd put the pins and voodoo doll away.

Trevor had left during the commotion, so I didn't have to fend him off, thank goodness. Arlo walked Marlys out, and Stanley followed me around as I cleaned up the studio, even bending down to pick a few bobby pins up off the floor.

When everything was clean, we turned off the lights, I locked the door, and Stanley and Arlo did their Mafia-princess thing, swooshing me off to Tate's house. We had settled into a routine, and I hated to admit it, but I was getting used to feeling safe and protected. I would miss the two guards when they were gone—well, a little bit, anyway.

After passing me off safely into Tate's home—and arms—the two men left. And my cell phone rang. If it was Tamara Williams, I was going to strangle her. I looked at the caller ID. It was my parents' number. I was going to have to strangle myself.

Tate kissed the back of my neck as I answered the phone.

"Jennifer, what in tarnation have you got yourself mixed up in this time?" my father asked.

I wasn't quite sure how to answer that. "I thought I explained what I knew, Dad."

"Well, yes, but your, uh, friend Tate delivered Bessie to me tonight. Explained she had been detailed. Detailed! Someone else was touching her, and he didn't even have the courtesy to apologize. One does not detail another man's vehicle, unless something untoward has gone on in the other man's vehicle!"

Tate could make out some of my father's angry words, and he pulled away from me and watched with a puzzled look on his face.

"Generally, Dad, whenever someone does something nice for you, like, say, having your vehicle detailed, you say thank you. Those types of things don't require apologies."

"No one, and I mean no one, has ever touched Bessie but me! No one."

I put my hand over the speaker of my phone. "Apparently, my father thinks you were having an affair with his truck." Tate just shook his head.

"Actually, Dad, I was driving Bessie for quite a while."

"You know what I mean," he roared.

I put my hand over the speaker again. "You didn't tell him about the gorilla?"

Tate shook his head. "I thought that might be best coming from you."

I sighed. "Dad, the reason Tate detailed your truck was because someone was apparently trying to make a point to me, and they chose to make that point by putting a dead guy in a gorilla suit in Bessie. Tate didn't want you to have death germs in your truck."

My father was silent on the other end of the line. After a moment or two, he calmly said, "Well, we better not tell your mother this. Tell Tate thank you very much. And perhaps you would reconsider getting a gun?"

"No, no gun. I'll be okay. Tate has two guys guarding me all the time."

"Are you sure, Jenny?"

"Yes, Dad. I'm sure."

After I disconnected, Tate looked at me with that warm amusement in his dark blue eyes—the look that always made my entire body go on alert. "Death germs?"

"Yeah, you know."

"Yeah, I know," he answered and then pulled me into a warm embrace.

TWENTY-THREE

WEDNESDAY'S PRACTICE WENT AS WELL AS could be expected, and Malece's Company team costumes turned out to be fabulous. She was magic. She actually smiled at me as she left. Thursday night Tate took me out to dinner. I was relieved to leave Stanley and Arlo behind. I imagined they were just as relieved not to have to escort me around and watch little girls dance.

Friday morning dawned sunny and bright, and I was in Tate's bed, all alone. Maybe things really were getting back to normal. I could hear two low, rumbling voices, and figured Stanley and Arlo were already on duty. Okay, so not totally normal.

I spent the day running small errands, like visiting a local dance store to get extra hairnets and scrunchies and a few extra pairs of tights. A grocery store stop provided bobby pins and hair spray, because someone always forgot those necessities. I considered stopping at a Victoria's Secret just to irritate Stanley and Arlo, but finally decided they already had to put up with enough.

Tate had promised to get off early to go to the solo competition with me, so when I was still waiting at 5 p.m., I started to get a little nervous.

I called his cell phone and got his voice mail. By five thirty, I had no choice. It was time to leave, which meant Stanley and Arlo were going to the dance competition with me.

My cell rang as we drove toward Bountiful High School, where the competition was being held. "You said you would get off early," I said into the phone.

"Complications," Tate said.

"I hate these complications."

"I'm sorry. But it's my job. Just like yours is dance. I'll meet you down there."

"You aren't just trying to get out of attending a dance competition, are you?"

He chuckled. "Nope. I promise I'll show up. Now I want you to consider each person you see, and think about if they have a good reason to hate you or want you out of business."

"Stanley and Arlo are really peeved at you." I looked at the two men, who really never changed expression. So I was kind of fibbing a bit, but hey . . .

"I doubt that," he said. "I'll see you soon."

So I walked into Bountiful High School at 6 p.m., flanked by Stanley and Arlo.

"Jenny, how are you?" Carla Finny asked as I stood in the line waiting to get in. As a dance teacher, I received a pass that admitted me, as well as most of my dance teachers. But I still had to wait in line. Carla ran a financially successful school in Layton, Utah. Financial success in dance terms often meant low quality. Not always, but the real way to make money as a dance teacher is to get lots of girls, lots of teams, lots of cash. If you didn't care what your dancers looked like, you could get tons of students and convince them all that they were the best. Carla's teams were a little lacking in the talent department, but she didn't really care, because they financed her second home in Park City and the Mercedes SUV she drove.

"Hello, Carla. I'm well. How about you?"

"Great, great, just got back from Hawaii. Second time this year. Love that place."

"Yeah, I know what you mean," I answered. But I didn't really. I'd never been much of anywhere, except for a few trips to Las Vegas and California, for competitions. Hawaii? Not even close.

After Carla wafted off, I looked through the crowd for other dance teachers and studio owners I knew. I saw Heidi Killian, who ran a small but respected studio, much like mine. She hated me because Carly and Maribel had started out with her and then found me at a dance competition. I mentally added her to the "people who might hate me" list.

Ann Tillery was another dance teacher who had lost about four dancers to me, but that wasn't my fault, either. She refused to emphasize ballet, and they were looking for more in their dance experience. She had never acted as though it was a problem, but I knew it had to sting. Still, we maintained a respectful dance relationship. She was more like Carla, and had to know that emphasizing quantity over quality might bring in more money, but it wouldn't earn her a good reputation.

I got to the front of the line and handed my pass to the girl at the check-in table, got my hand stamped, and then started to walk into the gym, where I could hear the first music starting up.

"Whoa, wait up," said the check-in girl as Stanley and Arlo tried to follow me. "Nobody goes in without paying."

"We're with her," Arlo said, pointing at me.

"Yeah, well, you don't have teacher passes. And you

sure don't look like dance teachers, so you're gonna have to pay."

The girl was about sixteen, pimpled and full-faced, and probably Holly Vendstra's daughter, since I saw more than a passing resemblance. Holly was a bulldog, through and through. She ran her competition like a drill sergeant. Too bad she didn't run her dance studio the same way, but she had figured out that the dance competition business was more lucrative, and so she put all her time and energy into it instead of into hiring good teachers to lead her students. Since she had two left feet herself, there was no question she would *not* teach her classes. But she came from a "Dance Dynasty" family, one of those that had always existed in Utah, how could she not continue on in the family business?

"Look, these guys are my two new, uh, hip-hop teachers. I didn't have time to get passes for them, but Holly always lets all my teachers in."

"Hip-hop," she said, snorting through her rather piggish nose.

"Yes. Street hip-hop. Real hip-hop, like the kind you see on the mean streets of Los Angeles or New York."

"I don't believe you."

Arlo looked like he was getting ready to pull his gun, but I did not have ten dollars cash in my purse to get these two in. I'd spent what money I had on my little shopping spree. Why didn't I think of this?

"Hello, Jenny," came a singsong voice. Holly herself.

"Holly, hi. I was just explaining to, uh . . ."

"Alexandria," the girl said sullenly. Wow, what a mistake of a name that was!

"Right, Alexandria, how I forgot the passes for my two new hip-hop teachers."

Holly looked over Arlo and Stanley slowly, carefully, her eyes traveling from top to bottom—and everywhere in between. She was a bit of a man-eater, Holly, even though she was about six-two and weighed in at around two-fifty.

Arlo and Stanley started to fidget, so she just waved her hand at Alexandria. "Let them in, Lexi."

They started to walk, but Lexi stopped them again. "You need your hand stamped."

"Stamped?" Arlo asked.

"Yes, so that no one else will bother you. You have to show you didn't sneak in."

"People actually sneak into these things?"

Lexi gave him a nasty look, and he put his hand out and she stamped it. He pulled it back and examined the little smiley face on the top of his right hand.

"Not cool," he said under his breath.

Stanley put his hand out and endured the stamp, then gave it the same sort of perusal that Arlo had. He just shook his head, and we went into the competition in the gym.

We found a seat on the front row of the bleachers, near the middle. The first soloists had already gone, and the announcer called out the name of one of my littlest soloists, Amy Frey.

Amy was only four, and she still had to rely on cuteness, because at that age, there wasn't much dance skill. Still, she was sharp, and her timing was good, and I knew she would do well as she grew. And the audience loved her, since she knew how to shimmy and shake her bootie with the best of them.

Arlo and Stanley were not moved by her performance. Of course, they had been subjected to it several times already, as they guarded me at the studio.

There were a few other little girls, and then the first-grade division started. I had two or three soloists in grades one through three, so I watched them closely, Stanley flanking me on one side, Arlo on the other. "Oh dear, she just fell out of that double turn," I said to Arlo. He just shook his head. If anyone wanted me dead, it was probably these two.

"So, your soloists are doing well," Holly said as she stopped in front of us during a brief break. She was carrying a sheaf of papers that I knew were score sheets. She was probably taking them to her little tabulating cubicle so she could mess with the results. Everybody knew the judges at Dance-o-Rama were amateurs, the results rigged, and the trophies cheap. I attended because everyone else did, and it was a good place to showcase my dancers.

"Yes, they are. So far, anyway."

"So, do your hip-hop teachers have names?" she cooed, which was a strange sound coming from an Amazon.

"That's Arlo and that's Stanley."

"Do you guys do master classes?"

Arlo looked at me with alarm.

"No, they are very, very loyal to me. They don't hire out for anyone else. They're only here for a few weeks, anyway. They live in, uh, New Jersey." Okay, I'd never been to New Jersey, but I figured given Arlo's and Stanley's resemblance to cast members of *The Sopranos*, it seemed plausible.

"Too bad. I'd like to help them master a few dance steps," she said, looking from one to the other, then settling on Stanley. She ran her rather large finger down his cheek, and winked. He looked like he wanted to bite it off. "Well, better go get these results turned in."

"Good God," Stanley said.

"Sorry, she's kind of a piranha."

Stanley rolled his eyes. I saw Tate standing in the gym doorway, and I waved at him. Two workers were holding yellow tape—like crime-scene tape—in front of the doorway, since the next number had started up and it was poor form to walk in during a performance. Frankly, the child dancing would have fared better if everybody in the place had walked in or out until the music stopped. She forgot her dance and stood there crying, then stuck her finger up her nose before finally running off.

When the yellow tape was removed, Tate came over to us, and Arlo and Stanley stood up and almost ran out. I guess Holly really scared them.

"What's with those two?"

"Oh, there's this competition director, and I think she had her eye on them."

"Really? Weird."

"You should have been here."

"I'll take your word for it."

We watched a few more of my soloists, and Tate patiently listened to me explain what they had done right and wrong, and what we needed to work on before the next competition.

Holly came wandering by with more of her score sheets, and she looked in vain for Arlo and especially Stanley. "Where did your hip-hop teachers go?" she asked.

"Oh, they had an appointment with an old friend," I said.

She looked terribly disappointed. "Oh well. Hope they come back tomorrow."

"Are they coming back tomorrow?" I asked Tate.

"How would he know?" Holly asked.

"Uh, he is their scheduler."

"Wow, they must be the very best!" she gushed.

"Yeah, yeah, they are."

"So, are they coming back tomorrow?" She looked hopefully at Tate.

"No, I'm sorry, they aren't. They have other commitments."

Her face fell. "Oh. Okay. Well, sorry to hear. I guess I better get these score sheets into the tabulation room. Good luck with your teams tomorrow, Jenny. I know they'll do well. They always do."

I waved good-bye, then muttered, "Yeah, they'll do well as long as no one else has paid more money to the competition. If that's the case, then they won't win."

"You mean this shit, er, stuff is rigged?"

"Most competitions, no. This one? Absolutely. I discovered it about three years ago. I got my score sheets back and just happened to get a look at those of the winning team, and I saw they didn't have scores as high as we did."

"So what did you do?"

"I complained, and she gave both of us a first-place trophy and acted like that was that. But my friend Toni, who runs a studio in Bountiful, had some of the same concerns. And we had teams competing against each other. So we got together for lunch, and compared. And found out it didn't matter how high the scores were, she divided the results evenly. Everybody who came and paid her money won equally. That way, she ensures everyone comes back."

"So what is the point of the competition, then?"

"There isn't one."

"Why do you come back?"

"Exposure. I get at least four new students a year from people watching my teams, whether they win or not."

"But—"

"Wait, wait, it's Carly. I have to watch her solo."

Carly's costume had obviously been jazzed up by Malece, because it shined and shimmered, and emphasized her strong, lithe dancer's body. She hit every trick, stuck every turn; she danced as if she were floating.

I clapped wildly, as did the audience. I turned my head and saw Malece standing by Sal, who was in a wheelchair. Both of them clapped and whistled. Malece looked over at me and gave me a thumbs-up. Either she was starting to like me, or she was planning to off me. I gave her a thumbs-up back, hoping for the "liking" and not the "offing."

"She's good," Tate said.

"Yes, she is." I craned my neck to look for Marlys but couldn't spot her. Usually, she was sitting right by me. Odd.

"So, back to this competition. When you discovered it was rigged, what did you do?"

"Well, we called a meeting of all the dance studios up and down the Wasatch Front, and found out it was really pretty much well-known. No one comes here to win, except studios that really suck, because where they lose everywhere else, they win here."

"And?"

"And Holly got wind of it and showed up. She cried and blamed the judges, of course, even though she does all the tabulating, and then promised to hire professional judges."

"And?"

"And everyone felt bad for her. So they all hugged her, and said it was no big deal, and they would all still attend her competitions, and that was it."

"Nothing else?"

"No, I wasn't going to stop coming, because I get students here. She probably lost four or five studios, but I bet some of the others are the same. And I do feel bad for her. She can't dance, her own studio sucks, and she is divorcing husband number four."

He considered my words as April pranced onto the floor. Her costume was shiny, beautiful, and unlike anything else we had ever seen. Unfortunately, her dancing was not.

"She'll win," I said.

"Uh, that was not very good."

"What, you're the dance expert now?" I asked, smiling at him.

"Hey, you rub off on me. So why will she win?"

"Because Carly won last year and the other girl against them won the year before."

"Are you kidding me?"

"Nope."

"I don't get this dance world."

TATE WATCHED, FASCINATED, AS ALL THE different soloists sat with their teams, danced around to the loud music, or played games while waiting for awards to be announced. As I had predicted, Carly did not win, even though she had clearly outdanced all her competition. April, however, did, and Tamara gave me a knowing look, her eyebrows low and furrowed.

Someone forgot to tell her this competition was not at all professional, and rigged to the hilt.

Marlys wandered up after the trophies were given out, accompanied by Roger.

Roger?

"So, no surprises," she said. "I think this is the last time I'm gonna fork out this money, Jenny."

"I understand," I said. "I saw people watching Carly, though, so if we get five calls next week, I will do her solo for free next year."

"You're on," she said.

Roger stood with his face turned away from Tate and me.

"Hey, Roger," I said.

" 'Lo," he mumbled without looking at me.

"Hello, Roger," Tate said. The other man nodded his head and then looked off into the distance. "He's embarrassed," Marlys mouthed.

Carly came running over to her mother and said, "Well, that was predictable."

"Yeah, I know," Marlys said. "But you did an awesome job."

We chatted as the gym emptied, and we followed the crowd out the doors and into the parking lot. Tate took my hand to lead me to his car, and I turned as I heard Holly's familiar, grating voice. "Lexi, put those in the back. Not there on the seat."

I froze as I watched Holly instructing her daughter to load some trophies into a silver Hummer.

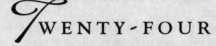

TWENTY-FOUR

TATE FOLLOWED MY GAZE, AND HIS FACE took on the cop look that was so familiar to me. I should not have to see that face as much as I did. I was a dance teacher, for Pete's sake!

I knew he was noting the license plate, and sure enough, he pulled a little notebook out and wrote the numbers and letters down. "So this person really *does* have a reason to want you gone, doesn't she?" he said softly.

"Well, I still come to her competitions!" I said. "I just let everyone know that she was—"

"Basically, you called her cheating out in front of everyone."

"Yeah, but it's not like it stopped. She's just more careful now. She instructs her judges to write in pencil, so she can erase and change scores."

"Definitely not a high-tech criminal."

"It's not really criminal, just unethical, right?" I asked.

"I don't know. I'd have to check in the dance competition statutes."

Holly walked around to the front of the Hummer and noticed me staring at her, in the throes of my Hummer phobia. Frozen in place. My mouth was working, but no other part of me seemed to want to move. If she chose this moment to jump in the Hummer and run me down, I'd be dead chicken.

"Hi, Jenny. Is everything all right?" Okay, so she wasn't going to run me down in front of all these people, but now, it all fit. It all made sense. It had to be Holly.

"Uh, I'm fine. Fine. I'm fine, right, Tate?"

"Yes, she's fine."

"Great competition, Holly. See you tomorrow!" I waved gaily, but my feet still weren't moving. Then Tate pushed me forward and I found my legs finally cooperating.

It was only after we got into his car that I took a breath. Then another. Then another, and another, and pretty soon, well, I didn't feel like I was breathing at all.

"Slow your breathing down," Tate said. "Slowly."

Hmm, interesting how someone who wasn't freaking out could tell you to slow your breathing down.

Mine just went faster. And faster, and then the world started spinning.

"If you don't slow down your breathing right now, I'm going to call the paramedics."

Whoa, paramedics. No thanks. Couldn't afford that. No insurance. I forced myself to breathe slowly in and out, in and out. After a few minutes, I was back in control.

"I take it you think Holly is a pretty good bet for the person who has been terrorizing you in the Hummer."

"Well, it makes more sense than Trevor or Tamara Williams. I mean, I did humiliate her. Kind of. She was crying and snot was everywhere, and it was a really, really ugly scene. But it's not like she lost a ton of business over it."

"Yes, but some people carry grudges for years. And certainly, seeing you out of business and having to leave the state would satisfy any need she has for revenge."

"Unless her revenge is to see me dead."

"Well, technically, if she were going to kill you, she wouldn't have sent all the warnings. She probably would have just done it. Maybe she thinks you have something on her, and she wants to scare you enough to keep you quiet."

"I think I pretty much told everybody what I had."

"Maybe she doesn't believe that."

"Maybe I have a headache."

"Maybe we should go home."

"That's the best suggestion I've heard all night."

While we drove, Tate called Holly's vehicle license into dispatch and asked for all the standard searches and whatnots the cops did on those things.

I concentrated on my breathing, willing myself not to hyperventilate.

"Has anything come back on any of the other Hummers?" I asked him when he was done.

"Nothing terribly interesting, except Trevor's Hummer is not a rental. It's registered to an R. J. Pickett, address in Salt Lake City."

"That's weird. I swear he said it was a rental."

"Well, I'm going to have to talk to him about it. He'll be there tomorrow, right?"

"He was planning on it."

We were silent the rest of the way home. Not a rental? Why would he tell me that if it wasn't true? I thought back to all the time I'd spent with him lately. Nope, I definitely couldn't see him hurting me, and he didn't have a reason to, anyway.

"I will be so glad when we get home. My head hurts from thinking too much."

Tate chuckled. "Home it is."

"Home. Home?" It had suddenly, in the space of a few days, become normal for me to consider Tate's place home. There was something wrong with that. What it was, I didn't know, but I still knew it was wrong. I was an independent girl. Woman. Oh, who was I kidding. I could barely find matching socks without holes in them, but still . . .

"You're thinking again," Tate said.

"It's just that I realized I'm thinking of your place as home, and that isn't right. I need to not get used to hot showers, fluffy towels, and soft beds. And food in the cupboard. That's not me. Not the life I lead."

"Is there really anything wrong with that life?"

"Nothing at all, except it doesn't belong to me."

"It does if you want it to."

I narrowed my eyes at him. "What do you mean?"

"I mean I like having you living with me. I think we should make it permanent."

Ulp. Ulp. Ulp!

"Uh, uh, you know, my mother is Catholic? And my dad? He's Mormon. And I know they don't go to church or anything, but they are having a hard enough time with this temporary arrangement. Long term? Sure to cause heart attacks and strokes, and who knows what other kinds of medical conditions caused by that kind of stress."

"Okay," he said slowly.

"And then there's the psycho dance moms. If they find out I'm living in sin, they would probably all pull their students out of my school, and I'd go bankrupt, and I sure couldn't help pay for anything if I had no students."

"Jenny, if you don't want to do it, just tell me." I could hear an undertone in his voice I'd never heard before, and guessed it might be hurt. But . . . suddenly I realized I was hurt, too. Because I knew he liked me. And I knew he liked having me around, and wanted to make it more permanent.

But not once had he ever said the "L" word; he'd texted "Love ya," but that wasn't the same as saying "I love you." I had an active imagination and had grown up with this dream, fantasy maybe, that one day my prince would come. I knew it was stupid, but I wanted the fairy tale, just like

Julia Roberts in *Pretty Woman*. Except I wasn't a prostitute, and he wasn't a gazillionare. At least as far as I knew.

When my prince rode up on his white horse, he'd look in my eyes and tell me he loved me, and only me. Tate must not be my prince, because he wasn't even talking to me. We rode the rest of the way in silence. That night, he slept in the guest room.

And when I woke up in the morning, I could hear the voices of Stanley and Arlo. I knew Tate was already gone. Maybe in more ways than one.

STANLEY AND ARLO DIDN'T ACT PEEVED AT having to escort me to the Saturday dance competition, but they really never acted much of anything. Holly would probably be excited they had returned, though, and thinking of her made me think of the Hummer, and then of Tate, and then I got a big old lump in my throat and some tears rolled down my face. Darn sneaky tears! I'd inherited them from my mother.

A hand patted mine, and I looked down to see Arlo's big mitt over mine, gently consoling, and for the first time, I saw the father his kids probably saw all the time. Usually he was all business. But now I knew he had a heart. And he knew mine was broken.

I pulled out my cell phone and made a quick phone call. Alissa answered on the first ring.

"I need a favor," I said.

"Okay?"

"I need a place to stay. Just for a few days. I can't go home. Can I stay with you?"

"Of course," she said. "Do I need to go shoot him?"

"No, that would put a real dent in your future plans."

"You want to meet for coffee?"

"Dance competition."

"Okay, see you tonight. You still have your key?" Alissa

and I had traded keys a while back. I'd had to get mine from her numerous times. She'd never once had to ask for hers. And that just about summed the both of us up.

"Yes, I have it." It was on a key chain, somewhere in the bottom of my purse.

After I disconnected, I watched the road as we turned onto 500 North in Bountiful. It was going to be a long day. And an even longer night. And I missed Tate already.

After we pulled into the Bountiful High School parking lot, Stanley drove to the front of the big gym and Arlo did his usual thing, checking things out, then ushering me out and into the competition. He waved my pass at the two guys standing at the door, and amazingly neither one tried to stop him. I wouldn't have tried to stop him, either. Even though Holly's daughter sure did. Probably came from living with her mother. Her mother who possibly wanted me dead.

I shivered a bit, and then about four little girls ran up and hugged me. They were all dressed in their costumes, hair slicked back and parted on the side. They wore mascara, lip gloss, and eyeliner. It didn't look great up close, but was totally necessary out on the floor.

Sometimes, the girls or moms overdid it and produced what I considered the "aging hooker" look. I usually waited until the offending mom had turned her back and then used makeup wipes and Q-tips until the dancer once again looked like a little girl—albeit one who was wearing light makeup.

I made my way to the dressing room assigned to us. As usual, it was the boy's locker room. I'd been stuck there ever since I'd alerted the other dance teachers to Holly's not-so-honest ways.

It smelled like urine, old tennis shoes, and stinky teenaged boys. Arlo and Stanley stood guard, both of them wrinkling their noses at the aroma. The girls ran around excitedly, the little ones entranced with their costumes and makeup, and the older ones looking a little nervous.

Trevor's Company routine would be later in the day, around the same time as the shows. Shows gave me hives. They involved a studio's entire roster of dancers, as well as props, parental involvement, and a lot of time. I didn't care for them, but my Company routine ended up as a "small show" here at Holly's competition. Most of the others had special categories for Company routines, which usually included girls of all ages.

Marlys walked up and handed me the schedule and then walked around making sure each little girl had received her wristband. We had handed those out earlier in the week, of course, but inevitably someone forgot theirs and ended up needing another. The compassionate doormen would usually let them through once, but getting in and out could be a problem.

I looked over the schedule, and then I lined up the Minis. They would go on first, and after an hour or so break, the Smalls would be on. Then the Petites, followed by the Seniors. And finally, the Company routine.

Some days it was nice not to have so many students, because I knew some studios had three routines for each group. I planned on adding a lyrical routine for the Petites and Seniors, and a Company hip-hop next year, but I believed in quality over quantity. I was trying to grow my studio slowly.

Of course, that meant I ate a lot of mac and cheese. And of course, that made me think of Tate's comment, and then Tate himself, and next thing I knew those darn sneaky tears were trying to well out of my eyes.

"Jenny, what's wrong?" I looked down to Maribel watching me solemnly, her eyes big and wide—and made even more so by the eyeliner and mascara.

"Nothing, honey, I'm just so proud of all of you."

"My mom doesn't cry when she's proud," she said.

"She does, honey. She just hides it."

"Oh. Okay."

Maribel turned around and skipped off. She waved at James as she passed him. I was relieved to see he didn't have the rat dog with him.

"Okay, I'm not trying to panic you," James said in a voice that was pretty much designed to set off panic, "but there are four Minis missing. They should have been here fifteen minutes ago."

"Which ones?" I asked.

"Brinley Shaw, BreeAnn Shaw, Destiny Morgan, and Avery Lang."

"Ah, yes. They'll be here about five minutes before we go on, probably without makeup and their hair in rats' nests around their heads."

The circus had started.

TWENTY-FIVE

THE MINIS, SMALLS, AND PETITES ROUTINES all went extremely well. There were some flubs, of course, especially in the younger routines. But they still had the "cute" factor to rely on, so people didn't notice as much. Of course, I did. But we would talk about it Monday at dance.

The Seniors were in line, waiting to go on, and the six Petites and two Smalls who had made the Company routine were getting ready. The Seniors had only about four routines in between their team routine and the Company routine, so the girls who were in both dances would have to move fast. They'd done it before, and the dressing room was full of psycho dance moms ready to help girls strip out of one costume and into another.

I turned and saw Arlo's bright red face, and realized that he had not really signed up for this. "You guys can wait outside. I'll be fine."

"No way," Arlo said, but he didn't look happy. "He's in here." He pointed at James.

"Well, he? He would be a menace in this place were it full of men, and as it is, he might as well be surrounded by store mannequins. Look, I'm surrounded by the craziest women in Utah. If someone came after me, they would all immediately attack. And there is only one way in here. You can guard that door, and everything will be fine." I decided not to mention that one of the suspects—possible suspects—was one of these moms. A rather well-endowed Petite ran in and began to strip down, and that convinced Arlo and Stanley to stand guard *outside* the locker-room door. That and the fact that James had caught them looking at him and gave them a little finger waggle.

"Okay, Seniors, line up." I ran the routine through to counts, the girls finding space wherever they could in the crowded locker room.

"Two routines, Jenny," Marlys said, sticking her head through the door.

"All right, let's go, girls. Make this one good."

And they did. The audience stood and applauded after the routine. I spotted Trevor in the stands, giving me a thumbs-up. He sat next to a skinny blond woman, who glared at me. Stand in line, sister. I was pretty sure she was the mother of a dancer on a rival team—one that had been trying to lure Trevor to their studio to choreograph routines for a year or more. He kept saying no. I was probably on her hit list. Down closer to the ground, I spotted Malece, and next to her, in his wheelchair next to the benches, was Sal. He gave me a thumbs-up, too. Malece gave me a nasty sneer.

Somehow, she had sensed Tate and I were . . . What were we? I didn't even know. Truth was, I didn't know what we were before, so what we were *now* was a total mystery.

The announcer called out my studio's name, and the girls entered onto the floor, in perfect cadence. They pulled the routine off flawlessly, and after they exited, they all broke into a full bore run for the locker room. I followed behind, as did a stream of moms.

Arlo and Stanley looked alarmed as the stampede of moms headed toward them.

"Quick change," I explained breathlessly.

"Uh, okay," Arlo said. Stanley winced. I suspected he would be asking for time and a half for this assignment. Of course, that made me think of Tate, and the fact that he was footing the bill for these guys, and those sneaky tears tried to get me again, but then I heard a scream from inside the locker room.

I pushed through the doors, Arlo and Stanley on my heels, yelling for me to stop.

"A mouse! A mouse!" yelled one of the Petites, running away from the lockers. Bountiful High School was old, so I wasn't really surprised.

"Ayyyyiiiii!" came a high-pitched scream, and James rushed out of the locker room, waving his arms and waking the dead. He probably never even saw the mouse. I sighed.

Stanley ran over and grabbed a popcorn bucket from the bench, dumped it out, and went into stealth mode, stalking the mouse. All he needed was some camouflage and a big knife, and we could call him Rambo.

He moved in, dropped the bucket over the mouse, and then stood up and turned around to applause and yells of appreciation from all the dancers.

And he blushed. I swear! His face went bright red. Then he smiled. I almost passed out. The man could smile.

A janitor came into the room, quickly slipped a thick cloth under the popcorn bucket, and then left with the mouse. Stanley followed him out, still smiling, with Arlo right behind.

"Two routines," Marlys said, poking her head in after the men had cleared the doorway.

"Jenny?" Sidney Clark said, a question in her voice. "I can't find Carly anywhere. We were here, getting ready, and she said she had to go to the bathroom, and then she just disappeared."

"Did you check the stalls?" I asked her. Since we were in the boy's locker room, there were a couple of stalls and some urinals. The younger girls—and sometimes the older ones—would giggle at the devices they never saw in their own public restrooms.

"Yeah, she's not in there."

"Carly? Carly?" I called out. "Who's seen Carly Fulton?"

All the girls raised their hands. Dumb question. "I mean, who has seen her in the last ten minutes?"

"One routine," Marlys said, poking her head in the door.

No hands this time. "All right, all of you, go out there. Line up. I'll find Carly. She might miss the routine."

"But Jenny, she has the solo role," Sidney pointed out.

"You'll just have to cover. Spread out. Don't leave big holes."

The girls took off, and fear and dread filled my heart. Carly was probably my best dancer, the daughter of one of my closest friends, and if someone wanted to hurt me, they couldn't strike much closer.

I ran through the locker room, but she was not there.

I heard the sounds of Trevor's music fill the gym, but all I could think of was Carly. Where was she?

"Jenny? Where's Carly?" Marlys had noticed her daughter was not in the lineup. And I had no idea how to answer her. Because Carly was missing.

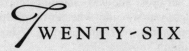

TWENTY-SIX

ALL THE GIRLS CAME RUNNING IN, FLUSHED and excited as Marlys and I stood staring at each other. I stepped outside the locker-room door and quietly told Arlo and Stanley that I thought something might be terribly, terribly wrong.

Arlo and I took off in one direction, while Marlys and Stanley took off in another. We scanned all the girls, looking for a better part of an hour. By the time we were done, the routines were over and the girls were sitting on the gym floor, playing games, and waiting for awards.

There had been no sign of Carly. No one even remembered her coming back from the Petites routine, and I figured that had to be the time she disappeared. I swallowed my pride and called Tate's cell phone. He answered on the first ring.

"Something's wrong. Carly is missing. Marlys's Carly. She missed the Company routine. She would never miss that. Never."

Tate told me to hang on, and I heard him talking to someone. "The local PD is on the way, and I'm on my way, too," he said. "Stay with Stanley and Arlo."

When I met back up with Marlys, I could see the terror and panic in her eyes. She was clutching Maribel's hand, and the little girl was sobbing, whether from fear about her sister's disappearance or from the pain of her mother's death grip, I didn't know.

"This is his fault, isn't it?" she asked me, wild-eyed.

"His fault?" I asked, confused.

"Roger. This is all about those damned Russians and the blackmail. It's his fault!"

Here I'd been blaming myself. I'd never even thought of the Twinkle Toes people.

"Yo, Jenny. What happened there? Where did my soloist go?" Trevor said as he walked up to me. His eyebrows were lowered and his mouth a straight line. "That solo was the best part of the routine."

"She's missing, Trevor. Missing, as in no one knows where she is. We've called the police."

Trevor's eyes widened. "Missing? Not as in missing the routine, but as in missing, missing?"

"Yes," I said impatiently. "Missing, missing."

"Whoa," Trevor said, looking around as members of the Bountiful Police Department started to stream through the doors. There were quite a few. I guessed that Tate had called out the Mounties. Not all of the girls noticed the uniformed officers, but most did, and silence soon spread through the gym.

Arlo approached the nearest officer and started talking to him, then pointed at me. Great. I was going to be infamous in Bountiful, too. Two officers came over to Marlys and me, and got a description of Carly. They asked us a bunch of questions, and I tried to answer them as best I could. Marlys had turned back into a crazy woman and was little help. I understood. Her daughter was missing. Her whole life was her children. And she thought Roger was responsible. I wasn't so sure. After all, Roger didn't drive a Hummer.

After a moment, a man in a suit coat and slacks went to the front and asked to borrow the microphone. Holly, who had been standing there with some of her tabulated results, probably getting ready to start awards, handed it over without complaint. She was wearing a gold sequin top and short shorts—not an attractive look for an Amazon. Actually, probably not an attractive look for anyone but a hoochie mama. She batted her eyelids at the police officer; looking alarmed, he turned to the girls, who waited patiently.

"Hello," he said into the microphone, and a loud *skree* sounded from the instrument. He jumped back a bit, then looked at Holly. "Just try again," she said, waving at him once more. He looked back at the microphone. "Hello, girls. We have a very serious situation going on right now, and so we need your help. A young girl has gone missing." This time there was no feedback from the microphone, but the room twittered as the girls began to talk nervously and as parents, listening closely from the stands, murmured to each other and looked around anxiously.

"Carly Fulton is thirteen, has shoulder-length blond hair, dark green eyes, and she was last seen wearing a . . . a black tutu, red pointe shoes, and a black embroidered and beaded corset." He stopped and looked down closely at the description he had been given, as if finding it hard to believe.

"If anyone has seen Carly, we would appreciate you approaching any of these fine policemen here and telling them what you know." He motioned around the room to all the policemen. He started to walk away, then said, "Uh, thank you."

He handed the microphone back to Holly, who smiled wolfishly at him. He scurried off, giving her backward glances. I watched her closely. After keeping the police-man in her sights for a few seconds, she returned her eyes to her score sheets. She thumbed through them, then turned to the person at the sound table, said something that made the man smile, then turned back to the score sheets. She looked at her watch impatiently and rolled her eyes.

All around us, people were walking up to the policemen and offering whatever tidbit they thought might be helpful, concern evident on their faces. Holly just looked bored.

A shout went up from the north side of the gym, on the upper level, and several policemen took off running for the stairs. Marlys and I followed closely, and then an arm pulled me back. It was Tate. Either he'd set a land speed record between Ogden and Bountiful or he'd been much closer than I'd realized. And of course that was it. He might not have let me know it, but he'd been nearby. He was Tate. He was Superman. But even Superman wasn't stopping me from getting to Carly.

"Don't keep me from her," I said to him as I struggled to get past him and through the doors that led to a stairway to the upper level.

"I'm not keeping you from her," he said, his voice tense. "I'm keeping you safe."

"Tate—"

"Just stay with me. Got it?"

I nodded my head, and together we ascended the stairs and hurried back behind the second riser of bleachers, where several policemen were bent over a small figure wearing black, the red pointe shoes standing out like blood.

I winced and ran to her. This time, Tate didn't hold me back.

I heard Marlys scream as though she were a million miles away, and as I reached Carly and bent down, I saw her face was as white as snow, a slight blue tinge to her lips. Blood seeped from a wound on her head, and I bent down and got as close to her mouth as I could. I could feel faint wisps of breath, and I sat back up, tears streaming down my face.

One of the policemen was giving instructions for medical help through his two-way radio, and Marlys dropped beside me.

"She's alive," I said, my voice barely a whisper. "She's hurt, but she's alive."

"Oh my baby," she moaned, leaning toward her and trying to scoop her up in her arms.

"Please don't move her, ma'am," one of the policemen said to Marlys. "She has a head injury, and we need the paramedics to get her stabilized so we can transport her."

Marlys backed off and put her hand to her mouth, sobbing over her daughter's prone body.

I stood up and turned, blindly, tears stinging my eyes, and walked into a solid wall of chest. Tate pulled me close to him, and I realized then how badly I was shaking, how scared I was, how angry I felt.

I let him hold me for a minute, even as the paramedics rushed in and began to stabilize Carly.

As they lifted her up and put her on the gurney, one of the policemen said, "Hey, what's that?" I turned to watch as he leaned over and picked up a small silver toy—a toy Hummer.

And that was all it took. I knew then exactly who was responsible for all of this, and she was going to pay.

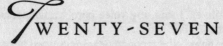

TWENTY-SEVEN

"JENNY, WAIT," I HEARD TATE CALL, BUT I had a purpose and a mission. I was going to tackle that Amazonian Holly Vendstra and slap her silly until she . . . I slowed down. Tackle Holly and slap her silly?

Not much of a plan, really. Tate caught up with me. "You think Holly is responsible for this?"

"Hello? Isn't it obvious? Her competition. She drives a Hummer. She has a serious hatchet to grind with me. It has to be her. Nothing else makes sense."

"Trevor Paulsen is here, too. Driving a Hummer he claims is a rental, and which we know is not. As is Tamara Williams, whose darling daughter doesn't get a lot of roles because Carly is so much better than she is. We need to follow all the clues, Jenny. And you need to let the professionals do it."

His words sunk in. Trevor was here, but it was his routine. He would want it to be the best. Unless he had some whacked-out agenda that included getting me to quit teaching dance and leaving Utah . . . Nah. And Tamara? She was crazy, yeah, but would she really hurt someone else's child so that hers could be in the spotlight? Her daughter won tonight, for Pete's sake, even if everyone knew the contest was rigged.

"It had to be Holly. She worships at the church of the almighty dollar. Nothing else matters to her. I threatened her livelihood, or she thought I did, so she's decided to threaten mine."

"That makes sense, and I'm about to go question her right now."

"I'll go with you."

"No, you won't. Arlo and Stanley are going to take you to the hospital where they took Carly, and you are going to be there for your friend Marlys, while you let me do my job."

"This is not your jurisdiction," I said. "You can't investigate here."

"Too much television, Jenny."

I sighed. Marlys needed me. Carly needed me. Roger probably needed me, too, the spineless . . . "Hey, what about the Twinkle Toes people? Could this have been them?"

"We will certainly be looking at them, as well as all the others, Jenny. Now, go with Arlo and Stanley. Tell Marlys I love her and Carly, and I'll be there as soon as I can."

My heart melted a little, until his words sunk in. He could tell Marlys and Carly that he loved them, but he'd never so much as said the word to me. And he wondered why I couldn't call him my boyfriend without swallowing my tongue! I turned and walked away without another word, Arlo and Stanley at my side.

After we walked down the stairs and into the entryway of the large gymnasium, I heard Holly's voice come over the loudspeaker as she began to announce awards.

"Aren't you going to stay for awards, Jenny?" asked the mother of one of my Minis.

"I can't," I said to her. "Would you do me a favor and

collect our trophies, and make sure the girls all get their individual trophies?"

"Well, sure," she said. "Avonlea is so excited for her first trophy, we wouldn't think of leaving."

I couldn't even bear the thought of looking at the trophies. Were they blood trophies, like those blood diamonds I'd always heard about?

Phew, Melodrama Queen. Chill. Usually, I heard Grandma Gilly's voice in my head. Today, it was Marlys's ironic tones, bringing me back to reality. She did that a lot. My turn to be there for her.

THE PARAMEDICS HAD TRANSPORTED CARLY to Primary Children's Medical Center in Salt Lake City. Although there were closer hospitals to Bountiful High School, Primary was the best in pediatric medicine. Me and my shadows found Marlys and Roger signing paperwork in a cubicle of the hospital.

"She's getting an MRI right now," Marlys said. "She regained consciousness on the way here. I rode in the ambulance with her, and she opened her eyes and looked up at me and said, 'Mommy.' That's a real good sign she's going to be okay."

I nodded my head. It did sound promising.

After she handed the paperwork back to the nurse, she guided me to the ER that had been assigned to Carly. Roger shuffled along behind us. Ever since he had been caught handing money over to the Russians, he had acted like a guilty man. Especially when he saw me.

We got back to the room just as Carly was being wheeled inside. Her wound had been cleaned and dressed, and although she definitely didn't look her best, she looked far better than she had just an hour or so before.

"Hi, Jenny," she said softly. "Sorry I didn't make it out for the routine."

"Oh my heck, Carly. That is the least of my concerns. Are you feeling okay?"

"My head hurts, and I'm kinda sick to my stomach."

"Concussion, I think," Marlys said.

"Do you remember what happened?" I asked her.

"Last thing I remember was putting on my pointe shoes, then I realized I needed to pee. I was nervous about my solo. I went to the bathrooms in the locker room, but they were being used, and so I went out and ran upstairs to the bathrooms by the racquetball courts. No one is ever in there. And that's all I remember."

"You don't remember who hit you?"

"No, I just remember going into the bathroom. Then it's all blank until I woke up in the ambulance."

A young Indian woman came into the room and nodded at us. "Well, Carly, it seems that you did not suffer any serious damage to your head, which is a very good thing. There is some slight swelling, and you have a concussion, so we would like to keep you overnight for observation."

"Okay," Carly said wanly. "I'm kind of tired."

"Don't let her sleep," Roger exclaimed, then flushed, realizing he was telling this to a doctor.

"We will wake her up every hour and will be monitoring her vital signs, Mr. Fulton. Please do not worry. She will receive excellent care here."

A nurse came in and prepared to move Carly to a room, and Marlys pulled the doctor aside. "Are you sure she doesn't have brain damage? She can't remember anything after she went to the bathroom."

"Memory loss is common with traumatic injury," the doctor said in her singsong voice. "We will take good care of her. Don't you worry."

"Can I stay?"

"Of course."

"Me, too," Roger said.

"No, you need to go home to the kids. My mom is staying

at our house until you get there. Maribel went home with Leslie Stevens, and she will keep her until tomorrow, but the boys will need you."

Marlys's voice was harsh, her tone strident, and I looked at both at them, feeling the undercurrent of something seriously awry. She had seemed so relieved the other day, I couldn't understand why she now seemed so angry at Roger. Unless she believed the Russians had done this to Carly.

Roger looked like an abashed little boy. He gave me an angry glare, then walked over to Carly, kissed her on the check, told her he loved her, and left.

"Marlys, is everything okay?"

"Not now," she said firmly. "We need to sit down and talk, but not now. Now, I'm here for Carly."

I told them both good-bye, then hurried out to find Arlo and Stanley hovering anxiously. Both men were throwing evil glances at the retreating back of Roger Fulton. I looked at both of them, then at Roger, and shook my head. What the heck was going on here?

"All right, you two, spill," I said when we were in the car on the way back to Ogden. "If looks could shoot, Roger would be a dead man."

"If looks could shoot?" Arlo said.

I rolled my eyes. "You know what I mean. Why were you guys so pissed at Roger?"

"You mean besides the fact he's a liar, a cheat, a scumbag, and a good-for-nothing . . ." I stared at the back of Stanley's head as he trailed off. That was the most I had ever heard him say.

"I don't get it. I don't understand. I thought we all believed him."

"You might have believed him," Arlo said. "We're former cops. We don't believe nobody. So we did some investigating on our own, and we found out that your friend's husband is lying through his teeth. There was more than dancing lessons going on there, and the only reason he paid up is because they had pictures to prove it."

"And you told her?" I asked Arlo.

"Stanley did. He doesn't like creeps like Roger cheating on their wives. It's his pet peeve."

I stared at Stanley, surprised he would put himself in a situation that had so much potential for emotional back-wash. He remained expressionless. He was an interesting man, and not at all what I had judged him to be.

I sat stunned. My friend Marlys's life was about to shat-ter into a million pieces, and I was helpless to stop it. I wasn't even that good at picking up pieces. I usually missed a few. Marlys was the one who could magically put some-thing broken back together again. Only this . . .

"And do you think they are the ones that hurt Carly?"

"Either them or him," Arlo said gruffly.

"Oh my God, no, Roger wouldn't do that, would he? He wouldn't hurt his own child. Would he?"

Nausea filled my stomach, and I rolled down the win-dow slightly to get some night air. Things weren't sup-posed to work out this way for Marlys. Me, maybe, if, say, I actually had a husband to cheat, but not her.

Neither man answered my questions. I didn't blame them. Nobody really wanted to hear the answer, especially if it was yes.

TWENTY-EIGHT

STANLEY AND ARLO HANDED ME OFF TO Alissa, who assured them she had plenty of protection. I assured them she did as well. I'd seen it, and I didn't want her pulling her gun out again to prove it.

I gave her a quick recap of the events of the past few weeks, and she made us chamomile tea, which I despised, as she listened. "Don't you have some hot chocolate or something?" I asked.

"Chocolate has caffeine, which is a stimulant. After what you've been through, you need to be able to sleep."

I gagged down the tea, with lots of honey, and then she made up a bed for me on her couch. I watched, unable to move to help.

My body felt leaden and old, my mind filled with questions I couldn't answer. The most important one, to me, was who had hurt Carly? It was one thing to threaten or hurt me. But not Carly. Not an innocent child. I almost wanted it to be Roger, because then it wouldn't be connected to me. Then I felt guilty for that thought.

"Quit thinking."

I looked up, half expecting to see that Alissa had morphed into Tate. Nope, still Alissa. "Get into bed, and don't worry about it. Tate's good. He'll figure it out. And you're safe here with me. Now go to sleep."

"He might figure it out, but what about me? What about us? Is he going to figure that out, too?"

"I don't know, Jenny. He's a complicated man. And I don't know the whole situation. You'll tell me tomorrow. For now, go to sleep. It's really late."

It was late. I was tired. But I couldn't nod off; instead I turned into my pillow and cried, missing the feel of Tate and the rhythm of his gentle snoring.

I missed him. I loved him.

And I was sleeping alone.

SUNDAY MORNING, I AWOKE ON ALISSA'S couch. The room was quiet. A clock hanging on her wall said the time was 7 a.m. I was not normally an early riser, but waking at this time was especially unusual because I had gone to bed late and tossed and turned until well after 3 a.m.

I heard mumbled voices coming from the small kitchen, and for a moment I was afraid Alissa had been, uh, entertaining when I showed up, but then I remembered I had made arrangements with her earlier in the day. She wouldn't do that.

She better not be doing that, as I recognized the voice of Tate in the other room. I rose from the couch and wrapped a sheet around me, traipsing into the small kitchen.

Both of them were fully dressed, and having coffee. They looked at me as I stood there, hair that probably resembled Bozo the Clown's, mascara probably all around my eyes, and I decided I should have made a bathroom pit stop first.

"Rough night," Tate commented, then looked back at his coffee. I wanted to smack him. Hard.

"Why yes, thank you, it was," I said snidely. Then I turned and walked away, eager to make my exit, get into the bathroom, and redeem myself. Too bad I tripped over the sheet and fell down on the carpet with a hard "oomph."

Tate picked me up, unwound the tangled sheet from me, and gave me that warm-eyed look that always turned me into a melted bowl of ice cream, even when I was trying to be the frozen ice princess.

"Don't even give me that look," I said.

"What look?"

"That look. You know darn good and well what you're doing."

"I miss you."

"Stop it."

"What did I do to make you so angry with me? Where did this distance come from?"

I wanted to cry. He didn't even know why he was hurting me.

After a minute of watching me, he turned away. "I thought I'd come over and tell you what we found out," he said without looking at me. "There were no prints on the Hummer, unfortunately—the toy one that is—so we couldn't find out anything from that. Holly Vendstra has an alibi for the time of Carly's disappearance. She was tabulating results with her assistant. Trevor was seen by about five people, sitting in the stands, waiting for the routine to go on, so he has an alibi, too. Tamara Williams claims she was in the dressing room, getting her daughter ready to perform, and April backed that up."

"Wait a minute," I said. "April was done. She isn't in the Company routine, remember? She was done and had nothing to get ready for after the Petites routine was done."

"Hmm," Tate said. "Interesting. I'll go have another little chat with her.

"And Roger?"

"Roger?"

"Yes, you remember him. Marlys's husband, the Twinkle Toes client?"

"I assumed Roger was sitting with Marlys."

"Well, you assumed wrong, mister, and you know what happens when you assume. You make an ass out of you and me. Ass-u-me." Boy, I'd been waiting my whole life to use that one. Judging by the look on Tate's face, I'd picked the wrong person to use it on.

"Clichés aside, do you have information about Roger that you are not sharing with me?"

"Talk to Stanley and Arlo. They've been doing their own investigating. I thought they had talked to you."

"I guess I need to go speak with them now," he said tersely, and without another word, he walked out the door.

"You weren't very nice to him," Alissa commented.

"I'm mad at him."

"Gee, I never would have guessed."

I gave her a look, but unfortunately, my looks never had much impact and she ignored it.

"So, are you going to tell me what he did?"

"He asked me to move in with him permanently."

"Hmm, yes, I can see why that would upset you and permanently endanger this relationship."

"Stop being a smarty pants."

"Smarty pants? Jenny, it's time to grow up. What bothered you about him asking you to live with him?"

"The whole 'why buy the milk if you can get the cow for free' thing."

Alissa pondered that for a moment and then smiled at me. "You love him, and you want him to love you back."

"Is it too much to ask?"

"No, but maybe he doesn't know what you need to hear."

"Why doesn't he know?"

"Hello? Guy? Never married guy, to boot. They are walking idiots."

"Are you trying to say I need to tell him that he needs to tell me that he loves me?"

"Something like that."

"Doesn't that defeat the purpose?"

"This isn't the movies, Jenny. This is real life."

"I don't like it."

"Deal."

Great. Tough love about love. Just what I needed early on a Sunday morning.

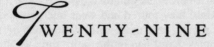

TWENTY-NINE

ALISSA AND I SPENT SUNDAY WATCHING movies and lounging. We watched my favorite, *Pretty Woman*, and I gave her a pointed look when it was through. "See? Fairy tale."

She just rolled her eyes.

Monday morning Arlo and Stanley were at Alissa's door at 11 a.m., the time I'd arranged to head over to Marlys's house to visit with Carly.

We did the Mafia-princess routine that we all had down pat, now. At Marlys's, I chatted with Carly, who was hanging out on the couch and texting friends on her phone. She looked really good, and even better, I found out that she had been cleared to dance Saturday at UDC, as long as she took it easy during the week.

Stanley hung back and chatted with Marlys in the kitchen, which I found totally amazing, since he never said more than two words to me.

At my parents' place, we repeated the Mafia-princess routine and then went in to make sure my dad had no hard feelings about the death germs in Bessie, and that my mother wasn't knocking over drugstores.

Mom served Stanley and Arlo coffee, and asked them about their jobs. I found out that they had both served in the Army Special Forces, as well on the police force for quite a few years until they retired and went into private security work. My mother got more information out of them in twenty minutes than I had in the entire time we'd been together.

We'd been together? *Sheesh.* That made us sound like some sort of perverse couple . . . trio? Double *sheesh.* I mean, this was Utah and all, but still . . .

After we left the Partridge household, they drove me to the studio, where I did some paperwork, returned phone calls—ignoring the forty million from Tamara Williams—and then I realized I had nothing to do until my first class.

I decided that if Stanley and Arlo could chat with Marlys and my mother, then they could darn well hold a conversation with me.

"So, tell me more about your work," I said as I walked out of the office to the front studio, where the two sat on their usual chairs. The gave each other a look, and then both looked at me, faces like stone.

"More as in what?" Arlo finally said.

"Do you guys own your security company, or what?"

"Yes," Arlo answered.

"And you're based out of Ogden?"

"No."

"Salt Lake City?"

"Yes."

"And what kind of work do you do?"

"Security work."

I sighed. "How come you talk to everyone else, but the two of you don't say two words to me? Am I that bad?"

"You're the assignment."

"I'm the assignment. Great, now I sound like math homework."

Arlo quirked a smile. I remembered his big hand over mine when I'd been crying as we left Tate's house, and I decided that would have to be enough.

"Okay, well, I guess I'll go return Tamara Williams's forty million phone calls, because she talks enough for everybody."

TREVOR SHOWED UP FOR OUR PRACTICES AGAIN. He helped fine-tune the routines, and I wondered about him still being in town.

"So, how long are you here for?" I asked him.

"I want to see you win the UDC and get that money. And I didn't get to see Carly in the lead solo role. So I need to be here for that."

"Thank you," I said to him. He just smiled that breathtaking smile, but for once, my breath wasn't taken. I missed Tate too much.

When Avonlea's mom walked in carrying a huge trophy, the girls all gathered around excitedly and started chattering about the ice cream party I owed them.

"Which routine was this for?" I asked her.

"Actually, it's only the first one. I have five more in my car. You took almost every category you were entered in."

"Really?"

"Yep."

That was unheard of at a Holly Vendstra competition.

"Yeah, well, it was pretty obvious that all your routines were so far above everyone else's. There just wasn't a comparison," Trevor said.

The girls were still clamoring for ice cream, so I told them that if they worked really hard today and tomorrow, we'd run each routine twice on Wednesday and then have an ice cream party.

A roar went up around the room. Everybody loved ice cream. It even made me feel just a tiny bit happy. A tiny bit. James came over to me and smiled. "You did good, Jenny. This is going to be the best year ever. Things are really going to change for you."

His words rang in my head. Things had already changed, and it wasn't the way I'd thought it would be. These weren't the changes I wanted. Why did one thing changing have to make the other thing change? That made no sense. I was even thinking rubbish. I tried to clear my head. When one thing worked out, why did something else always have to be not working? Or something be missing? Or was it some*one* be missing?

Definitely someone.

THIRTY

I'D GONE ALMOST AN ENTIRE WEEK WITH NO signs of a silver Hummer, no assaults, no missing dancers, and no Tate. I was almost willing to put up with all the others if I could just have ten minutes with Tate. But then I remembered Julia Roberts. She stood firm. She wanted the fairy tale. Me, too.

The Ultimate Dance Championships came up quickly, and Friday night's solo competition went great, with Carly winning despite the bandage on her forehead. She looked incredible in her costume, and after she performed, I turned to Malece, who stood by Sal's wheelchair, and told her she had a job, making all my costumes in the future. If she wanted it.

"What's up with you and Tate?" she asked, instead of replying to my comment.

"Nothing."

"Nothing?"

"No, nothing."

She just shrugged and turned away. Then she turned

back. "If you hurt him, I'll come after you and make sure you were sorry you were ever born."

Great. Death threats from Tate's sister, the woman I wanted to design my costumes. A woman who worked with sharp objects. Maybe there was another opening at the sheriff's office.

SATURDAY DAWNED BEAUTIFULLY. I WAS STILL sleeping on Alissa's couch, so it wasn't the ideal living situation, but the sun was shining, the birds were singing, and I'd turned into a Disney commercial.

"You seem happy," Alissa said as she came out of the bathroom in her robe.

"I'm optimistic. I think my teams will win that money at today's competition. And then maybe I can get a little dance store going and finally have more than twenty cents in my pocket at a time."

"Wish I could come see your teams. I have Saturday classes, though."

I understood. Alissa's desire to become a police officer was as strong as her determination to show every man that she could hold a gun as well as he could. And look a darn sight better doing it, since she was tall and dark haired and drop-dead gorgeous.

After I showered, I blew my hair dry and straightened it, cursing at the little wispies that kept escaping no matter how many times I fried them with the straightener. I decided I better stop before I burned all the hair off, and put some light foundation on my face, a bit of blush, eyeliner, and mascara.

After I was dressed in my Lucky jeans and T-shirt from Buckle—a Christmas present from my mother, of course, since I couldn't dream of affording such expensive clothes—I surveyed myself in the mirror. I looked cute. Not pretty, of course, but cute. Reasonable weight, probably because I had no money to eat, but hey, I'd take whatever luck I could get. My height—short—was out of my hands, so that would have to do. My red hair and china-doll skin would also have to do.

I was not drop-dead gorgeous like Alissa. Tate had always seemed to like me anyway. Maybe I was the kind of girl that guys would always like, but never the kind that would inspire undying love. Maybe that was all I could expect in life. I felt my confidence begin to sag.

That wasn't enough. It just wasn't.

The doorbell rang, and I looked through the peephole to see Stanley and Arlo standing there. I grabbed my bag, made sure my cell phone was inside, and opened the door.

And that's when the gunshots rang out.

Arlo tackled me, pushing me inside the apartment, and Stanley hit the ground. Why did Stanley hit the ground? "Stanley, are you okay?"

Arlo roughly pushed me to the ground, grabbed Stanley's shoulders, pulled him inside the apartment, and shoved the door shut.

"You're hit," Arlo said to Stanley.

"Yeah, hurts like a motha," Stanley said, wincing and gasping. He groped around with his hands on his chest and then said, "Hit the vest, though. I hate gunshots."

That made two of us.

Alissa was on the phone, down low by the base of the couch. "Shots fired at 2240 Eccles Lane. One security officer down, but he's apparently wearing a vest, so no serious injury."

A few more shots rang out, and we all stayed close to the ground. Soon, we could hear sirens wailing; Arlo cautiously made his way to the front window, gun drawn, and peered outside.

After a minute, he determined it was clear, and Alissa told the dispatcher that we were inside and the assailant appeared to be gone.

The usual chaos ensued, and Tate showed up, as always, but this time, he pulled me to him and held me close. It made tears come to my eyes.

"I want you back with me, where I can keep you safe," he said.

"That's not enough," I replied, unable to fight back the tears.

"What do you mean?"

"I need it all. I need to be loved."

"Jenny, I do love you. Are you kidding me?"

"You do?"

"Of course I do. You think I would change my life like I did for just anyone? Until you came along, no one even came close to making me want to be anything but a bachelor. But I can't stand being away from you, because I never know who is going to be shooting at you, or trying to get you into bed with them."

"Now wait a minute. Shooting me and getting me into bed are two totally different things."

"Yes, I know, but with you, it seems like one or the other is always happening."

"You're crazy."

"Isn't that the pot calling the kettle black?"

"That makes absolutely no sense," I said to him. "Why would pot call a kettle black? I've never understood why people say that. I mean, it's a racial slur, too, isn't it? Assuming that only black people sell pot."

Tate chuckled and pulled me close to him. "I love you, Jenny T. Partridge. I want you safe, and in my bed, and—"

"The declarations of love are nice and all," Alissa said, "but Jenny has a competition to get to, and we have reports to fill out, and I happen to be missing a very important class."

"She isn't going anywhere."

"Whoa, slow down there, Tate. What do you mean?" I asked him. "You know how important this is to me."

"Yes, and obviously, so does someone else," he said. "And that is why it is too dangerous for you to go to this competition. James can be there, and he can give you hourly updates, if necessary, but you can't go."

"I have to go."

"You can't."

"I can."

Tate sighed. "Jenny, can't you see how dangerous this is? It's obvious now, with the attack this morning, that someone does not want you competing your teams. Especially after Carly was hurt. Do you really want this to happen to someone else on your team? Somebody else's daughter?"

"That is not fair," I said to him. "You are using that emotional blackmail crap, and it's not fair."

"She's going," Arlo said, steel in his voice.

We both turned to him.

"Excuse me?" Tate said.

"Look, whatever it is, it's going to come to a head today. And that means she needs to go. But not alone. We'll call in reinforcements. We need extra guys to make sure nothing happens to the dancers."

"I . . ."

"This one is on us, if you're worried about the money," Arlo said. "It's personal now. Nobody shoots my partner and gets away with it."

I felt as though I'd morphed into one of those old Westerns. Or maybe an old cop show.

"Look, this is—"

"This is it, Tate. Like Arlo said, whatever has been going on is going to come to a head today, and it's going to happen at the dance competition. But it won't happen if I'm not there. And we have to make this stop. It has to end."

He looked at me, then back at Arlo and Stanley, who had managed to stand even though he was still clutching his chest. He'd brushed off any attempts to get him medical help. That didn't surprise me.

"Detective Wilson?" said a young uniformed officer.

"Yes, Johnson."

"Neighbors said they spotted a silver Hummer out front right before the commotion. Man noticed because he's always wanted one, and he said the motors have a distinctive sound. Knew there was a Hummer out there even before he saw it through the window. He didn't get the plate, though. Said it all happened really quick."

"It always does," Alissa said, irony lacing her voice.

Tate turned to me. "Jenny, whoever it is did not want you going to this competition today. And you very well could have died this morning. Maybe that's what they intended."

"Someone could have died this morning," I said, looking at Stanley, who was still a little pale. "And that's why I have to go. Because I only have two choices. Quit and run, which I can't do. You know that, right?"

He nodded.

"And the other choice is to face it head-on. So that's what I intend to do."

"What you don't seem to realize is that you are endangering other people's kids, Jenny. There is a lot at stake here, and it's not just your well-being and that of your dancers. There will be a lot of teams there, and a lot of people watching. Maybe the entire competition should be shut down."

"Look, there's no guarantee you could even get the UDC people to shut their competition down," Alissa said. "I mean, it's been planned for a long time, and there are thousands of dollars invested. The only real answer is to convince them of the need for security. If you walk in there with lots of reinforcements, lots of security, how is anyone going to get through?"

"It just seems too risky."

"It's too short notice to shut it down, anyway," I told Tate. "This competition gets teams from all over the Intermountain West. And like Alissa said, it's a big-money competition. They are not going to willingly go along with shutting it down just because someone is shooting at me. The only real answer is security."

"All right, all right. Fine. All I have to say is, whoever it is will be walking right into a big fat trap, because there will be cops everywhere today."

"May I suggest undercover?" I said.

"Yes, Jenny." Tate smiled. Evidently, Officer Aaron had told him about my problem with him being in uniform.

"Our guys will work in tandem with your guys," Arlo told Tate. "We need to get there and set up a command center. We have a motor home we use. I'll arrange to get it set up on the site."

"Won't it stand out?" Tate asked.

"Actually, lots of teams come into town and bring motor homes for their girls to change in and take breaks. So it will just look like one of the crowd," I told him.

"I still think this is a bad idea."

"Think away, thinking man. But I have a good feeling about this. I think today is the day my nightmares end." *And Tate loved me, too.*

THIRTY-ONE

MORE THAN HALF OF MY TEAMS HAD ALREADY competed, and nothing even slightly out of place had occurred. The girls had done well—better than any of our competition, as far as I could see—and the entire event was running smoothly and on time. Every time someone sneezed I jumped about forty feet, even though I knew that Arlo, Stanley, and about twelve of their men, along with some undercover policemen from Ogden, were on the alert, keeping an eye on all of the proceedings.

The Ultimate Dance Championships were being held at the Eccles Conference Center in downtown Ogden, not too far from my studio. UDC was a national competition that came through town every year. Unlike Hollywood Star-Makers and other similar events, UDC was strictly a competition, and not a convention as well.

And unlike a lot of the others, UDC gave prize money to the team with the highest overall studio average.

"Uh, Jenny?" Carly said to me. I looked over to see her on my right.

"What's up, Carly?"

"April is crying in the dressing room, and she won't come out. And we are supposed to be on in about four routines."

I rolled my eyes, then headed for the dressing room. I had given Marlys that duty today, since Tate wanted me out in the open at all times so that I could be watched over closely. As I moved, I sensed about four guys behind me moving as well, and I sighed. I used to dream that men would follow me around. Little did I know . . .

I walked into the dressing room with Alissa on my heels. She was working special duty for Tate today, and was practically glowing she was so excited to be in the mix. I should have told her to tone down the gleam. It didn't work that well for undercover.

"All right, April, what's going on?" I asked her. I looked around for her mother but didn't see Tamara anywhere. That was odd.

"It was an accident," April sobbed.

"What was an accident?"

"She just looked so cocky, and so sure of herself, and when she put on those red pointe shoes . . . well, I wanted them. I knew that was supposed to be my role, and I didn't get it because of her. And that made my mom really mad, and now she isn't going to get me the new iPhone like she said she would. So when she came out of the bathroom, I just shoved her, sideways, and she fell and hit her head on the garbage can. So I ran and got my mom, and we carried her to the place behind the bleachers and left her there."

"Whoa, whoa, are you talking about Carly? Are you the one who hurt her?" I asked, stunned by the confession.

"It was an accident," she sobbed again. Just then, Tamara came running into the dressing room and stopped, aghast as she saw April's tears and my accusing stare.

"I . . . you . . ." For once, the woman was speechless.

For a minute, no one said anything, and then she said, "You sent me out of here on purpose, April. You did, didn't you? I told you not to tell them, and you threatened me. Said you were going to tell them that I helped you if I didn't get you the new iPhone, and . . . Wow."

April's tears dried up and she suddenly looked remarkably guilty, slightly cunning, and incredibly weasel-like. "I just told the truth. I had to tell the truth. It was eating me alive." Now if those words didn't sound choreographed, I didn't know what did.

"You hurt Carly?" I heard Marlys's voice and jumped forward to shield April, knowing that if possible, Marlys would do some serious damage to the little b—, er, brat.

"It was an accident," she said, even though the tears were long gone.

"It was no accident," Tamara Williams said, her voice haughty and angry. "The little ingrate shoved her on purpose, because she was so mad I wouldn't buy her an iPhone. I told her if she got the solo role, she could have the phone, but she didn't even try. She shoved Carly and hurt her and then came running to me for help."

By this time, Tate had been called inside by Alissa, and he was listening to the entire story.

"Um, Jenny, I hate to break into this little repartee, but the Company team is due to go on in two numbers," James said.

"Company, let's go," I yelled, clapping my hands. The girls had all been standing around, mouths wide, watching the drama unfold before them. Never a dull moment in the world of competition dance, I'm telling you.

The dancers lined up, and I watched April try to slide away without notice, but it didn't work. Alissa bumped up behind her, and when the girl turned angrily to glare, Alissa gave her a look that could melt plastic. She sat back down on the bench with a thump.

"I have to watch this routine," I told Tate and Alissa,

and they told me to go. I followed my dancers out and looked on as they lined up.

The announcer called out our team, the Jenny T. Partridge Company, and they made their way onto the floor and hit their opening pose. From then on, it was sheer magic. The music was perfect, unique and unforgettable; Malece's costumes were stunning and eye-popping; the choreography was innovative and sharp; and Carly's solo, done on the red pointe shoes, was perfect. No one would have guessed that just a week before she had been hospitalized with a concussion.

When it was over, the crowd stood and roared approval, and I felt tears pour down my cheeks.

When we got back to the dressing room, Tate had arrested both April and her mother, and both were in cuffs. April was spitting mad, nastier than I had ever seen her be. Tamara didn't seem the least bit surprised about her daughter's behavior.

"Why are you arresting me?" she asked Tate. "She's the one who did it."

"We'll start with accessory to attempted murder and go from there," Tate said.

"Murder?" Tamara gasped. "She wasn't trying to kill her. She just wanted her out of her way so she could dance in the solo role." She sounded so sane while she said it, too.

Like the last competition, the Company routines had been last, and I heard them announce over the loudspeaker that awards would be starting.

"Are you going to stay?" I asked Tate.

"No, I'm going to make sure these two go where they belong. But until I have all the details, you keep Stanley and Arlo close, okay? I'm not convinced this is over."

"Of course it is," I said. "It all fits. Just like with Carly. April knew she couldn't take over the role, but she was angry, so she hurt her anyway. Probably the same thing her mother did to me."

"Well, just keep them close, okay?"

I agreed, then went out and sat by James, Marlys, and some of the other dance moms as we waited for awards. Trevor walked in with some nachos in his hands, and I waved him over.

"Did you see it? It was perfect," I said.

"I know! I can't believe how awesome they did. It's almost enough to make me want to move back here and teach at your studio all the time," he said. "Your dancers are so good and so well trained."

"Shh, they're starting," Marlys said.

They started the awards with beginning teams first and then made their way to advanced and professional teams. All of our team routines won first-place Gold, and several took High Gold, and one, the Company routine, took Platinum. We jumped off our seats, and everyone was clapping and screaming.

I sent Carly up to collect the plaque, since she deserved it more than anyone else.

After all the individual awards were given out, it was time for the high-point and overall awards, and of course, the grand prize given to the team with highest overall point average.

"Please be us, please be us, please be us," I chanted under my breath.

Two of our team routines, the Minis and the Petites, took the overall awards for their division.

"This next routine is our grand champion, and the studio the winner of this year's UDC Overall Studio High-Point Cash Award. The winner of the Company division, with a Platinum, and overall award is the Jenny T. Partridge Dance Academy!"

I'd like to thank my parents, who have always supported me, often more than they had any desire to do, and of course, my friends, and my . . .

"Uh, Jenny? Are you going to go up there and get it, or what?" Marlys asked me.

I jumped up, grabbed Carly's hand, and took her with me. I was crying when they handed over the check and the big plaque. She helped me hold it up, and the audience clapped. My psycho dance moms and dads clapped the loudest, of course.

I'd really wanted this, and now it was finally mine. And Tamara and her Hummer were going to be put out of business, and never again would I have to try to teach April Williams a solo lesson, when it was very apparent she had little desire to dance, and probably would soon be the head of a prison gang.

Oh, and did I mention, Tate loved me?

THIRTY-TWO

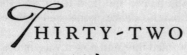

AFTER THE EXCITEMENT FADED, I FOUND MY-self in the dressing room, making sure that all of the girls had packed up their costumes, tights, clothes, and accessories. Marlys and Carly were there helping, and people kept coming up and congratulating me. The room was nearly empty when Trevor came in and walked over to me. He gave me a big hug, and I thanked him for all his help.

"I want you to come back every year, Trev. You did an awesome job with this. Awesome."

"Hey, it was fun. And I really like your girls. I would love to come back."

"Then it's a plan," I said.

"Are you sure you wouldn't consider coming out to L.A. and working with me there?" he asked, giving me that trademark Trevor smile. "I could pay you a whole lot more money than you make here. And you know how California is—all that glamour and movie stars and lots of bling."

"I have enough excitement here, Trev," I said. "But thanks for the invitation."

He gave me a kiss on the cheek and a rueful shake of his head and then headed for the door.

The room was nearly empty, and Marlys put her arm around Carly. "Well, we have a lot of talking to do at home," she said. "But I'm glad it worked out this way, Jenny."

"Are you going to be okay?" I asked her, thinking about what Arlo and Stanley had said about Roger and his involvement with the Twinkle Toes lady.

"Yeah, we are. One day at a time, but we'll be okay."

Both Carly and Marlys looked sad, and I didn't want to question them further, but I knew that in the next few days I would be sitting down for coffee with Marlys and talking things through. The days when she was there for me—and that alone—were over. I intended to be there for her, too.

Stanley and Arlo had been watching us clean up the room—even now, the two weren't far from us—and as Marlys left, I watched as Stanley took Carly's dance suitcase and told them he would walk them out to the car.

Arlo asked me what else needed to be done, and I told him that I just had to turn my fake check in for a real one before I headed home.

"Fake check?"

"Yeah, they don't give you the real one onstage. You know, in case it gets lost or something happens in the excitement."

"How do you get the real one?"

"I need to get our dressing room clean, then someone will be here to inspect it and hand over the check, plus the deposit I had to pay for the dressing room."

A tall blond woman poked her head in the room. "Dressing room check."

"Speak of the devil," I said to Arlo. "I'm ready," I said to her.

She stepped inside the room and walked toward us. She reached out to Arlo, and I gave her an odd look and opened my mouth just as he went down, hard. She pointed a gun at me and told me to move quickly.

"Uh, the room's clean. You don't have to get so nasty."

"Shut up, Jenny. Move. Out that door, now. Move quick." Her voice was high and yet I knew I'd heard it somewhere before.

Her face was attractive, and yet something was off about her. She was also vaguely familiar to me, but I couldn't quite figure out why.

"Move!" I moved.

"What did you do to Arlo?"

"Shut up. Just walk."

I could feel the gun poking in my back, and so I shut up and walked. She pointed me down a corridor and to a back exit, and I turned around, wondering if I could yell for help, and if anyone would hear me. Shouldn't have turned around.

I felt a sharp pain and my whole body felt as if it were on fire, then all my muscles decided to stop working and the world went black.

THIRTY-THREE

I KNEW THAT I WAS NOT REALLY UNCON-
scious and that I was being carried by the woman—
carried?—like a sack of flour, over her shoulder. Despite
the fact I knew what was going on, I didn't seem to be able
to control any part of my body. Or the moaning that came
out of my mouth.

I heard a car door open and a thump, and then I was
dumped into the back of a vehicle and there was another
clank. I tried to focus; I could tell I was in the back of some
vehicle, an SUV.

I knew right then I was in the silver Hummer. But who
was this woman? And why had she seemed so familiar?

I moaned again, and it didn't get any reaction from the
woman, who started up the vehicle. We roared away, and I
slowly moved my muscles, realizing that I was getting the
function back in my arms and legs. The woman driving
was in one heck of a hurry, and I kept slamming into the
sides of the SUV as she zoomed around corners and made
a couple of hard lefts.

After about five minutes, the turning stopped and I sensed we were on I-15.

I got on all fours and then peeked up over the seat, and saw the back of Trevor's head . . . and a blond wig over the back of the passenger-side seat.

Trevor?

I slunk back down and tried to consider my options. We were traveling way too fast for me to attempt opening the back hatch of the Hummer and jumping out. I'd die on impact. If I could get over the seat and sneak up on him, then maybe . . .

"I know you're probably plotting back there, Jenny, and let me tell you, it won't do any good. A stun gun only puts you out of business for a few minutes. So I know you are able to talk to me. But I don't suggest you try anything."

"Why are you doing this?" I said, still not looking over the seat.

"Why? Are you kidding me?"

"Yeah, why?"

"How many times have I asked you to come to L.A. with me? Or just to have a drink with me? You are ruining all my plans. You and that stupid Tate."

"Uh, you only asked me to come to L.A. once, and that was about five minutes ago."

"Oh no. I've talked to you about it many, many times. About how great it would be and how good we would be together, if you would just give us a chance."

"Is it possible you are thinking of some other Jenny?"

"Don't get smart." His voice sounded high-pitched, off-kilter, and more than a little out of control.

"Look, Trevor, you've joked about it before, I mean, we've joked about it, but it never went further than that. It was always innocent."

The Hummer took a hard right, and I smashed up against the side of the vehicle, making my body, which was still trying to recover from the effects of the stun gun, ache even more. We drove on farther, stopping at one point, then starting up again until he took a left and I could tell we were no longer on pavement, but on a gravel road. The vehicle hit an incline and I hoped we weren't headed up into the mountains somewhere, although from all the turns we had made, I'd assumed we were headed west, toward the Great Salt Lake.

He slowed down and then came to a stop, and I heard him open the door. Frantically, I looked around for something to defend myself with, and I spotted a hard metal CD case. It wasn't much, but it was all I could find, so I grabbed it and stuck it behind my back, just as he opened the hatch.

He glared at me, still wearing the woman's shirt and jeans he had adorned as a disguise to catch me, and Arlo, off guard. I guessed this was the same disguise he had used to get the upper hand on Officer Aaron as well. He must have left the studio after telling James he needed coffee, waited until Officer Aaron showed back up, then donned his disguise, attacked the policeman, and then returned to the studio. Today, his mouth was covered with a glossy lip gel, and his eyes had liner around them—although I was close enough now to see it was pretty hastily applied. "I was waiting for you. It was innocent, because you wanted it that way. Old-fashioned and romantic, like in the movies. Innocent, until you had to come to your hero for help and safety. And instead, you turned to the cop. You weren't supposed to turn to the cop. I was supposed to be the hero."

"You look sort of pretty as a girl," I said, the first thing that came to my mind. Not, apparently, what he wanted to hear.

"Dammit, Jenny, you are pissing me off. I tried to do this the right way, and you just ignored all the signs. You were supposed to leave Utah, to realize your fate was with me, in L.A. We were going to make it in California, two kids from Utah with big talent and big dreams."

Big talent and big dreams. *Big Talent and Big Dreams.* Trevor's screenplay! The one he'd given me to read, and the one I'd never even opened, because reading was right up there with going to church on my list of things to do.

"Uh, well, I guess I'm just a Utah girl. I've never had a real desire to live anywhere else."

He shook his head at me, then reached in and grabbed me by the shoulder, pulling me out of the back and making me stand up on the road. I could see we were on a hill somewhere close to the Great Salt Lake. There were marshes and grassy knolls all around us, and I could see birds flying overhead. The competition had ended around 5 p.m., so the sun would be headed down soon, and I shivered at the thought of being caught out here in this desolate area—provided I was still alive when the sun set.

I still had the CD case tucked behind me. I doubted I'd be able to hold on to it for long, so I knew I'd better find an opportunity to use it before he looked at me too closely. Up until this point, he had been telling his story with his hands and rolling his head around, and yelling, and not paying a lot of attention to me.

There was a sharp breeze coming in off the bay—the bay! That's where we were, the Farmington Bay bird refuge. I'd been here many times with my father, who had grown up in the fields and hills that surrounded the small Utah town, and he'd taken a lot of time trying to impress upon me the beauty of the bay. Time that was mostly wasted, because I didn't like mosquitoes, birds, and at times, the entire place smelled like the world's largest rotten egg. Farmington Bay was the entryway to the Great Salt Lake, and today was a protected bird refuge. This was in my favor, as it was regularly patrolled by the Division of Wildlife Resources, who carried guns and radios. Fish cops, as my dad used to say.

"Jenny, can't you see that I did this for us? I wanted to give you the fairy tale. The fairy tale you always wanted."

I stopped cold, just as I was about to bonk him on the head with the CD case. "The fairy tale?"

"Yes, don't you remember? One night we went out for drinks, and you had two glasses of wine and then told me you were waiting for your knight in shining armor. For your prince. And until you met him, you weren't going to bend. You wanted the whole thing. The fairy tale."

"What was I thinking?" I said aloud. "Fairy tales are just stories. Stupid stories that people make up. I want a real life."

Anger filled his handsome, er, pretty features. "I did this for you. Created all of this for you. I put myself on the line for you, to create your dream. To be your prince. Are you trying to tell me you've changed your mind?"

"Uh, well, kinda? I mean, I never meant for you to do this. I never thought of you that way, because you were this big successful L.A. choreographer, and I was just this little Ogden dance teacher. I never thought you would go this far . . . I never . . ."

"I even killed someone for you," he said, and I winced.

"I never asked you to do that."

"Yeah, well, I had to prove how serious I was—actually, prove how dangerous Utah really was for you. And that stupid Gorilla-Gram guy recognized me anyway, even though I'd been in drag. He saw me going into your studio, and he wanted more money. Always about more money. The whole thing just worked perfectly."

His features relaxed as he considered his plan. "Jenny, I need you in my life. I need grounding. The women in L.A. are piranhas. Fake boobs, fake hair, fake eyelashes. I need someone real. Curly red hair, average body, awesome dance skill . . ."

"Average body? *Sheesh.* You really know how to charm a girl."

He smiled that drop-dead, make-your-stomach-tickle smile, and I suddenly realized I did not want to drop dead.

I took that moment to use the CD case and bean him hard on the side of the head. He dropped to the ground and I dashed off, heading down a small rough trail, dirt and pebbles rushing in front of me. I skidded and fell on my butt, but I jumped back up and followed the pathway down to the road and started to run down it, gasping, until I heard a big roar behind me. He had the distinct advantage. The only thing I'd seen out here so far were some birds, and they weren't going to save me. I was going to have to dive into the marsh and hide, and that idea did not thrill me. Not only was it not entirely warm just yet, but I'd been out here a fair share with my dad, and I knew that little rodents called weasels lived inside the marshes, and they were not attractive furry little creatures. Not only that, but water snakes were abundant and mosquitoes lived here in swarms, and it had been just warm enough today that I was sure more than a few had woken up.

Hummer tire tracks up my back or rodents and mosquito bites? The roar convinced me. I dove into the marsh and made my way through water that was first ankle high, then thigh high, and tears poured down my face. I made myself cry silently as I waded through the tall marshes, swatting at the mosquitoes that buzzed around my head and bit my bare arms and hands. The roar stopped, and I heard Trevor's voice calling, "Come out, come out, wherever you are. Come on, Jenny. I'll forgive this lapse. We can still live happily ever after."

"Not bloody likely," I cursed. Wow, where did I pick that up? Oh yeah, probably too much television.

I gasped as a water snake uncoiled and swam right in front of me, slithering against my thigh, and I said a quick prayer of thanks that I was in long jeans. I shivered and knew that I couldn't hide out here too long. If the mosquitoes didn't get me, the night air would.

"Jenny, come on. I'm not in the mood to come diving into that marsh, but I will if I have to."

Come on in, I willed him. I eyed the front of the marsh and knew I could find my way back out to the road. I could shove him into the water, maybe stand on his back for five minutes or so, then make my way out and steal the Hummer.

I was not going to die here.

I backed up, peering at the front of the marsh, squinting in the darkening sky, and then hit a solid mass of muscle. A hand covered my mouth; my eyes nearly popped out of my head. How did he get behind me? I stiffened and waited, but after a moment, I heard Trevor call again from the road. My captor loosened his grasp, and I turned to see Stanley, dressed in Rambo-like camouflage gear, minus the bare chest. He let me go, motioned for me to be silent, and then led me to the back of the marsh, where there was a small outlet of water and an open grassy area. He counted to three using his fingers, then threw some kind of apparatus into the bog. After a minute, there was a large explosion and I heard Trevor scream and swear.

"What the hell? What the hell just happened? Jenny, are you okay? Are you okay?"

We waited another minute, then Stanley pulled me to the gap in the brush, and I looked through to see Trevor pacing, his hands rubbing through his hair. He'd take a step forward to the marsh, then back again.

The whole time I'd been only about twenty yards from the road, although in the marsh I might as well have been in the middle of a forest.

"Damn sissy California boy," Stanley whispered, then smiled one of his rare grins.

We waited there, watching as Trevor considered diving into the marsh, then stepped back time and time again. Moments later the road filled with flashing lights and sirens, and Trevor looked around, seemed to contemplate running, and then just dropped his arms to his sides.

"Don't scratch those," Stanley said as I itched one of the trillion mosquito bites I had.

"I'm probably going to get that South Nile Virus," I said. "Hey, thanks for saving me. You were cool. How did you know?"

"Arlo dropped a tracker on you. He's not a big believer in leaving things up to chance."

"Where did you get the Rambo gear?"

"Rambo gear? I carry this sh—, er, stuff in my trunk all the time."

So much for fairy tales. I'd gotten the action-adventure version; I decided I much preferred it.

THIRTY-FOUR

STANLEY TOOK ME TO THE MOBILE UNIT THAT served as an office for the Division of Wildlife Resources and then gave me a towel and a cup of really bad, really bitter coffee. I wasn't drinking it, just holding it to get warm. I'd tried one sip but then remembered I'd sworn off police department coffee the first time I ever tasted it.

Seconds later, Tate walked in. He pulled me into an embrace, then asked me that familiar question. "Why am I always having to do this?"

"Well, now that we know who was driving the Hummer, I'm hoping that all my adventures are over and that nothing like this will ever happen again."

"You look like you have the chicken pox."

"Mosquitoes."

"Damn, you are covered."

"Yeah, in places that I wouldn't think they could even reach."

He smiled, then sobered. "I'm sorry this happened."

"Hey, you thought it was Tamara."

"Well, it certainly looked like her, but it's never that easy with you. I should have remembered that."

"You were doing your job, and I was doing mine. And then Arlo got hit with that thing—what was that thing?— that knocked us both for a loop."

"A stun gun."

"Well, I don't like those things. I think I'd prefer a real gun."

"You wouldn't."

I just shrugged, and he loaded me into his car and took me home.

HERE'S THE THING ABOUT FAIRY TALES, ONLY the genuinely mentally ill believe in that kind of thing. People like Trevor Paulsen, who now had a very special room in a very special section of a very special hospital in Salt Lake City. He had earned a fair chunk of change in his time in L.A. and could afford the very best care. Good thing. He was going to need it.

Turned out Trevor's real name was Robert James Pickett, aka R. J. Pickett, and the Hummer was no rental. He kept it here, in the garage of a condo in Salt Lake City, specifically to help convince me that Utah was not a safe place for me to live and that I really should relocate to sunny Southern California.

Tamara and April were facing charges for the attack on Carly, even though they were now both claiming it was an accident. And as far as we knew, the fact that Holly Vendstra drove a silver Hummer was just a coincidence. Although in my world, one never knew.

And the toy Hummer that turned up on Carly? A little gift from Trevor, who had seen the spat between Carly and April, and found an excuse to throw in a little extra fear for me—in the shape of a small toy Hummer. The fact that he knew Carly had been hurt and had done nothing to help her made me want to beat him with a baseball bat. Good thing I was a nonviolent sort of person and did not have access to basic sports equipment.

Tate picked me up at Alissa's house on Monday afternoon. He'd insisted I go back and stay with her, until we ironed out our "fairy tale" details. It didn't matter how many times I told him I'd changed my mind and that action-adventure would do just fine. He wasn't listening.

"So, where are we going?"

"I thought you would want to be there when they arrest the Twinkle Toes people."

He thought right.

He made me wait outside, of course, during the good stuff, and then when he received a call, we went inside the building. Arlo and Stanley had turned over the information they discovered, and then two undercover officers set up a sting. The Friday before, one of the two men had connected with the same temptress that lured Roger astray, and photographs were taken. Although the situation didn't go as far as Roger's, it was enough for the blackmail to take place, the money to exchange hands, and arrests to be made.

Four women and two men—who apparently did the picture taking and any muscle work—were arrested.

I got to watch that part. Or at least see them get read their rights.

"You people give dance studios a bad name," I told the tall woman I knew as Svetlana. "The Russian Mob should keep their fingers out of the dance business."

"Ve are not Russians. Ve are from Ukraine."

"There's a difference?" I asked.

"Please. Of course." She gave me a snooty look as they led her off in handcuffs. Guess I should have kept up on my geometry lessons.

"So, it's an ending. Not a happy one necessarily. Will Marlys get the money back for her kids?" I asked Tate.

"We're hopeful. Is she okay?"

"She kicked Roger out. He's living with his parents again, I guess, and calling her every twenty minutes begging to be forgiven and come home."

"But is she going to be okay?"

"Marlys is strong. And if she wasn't, she'd make herself be, just for the kids."

After the excitement was over, Tate drove me to Rooster's Brew Pub, my very, very favorite place to eat, and the sight of our first, uh, well, not really date. First dinner together? I ordered the fish tacos and a Diet Coke. Tate, as usual, ordered some healthy salmon and vegetables, and a beer. The beer was not so healthy. I was glad he had a few vices.

After we finished eating, I leaned back and sighed. "That was good food. Not as good as your grilled cheese sandwich and tomato soup, but close."

He smiled, and then our waitress appeared with a dessert and a sparkly candle burning on top.

"What's this for? It's not my birthday."

"It's a celebration," Tate said, and thanked the waitress. She walked away, and he leaned into me. "This is an 'I love you' candle. If you'll forgive me for not saying it soon enough, I promise to provide you with a different 'I love you' surprise at least once a month for the rest of your life."

"The rest of my life?" I squeaked. How did I get myself into these things?

"Yes."

"Are you—"

"Jennifer, thank God I found you here!" James came running dramatically toward me.

"Please, not tonight," Tate said, but James ignored him.

"You will not believe it. I've been called for a show! A show! It's in Wendover, of course, which is not quite Vegas, and not even close to Broadway, but still, they want me to do a show."

"And this has *what* to do with me?"

"Well, of course, we're a package deal. Apparently, a brother of the owner's sister saw your routine at UDC, and they want an entire show themed around it, and they want the creative team that put it together, so I told them—"

"James, one half of the creative team is in the loony bin, and the other half, me, is staying firmly put in Ogden. And you had nothing at all to do with it."

"Oh please. Would you stop? I was there for rehearsals. I made suggestions. I can't believe you are trying to downplay my input. And with Trevor riding the c-r-a-z-y train, you will need me to help you get the thing going."

"I don't want to get the thing going."

"Jennifer! This is my, er, our chance. The big time. Well, the semi–big time. Maybe the pathway to the big time. But this is it!"

"No thanks."

James stopped and looked at me, eyes wide. "You can't say no."

"I just did."

"But . . . but . . . they are expecting us."

"James, what did you do?"

"Just signed a weency little contract, and sort of put your name on there, too. Sort of . . ."

"James!" Tate and I said in unison.

Somebody get me one of those stun guns.

GET CLUED IN

Ever wonder how to find out about all the latest Berkley Prime Crime and Signet mysteries?

berkleysignetmysteries.com

- *See what's new*
- *Find author appearances*
- *Win fantastic prizes*
- *Get reading recommendations*
- *Sign up for the mystery newsletter*
- *Chat with authors and other fans*
- *Read interviews with authors you love*

MYSTERY SOLVED.

berkleysignetmysteries.com

ISBN 978-0-425-22128-0

The buzz of competition is in the air and Jenny T. Partridg is training her budding prima—and not so prima—balleri nas for the big dance championship. She knows these co tests can get ugly, but this year it seems someone is real shooting to kill...

Pliés and arabesques don't pay the bills, so Jenny's looking expand her studio to include a new dance shop. She know that her moms will spare no expense for pink satin slippers ar fluffy tutus, but start-up costs are really adding up. Jenny hop her girls will win the Ultimate Dance Championship and pirot ette their way to the twenty-five-hundred-dollar prize.

U f uation just might stand in her wa ps by the studio to deliver Jenr ds up dead in her father's truc Dodging bullets and a mysterious silver Hummer, Jenny realiz that even dreamy Detective Tate Wilson can't save her from th one. She'll have to do some fancy footwork, and fast...

ISBN 978-0-425-22128-0

5 0 6 9 9 >

9 780425 221280

$6.99 U.S.
$7.50 CAN

www.penguin